Season of Apples

Also by Ann Copeland

At Peace
The Back Room
Earthen Vessels
The Golden Thread
Strange Bodies on a Stranger Shore
The ABC's of Writing Fiction

Season of Apples

ANN COPELAND

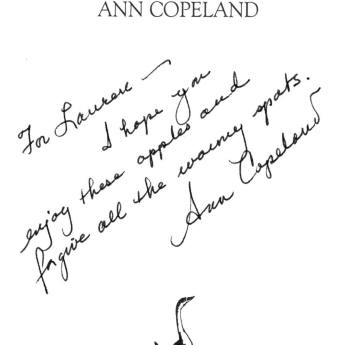

For Lauren —
I hope you
enjoy these apples and
forgive all the wormy spots.
Ann Copeland

GOOSE LANE

Published by Goose Lane Editions with the assistance of the Canada Council and the
New Brunswick Department of Municipalities, Culture and Housing, 1996.

The following stories have appeared in slightly different form in the following journals
and anthologies: "Mother Love," "With the Continuing Ed Teacher," and "Crossing
the Border" (as "Border Crossing") in *The Fiddlehead*; "About Billy" in *The Nashwaak
Review*; "Getting the Picture" and "Parting" in *The University of Windsor Review*;
"Sin" in *Matrix*; "I Only Teach Comp" in *The Uncommon Reader*; "Remembrance Day"
and "Trick or Treat" in *Turnstile*; "On the Other Side" in *Wild East*;"The Day the
Grocery Story Fell In" in *The Pottersfield Portfolio*; "Portfolio" in *The Southwest Review*;
"Another Country" in *The New Quarterly*, *Vistas*, and *Best Maritime Stories*;
"Season of Apples" in *Green Mountains Review*.

Edited by Laurel Boone.
Cover illustration, "Adam and Eve" (detail) by Lucas Cranach the Elder (1472-1553)
Back cover photo by Daniel St. Louis.
Book design by Julie Scriver.
Printed and bound in Canada by Imprimerie Gagné.
10   9   8   7   6   5   4   3   2

Canadian Cataloguing in Publication Data

Copeland, Ann.
Season of apples

ISBN 0-86492-210-8

I. Title.
PS8555.05925S42 1996   C813'.54   C96-950148-X
PR9199.3.C647S42 1996

Goose Lane Editions
469 King Street
Fredericton, NB
CANADA E3B 1E5

For Dr. Albert Spatz
friend and keyboard partner
for many years

Contents

The man who finds his homeland sweet
is still a tender beginner;
he to whom every soil is as his native
is already strong;
but he is perfect
to whom the entire world
is as a foreign land.

Hugh of St. Victor, *Didascalicon*

Mother Love

HAMP SPITSKY WISHED ALMA wouldn't wear a hat to the affair, but he knew better than to say so. She was standing in the front hall adjusting the aqua velour cloche, pulling it first to one side, then the other. He had bought it for her in the January sales, remembering her admiring notice of it in a store window on one of their December shopping excursions. Soft and fuzzy, its narrow brim was malleable according to one's mood. Tonight, evidently, Alma felt jaunty.

"Is it cold out?" he asked, squeezing by her to extract his trench coat from the hall closet.

"It's not a question of cold, Hamp. This will be a rather dressy affair." She pulled the brim lower over her left eye.

He belted his coat, resigned. Obviously the evening was important to her: she was sacrificing the final episode of *Masterpiece Theatre*.

"It's good we're going early," she said, picking up her purse from the hall table. "It'll be mobbed. The gym seats two thousand, Marilyn was telling me, and all the advance tickets were sold."

Every Tuesday, Alma played bridge with Marilyn Ross and "the girls," an afternoon they rounded off with coffee and a guilty caloric binge. Tuesday night at Spitskys' often featured a special leftover dessert.

As Hamp backed out the drive and headed toward Main, he was aware of the aqua fuzz framing his wife's freshly tinted hair. Sometimes he tried to imagine her head covered with gray or white. Impossible. He'd seen only the carefully maintained reddish brown that in a bad week came out bronze. This was a good week. He had yet to discern the full dimensions of her vanity, but he already knew that hair and clothing counted. Oddly enough, his own baldness seemed to attract her.

Who, in a crowd of two thousand, would notice either of them tonight? More than a few would get a whiff of her Chanel, though. Should he tell her it was a bit strong?

He cracked the window on the driver's side.

"I'd park a distance away," she offered when they were about three blocks from the college. "That way we'll be able to get out afterward."

Actually, Hamp knew his way around campus fairly well. It was a small college, about twelve hundred students, its ivied brick buildings dominating the far edge of town on a preserve of gleaming dogwoods and ponderous oaks. This year, looking about for an activity they might enjoy together, Alma and Hamp had subscribed to the college's musical series. The first concert had featured a preternaturally endowed soprano belting out arias in Italian and German to a piano accompaniment. Despite the fascination of that heaving bosom, the evening had left him numb.

The previous fall, LeMar's business department had offered a weekly course in investing. Encouraged by Alma, Hamp took it. They met in a windowless room with fluorescent lighting, five men over sixty and a young woman of the liberated variety determined to learn about money before she woke up in middle age to find herself dumb, uninformed, and poor. Hamp was convinced that would not be Corinne's fate: her ankles were too trim. She showed them off with iridescent socks or subtly patterned hose, and a rainbow of soft feathers dangled from one ear against her long lovely neck. Her presence had redeemed the arid atmosphere of aging males bent on protecting their assets. In any case, he'd sat through a semester of learning the ins and outs of IRAs, treasury bills, mutual funds, blue chip stocks, CDs — how to calculate the risks of gambling against the pleasures of winning — and had ended up feeling better about decisions made two years before, when he'd finally risked the big gamble and proposed to Alma Harrison.

⊰⊱

Hamp eased their Chevy in behind a pickup truck on a side street two blocks from the gym. Several years ago, against considerable opposition from nearby residents, LeMar had erected a huge dome, called simply The Dome, to shelter its many sports activities. Toward this Hamp and Alma now headed, joining others already crowding the sidewalks leading toward the open doors. Even from this distance you could see hundreds, thousands of small dark figures swarming in the radiant hive — for so the glaring lights inside made The Dome appear against the darkening spring night.

Alma had the tickets. She'd arranged the whole thing after she read about it in the paper. "Famous Opera Star to Visit LeMar College."

Candace Lillaberro had retired from the Metropolitan. She would talk, not sing. Why, he'd wondered from the outset, would so many people come to hear an opera star *talk*? The key word was *star*. That was it, the contemporary disease, suckers for stardom, kids, adults even, willing to sell their souls for a gawk at stardom. Had they ever really listened when stars opened their mouths to talk?

He'd put the question to her squarely but tactfully.

"Bobby'd never forgive me if I missed this," she said.

He heard the absolute. This was one of the things about coming to marriage late: turn a corner and you bumped into habit become rock. Little things, like preferring tooth powder to toothpaste or liking the toast light. On their first morning at home after the honeymoon, he'd manfully stifled a spasm of irritation at the specter of nearly charred toast. It was trivial and he knew it, knew too that trivialities could bundle to significance.

Her son Bobby, however, was not trivial.

Neither was tonight's excursion. Hamp sensed that. Such were Alma's enthusiasms that she could sometimes lift and carry him along, for a time. A thoughtful man, widowed young, schooled by the silence of long singleness, he was not easily impulsive. He valued his wife's capacity to desire and *do* — uninhibited, or so it seemed, by the restraint of too much thought. Before they met he'd thought himself dull. Alma was beginning to persuade him otherwise.

And what was the acceptance of darker toast or minty toothpaste weighed against the draftiness of his former life? Gladly would he squeeze out the Colgate for Alma's sake. He'd watched his calories and was now, at sixty-two, trim. She appreciated his every inch.

⌗

Near the door the crowd narrowed, pushing to get inside. A small woman in furs knocked against him. Everyone, it did seem, was quite got up. April in Oregon hardly called for furs. Alma had settled for a light coat, despite her rather wintry cloche. An old man with a withered face squinted at Hamp. Was it dandruff on the collar? A thread on the coat? Hamp looked away and grasped Alma's elbow as they pushed through and were finally inside.

Clearly, a large crowd was expected. In addition to the bleachers, rows of chairs filled the floor. On one side of the gym a stage had been set up, empty except for microphone, two chairs, and a small table holding a pitcher and a glass. College girls, slender clear-skinned gazelles in long black skirts and frilly white blouses, were directing people through the aisles. The main floor appeared filled. Hamp and Alma joined those swarming up the bleachers. "Let's go up high," whispered Alma, climbing ahead of him. "Better view."

They settled themselves in the center bleachers, two rows from the top. Others were moving in on either side, nodding, chatting, bumping knees, shedding coats and jackets, arranging themselves. A narrow-faced woman in cerise pushed in beside Hamp, smoothed the emptied sleeves of her pale pink jacket, and set it carefully on her lap.

"What a mob," she said, crossing her legs.

Her bright skirt rode high above slender calves, bony knees. Small dark nylon diamonds trailed across her ankles.

Hamp nodded.

"But then how often does a star come to Oregon?"

He nodded again.

Idiocy. He wouldn't walk across the street to hear an opera, all that bleating and screaming, all that wasted energy. He played banjo himself, bluegrass, and loved nothing better than picking the old tunes. Alma seemed to enjoy this novelty. She showed him off to guests, bragged about his musical ability. She couldn't carry a tune herself.

Leaning forward, she was talking across him to the woman.

"My son is studying for an operatic career," she said in a loud voice. "We just had to come."

A red-haired young man in the row ahead turned to look at them over half glasses. Oblivious, Alma went on. Hamp studied the small gold stud gleaming in his wife's earlobe. He wished she'd stop.

"Alma," he whispered.

She glanced at him and sat back, squirming herself to relative comfort on the hard bleachers. Alma had been trained to please.

"Look, Hamp," she said, nudging him. "There's Marilyn."

Sure enough, Marilyn and John Ross had just come in the door and were slowly pushing through the crowd. John Ross, recently retired and loving open collars, looked unhappy in his tie. They stood in the aisle at the bottom of the center bleachers, their eyes combing rows for a couple of empty places. Alma began to wave.

"They don't see you," said Hamp. "And there isn't enough room for them up here, anyhow."

She dropped her arm as the Rosses moved on toward the far end of the gym.

"Marilyn was telling me at bridge that she went to the Met last year," said Alma, her eyes following the Rosses as they finally located seats and began climbing toward them. "Said it was marvelous, Hamp. *La Boheme*. You know, the one where the girl finally dies in the end."

That, it seemed to Hamp, might be almost any opera. Now that Bobby was headed for vocal fame, Alma had begun to pick up details that might keep her in touch with his future. She'd tune in to the Met on Saturday afternoons, then diligently distract herself by baking something complicated, preparing dinner, chopping vegetables — anything to blur the focus on all that music. It amused Hamp. She was like a moth fluttering about the distant edges of a world of glamor, a world of passion and color far removed from the softer austerities of Oregon drizzle, benign mountains, and forests. On that great gold-curtained stage, oversized lovers sang of oversized loves. Enough to know it existed. Against such splendid vibrations could she happily run her Mixmaster, dip into her flour. For life had connected her, or soon would, to that very stage through the person of her own Bobby. She tried out German and Italian titles, practising them aloud. When someone corrected her pronunciation, she suffered it with grace. After all, she was attached by blood to one who would have to get it right. For all her twenty-five years in the west, Alma Spitsky, formerly Harrison, née Grindel, never forgot she'd come from back East, upstate Vermont. For her high school graduation her parents had taken her to New York: the Automat, Radio City, the Rockettes, the Empire State, a Broadway show. That was 1948. She had never been to the Met.

Hamp had never seen Manhattan and didn't intend to. Oregon was heaven.

✦

"Look, Hamp," she whispered, putting her small manicured hand against his sleeve, "that must be Candace Lillaberro herself."

Indeed, almost without being noticed, a white-haired man in a dark suit and a woman in bright yellow had climbed the stairs to the stage and taken a seat on either side of the table. They sat there chatting, looking out at the crowd.

"Must be. Who's with her?"

"The president of LeMar," murmured the woman on his left.

Alma was rustling in her purse. She extracted small binoculars and held them to her eyes. "Yes, that's Candace Lillaberro, all right. I saw her picture in the paper. A little heavier than I expected. Want a look?"

He took the glasses and focussed them. Into his vision floated the face of a woman who might have been his own mother: round cheeks, double chin, eyes dark behind her glasses, blonde hair curled about the forehead. A face as ordinary as pie. Alma was far better looking. She'd kept her figure; her face knew how to look happy. She'd been blessed with good bone structure — high cheekbones, beautiful eyes.

The short dapper man sitting beside Candace Lillaberro was watching someone or something in front of him. As Hamp gave the glasses back to Alma, a young man in jeans jumped onstage and barked thorugh the microphone, "One, two, three, testing . . ."

People grew quiet.

"How long has your son been studying?" asked his neighbor, shifting her weight and recrossing her knees.

"It's my wife's son," he murmured. "I'm not sure — "

Alma leaned across him. "He went back East three years ago, after he finished at the University of Oregon. Of course, he'd spent four summers at music camp in Interlochen."

"I heard on the news last night that Miss Lillaberro's real name —" began the woman, but quieted down as the president stepped toward the microphone and stretched out his hand.

Gradually, people stopped talking and rustling.

"We are very pleased tonight," said the president, grasping the microphone, "to have with us a distinguished woman, an opera star well known to you all, practically a household name. We have enjoyed her silken tones for years, and tonight she will speak to us about her life. She really needs no introduction."

Someone down in front had started clapping. Hesitantly, then more enthusiastically, the crowd took it up. The star smiled.

"And so I will not keep you all in suspense. I am certain Miss Lillaberro will have words of significance for all here tonight. We know well the story of her personal industry, her early hardships, her meteoric rise, her concern now to help those struggling toward a musical career. Miss Candace Lillaberro!"

"She changed her name to sound more operatic," whispered Hamp's neighbor.

Candace Lillaberro rose and approached the microphone. Somehow it was a surprise to find her short.

"Thank you all, thank you so much." She smiled out at them. "I am indeed happy to be here tonight at . . . LeMar College, not to sing for you, but to talk to you about the world of singing . . ."

⫘

Five rows ahead, to his right, Hamp spotted a familiar neck. Against it swung one long multicolored earring. What would *she* be doing here? Beside her sat a fellow in a jean jacket, his hair cut short and square in the style so many favored this year, a throwback to the fifties. Hamp couldn't make out his profile. Alma was leaning forward. Her earnest bones rubbed against his thigh. The opera star had begun narrating the years of her childhood: backwoods, southern, poor.

". . . and then, one day when I was eight or nine, I happened to go back to school on a Saturday afternoon. A one-room schoolhouse, a bygone phenomenon," she cooed into the microphone, "and there was my teacher, Miss Sheniby, listening to the opera. I was spellbound. Captivated . . ."

Alma turned to him. He knew that expression. *See,* she was saying with her gold-flecked, deep-set blue eyes, *see, Hamp? Just what I've told you. Environment does change people. It makes all the difference. If that young girl hadn't met that teacher . . .*

17

She turned back to the stage.

"Can I have the binoculars?" he whispered.

She handed them to him without turning. He trained his eyes on the crowd, barely hearing as Candace Lillaberro drawled her way through childhood, adolescence, good teachers, sympathetic parents, meteoric rise, invaluable mentors, hard work rewarded, and the rest of it.

⬧

Hamp Spitsky had been married to Alma Harrison one full week before it dawned on him that he was permanently attached to a rather silly woman. Loveable, but silly. Perhaps he should have recognized it earlier, but the camouflage of a heart that was genuinely affectionate, sensitive to his needs, grateful for his attentions, and in every way designed to fill those vacancies he'd almost come to accept as destiny, such camouflage had made her occasional lapses into the ridiculous seem trivial. What was a silly mind compared to a loving heart? Her absurdities were not inflictive. She let him be. She was sincerely proud of him.

She saved everything — letters, bottle tops, plastic containers, coupons, Bobby's baby hair and first tooth, shoes she would never wear again. She was superstitious about inane things — spilled salt, a dropped spoon, walking beneath a ladder, Friday the thirteenth, and though she was the most consistently cheerful woman he'd ever met, she harbored continuous anxiety that bad luck was just around the corner. She wouldn't miss her daily horoscope and credited Bobby's promising future to the fact that he was a Sagittarian.

Hamp had not known her husband, a successful stockbroker, but John Ross (the only leftover friend from those days who really connected with Hamp) had once confided, after too much Scotch: "He was a cold son-of-a-gun, Hamp, would've murdered his grandmother to save a buck. How he ever picked up a loveable fluffball like Alma beats me." She'd weathered John's sudden stroke and death five years before, pulled herself together, and gone on. Alma was a survivor.

⬧

These origins were prehistory, inaccessible to Hamp who, fifteen years earlier, reluctantly resigned to permanent childlessness, tired of teaching high school math, had taken a chance and bought out the local stationery and art supply store. He'd always wanted to run a business and, at forty-seven, discovered in himself new talents. Customers called him personable, diplomatic. Salesmen called him shrewd. His staff called him fair. He could have lost his shirt as his perhaps envious fellow teachers predicted, but in fourteen years he turned a substantial profit, opened a second store in the new mall outside town, and retired — to Alma, whom he met over a customer complaint. She was the customer. As a dissatisfied consumer she was a bubbling tiger. He admired her spunk, replaced the defective desk lamp, and asked her out for dinner.

In bed, he discovered, she was wonderful: inventive, untiring, tender, and giggly in a way that excited him. The very silliness that by daylight irritated, in the dark captivated.

Most troubling of all her daytime preoccupations, to Hamp's mind, was her obsession with Bobby, a tall, skinny, pimply-faced fellow of twenty-four who had spent two weeks with them last summer, home from the East and full of it, name-dropping left and right, patronizing these poor benighted Oregonians. He'd been easternized and urbanized; it made Hamp's flesh crawl. Alma, blissful, seemed not to notice. During those weeks Hamp watched his new wife worry whether the meat was too rare, the carrots too soft, the house too hot, the bed too hard, and on and on in her efforts to create for Bobby, her budding star, a stress-free environment. Hamp, meanwhile, coming upon dirty socks on the sofa, cigarette butts in the bathroom (a singer smoking?), and empty beer cans making rings on mahogany veneer, wondered just what Bobby was doing back East. He seemed perfectly content to let his mother wait on him. When Hamp gently pointed this out to Alma, her eyes widened in surprise. "But Hamp. We only have him for two weeks."

The logic of a mother's devotion eluded him. He shut up.

Laughter. Applause.

He must have missed something.

The president stepped forward and shushed the audience.

"Miss Lillaberro has graciously agreed to answer questions," he said, over dying applause. "Can you all hear?"

Heads nodded.

The predictable silence fell as everyone waited to see who would dare.

"Hamp," whispered Alma, "isn't she wonderful? So human."

He nodded. The lovely neck five rows ahead was bent forward, her soft dark hair close to the flathead's ear. When she turned that way he could see her profile, a profile he'd studied many a night while supposedly calculating the advantages of deferred interest and long-range planning.

"Maybe she would help — " whispered Alma.

He barely heard her. His attention was riveted on the long lovely neck.

⊰ℲℲ⊱

On the last night of class he'd come upon her down by the front door of the building, lighting up a cigarette. "Could you give me a lift, Hamp?" she asked, with such simplicity his heart bounded. Had she been waiting for him?

"Of course. No problem."

"Supposed to have the car tonight," she grumbled as he opened the door on her side and wished Alma didn't let Soopsie, her long-haired mutt, ride in the front seat. He felt gallant, protective, old.

She directed him to the opposite end of town, a new development with rows of attached single dwellings and tiny front yards.

"How'd you like the course, Corinne?"

Boring topic. She wore a light fragrance, something clean and sweet.

She looked out the side window. Streetlights had come on and a fine light Oregon rain had begun. "So-so. Kinda boring, really." She laughed, a musical laugh. "At least I'll know what to do with my millions."

They pulled up in front of her small clapboard house.

She ground out her cigarette in the ashtray but made no move to go. He saw that she bit her nails.

20

"My boyfriend took the car tonight without even telling me," she frowned. "Had to call a taxi to get to class. Didn't want to miss the last one."

She sat there quietly, curled into herself, and responded to his few innocuous questions. She was from the town, had never been far out of it, wanted to travel back East next year, wanted to see it all.

"And you?" She eyed him.

"Me." He half smiled. Alma was home waiting. She'd be watching television. "I'm a newlywed." He loved to say it.

"You never got married till now?"

Her eyes, large and gray, widened — as if everyone over thirty must have at least tried out that state.

"Just briefly, when I was younger. My wife died very suddenly." She would have been, he wanted to add but didn't, about your age.

The girl's face softened. "I think I'd better go in," she murmured, as if they'd crossed some invisible line and she wished to go no further. "But thanks a lot, Hamp." She turned her full face toward him and reached out one hand to touch his, lying beside him on the seat. "It's been a pleasure meeting you. Good luck."

So old fashioned, those words. "It's been a pleasure meeting you." So gentle. It pained him. He wanted to know everything about her, who she lived with, on what terms. Was she lonely? With those ankles? Did she weep in the middle of the night? Did she see him as foolish? Interesting?

It was like guessing about the dark side of the moon.

She slammed the door and hurried up the walk.

When he got home, Alma had the kettle on. She was in her housecoat, waiting to hear all about his final class.

※

A tremor stirred the crowd. Down in front, a woman had asked Candace Lillaberro a question. The star was explaining that it took years of hard work, years and years, patience, sometimes luck. The opportunities were there. She mentioned singers whose names had become household words: Gedda, Pavarotti, Domingo. He'd heard of Pavarotti.

When she finished speaking, again silence.

"I have time for only one more question," said Miss Lillaberro.

She'd been talking for fifty-five minutes.

Hamp was startled to feel Alma's elbow graze him as her hand shot up. A few other hands were waving here and there about the gym.

"What're you *doing?*" he whispered.

"Shh." She waved harder.

Candace Lillaberro looked around slowly, surveying. How to choose from among so many?

Suddenly Alma stood up, rising on her toes, straining to make herself seen. She waved her arm wildly.

Please, no, he thought, watching her behind wiggle with effort

"Put your hand down," he whispered, "please." Would she say something utterly silly before this whole crowd?

She ignored him. Or perhaps didn't hear.

Miss Lillaberro nodded in their direction. "Yes. Way up near the top of the bleachers, there. The lady in the aqua hat."

A few heads turned curiously toward the aqua hat. Alma cleared her throat. Hamp saw that her hands were shaking.

"Isn't she brave?" whispered his neighbor.

"I — " started Alma, but her throat grew thick and she had to stop. She cleared her throat, began again. "I have a son, Miss Lillaberro . . . " Her voice faded.

Oh God. What next? One year of marriage was not enough . . . he knew too little to predict.

"Yes?" Candace Lillaberro nodded encouragingly.

"I — " Again she cleared her throat, rested a second, tried to speak. "He has been trying for almost two years to get an audition, Miss Lillaberro. He is very well prepared."

Hamp saw Corinne turn and look up at this unbelievable mother. Did she spot him at her side?

"Yes, I'm sure he is," said the star, smiling at those close by. Everyone understands a mother's love.

Hamp had the sudden powerful sense of a cosmic complicity, a female plot which left him forever on the outside.

"And I wondered . . . you said you're putting all your efforts now into helping young people who want a musical career. That it made a difference in your life to have some experienced singers take an interest in you. I wondered — "

Her voice faded again. The gym had grown very still, people near them looking away, straight ahead, anywhere but at Alma Spitsky in her beige spring suit doing the unthinkable. Before two thousand people! Where would a mother stop?

"What should he do to get an audition? How would you advise me?"

Candace Lillaberro surveyed the crowd. Eyes were on her, the weight of them. She had proclaimed her dedication to the cause. Here was a mother. She was herself a mother. In her talk she'd made much of that.

"Where is your son now?" she asked.

"He's studying in New York."

Ah. No way out. Not even the whole wide country to cross.

Hamp wished he had the binoculars so he could study the dark eyes and round obliging face. Despite his anxiety (he did not want Alma shamed), he relished the vision of fatuousness punctured.

"Well, then," said Candace Lillaberro gamely, "the next time you are in touch with your son" — Bobby of the dirty socks and cigarettes — "you could suggest that he call me in New York. Perhaps I can help him arrange for an audition."

Hamp felt the breath leaving his wife. She was spent. She murmured a thank you and sat down. Limp. She took his hand. Her palm was damp. While she squeezed his fingers, she kept her other hand on her lap in a tight fist. He wanted to hug her, hold her tight, protect her. From what? Some danger out there, something hidden, ominous, all encompassing — from which, in fact, she seemed already to have escaped. Or perhaps she was immune.

People near them began to stir. The woman beside him unfolded her pink coat and shook out the sleeves.

"Thank you one and all," smiled the unflappable Candace as the president came forward to capture her. "You've been a wonderful audience."

Applause. Smiles. More applause. Nods. Murmured thank yous.

It was over.

People stood, stretched, began to put on coats, talk. The doors at the far end of the gym were opened onto the cool damp Oregon night.

The president and his guest began to descend the stairs, stopping here and there to greet someone, shake a hand, sign a program. And then the yellow dress vanished, a lifetime of warble swallowed by fans.

"I'll write Bobby tonight," said Alma, taking his arm. "Or maybe I'll call him." Her cheeks were flushed, her eyes bright.

They began their descent toward the floor.

❦

The long lovely neck with the earring had disappeared. Everyone was pushing forward. The briefly illumined dream of footlights and fame had already dwindled to a wisp of memory, a mere passing puff before the immediate challenge of finding the car. Getting out of here. Programs littered the floor, crumpled and stepped on. Against the bright yellow light above the approaching doorway, dozens of tiny bugs circled. Beyond that — silver drizzle.

Perhaps John and Marilyn would stop over for a drink.

Alma's happiness hugged his arm, connubial. He felt its contour, its weight, strangely comforting and firm, an elbow against the side, grazing his ribs.

They would go out there, into the night, through life, survive. Neither ignorance nor innocence would undo them. Given the moment, something else entirely could emerge. He felt it. He knew.

People brushed by them murmuring "Excuse me." The occasional one studied her discreetly — her velour cloche, her light coat, the ordinariness of her cheerful, unlined face. The woman with courage. Gutsy.

Yes, he longed to say to bold surveying eyes. My wife. Of one year. She's quite something. Don't be fooled. There's more here than a pretty face. Believe me, she can be a tiger.

But obviously they already knew.

About Billy

I'M EIGHTEEN YEARS OLD and still a virgin. The virgin part doesn't bother me, except that by the time she was my age my mother had already started on one of my four daddies.

She'd had at least one, maybe two. I'm not sure, because she's funny about telling her age. One, for sure. Earl. That's where I came from. "Earl got in too early," she used to say when she'd had a few too many or was stoned.

My real daddy is Billy. He's the one I think of when I want to talk over a problem. Trouble is, Billy's hundreds of miles from here and by the time I write him a letter and wait for an answer the problem's shifted or been solved. I wouldn't dare use the phone in this place. Kevin's weird, and as soon as I finish high school this June, I'm leaving. I've already told Jeanine. She says okay, she'll help me all she can. She's getting real worn down now with his two kids. They're a pain, nine and twelve. Girls. I find it hard to believe I was ever like that. She tells me I sure was, sometimes.

One of these days, maybe next summer, I'm going to talk to Billy about this virgin business.

It's on my mind now because last year my closest friend, Renée, got pregnant. She skipped taking the pill. So she had an abortion. She claims it wasn't too bad and she's going to finish high school this year on time and everything, but I don't like to think of it — maybe because I figure my mom could of done the same thing and then where would I be? Still, if I'd been in Renée's place I might of done it, too. So I'm gonna be careful.

Besides, the big problem in my life has not been finding a man to make me a mommy. It's been putting together all my daddies.

My first daddy, my real one if you want to look at it that way, was, as I said, Earl. I never knew Earl till I was twelve, in seventh grade. By that time I had other things on my mind. That was the year I got my period and the cramps were awful. Charlie Coopersby, a tough kid in eighth grade, was starting to look at me funny and it made me nervous. Jeanine wasn't paying much attention to me those days. She was on her third, depending on how much you know and how you count. It went this way, so Billy tells me . . .

Jeanine had me out of wedlock. That's the old-fashioned term. Actually, Renée tells me her mother had her that way, too. But she's from California. They've different attitudes there. I was from the Northwest. Know what Oregonians say about Californians? *Don't Californicate Oregon.* I've seen it on bumper stickers, and I know what they mean. Anyhow, Jeanine had been raised Catholic, so she was in big trouble. Left home. That was that.

They tell me I was healthy. We lived, Jeanine and Earl and me, in a tiny duplex just outside Boise, Idaho, near enough to the sugar beet refinery that when the wind blew wrong you were nearly gassed. So Jeanine would tell me later, after we moved north. I can't remember much about the house, but I think I remember that smell. And one other thing, this picture of me as a toddler. It stood on Jeanine's dresser. Me in a bonnet and swimming trunks, bare top, looking fat and happy. It was in a white plastic frame shaped like a heart. She said Earl bought it for her, and she kept it long after he was gone. Near as I can figure out, he left her just after I came along. "Wasn't made to be a father" is how she put it. She never seemed bitter, that's what used to get me. As if it didn't make any difference to her at all.

Maybe that's because she already had the Nerd. This one married her. Next to the picture of me in the heart frame stood this other picture (she put it in her top drawer after she married Billy, but I still remember it) of Jeanine with this little man, he looked about a foot shorter than her, and he had round glasses. His hair grew thick and straight and in the picture his ears looked low, as if they'd slipped. But what I remember most is the expression on her face. She looked . . . how would you say it? Gloating, sort of. The look that goes with "I told you so."

It didn't last long. Under a year. That's what Billy told me. "Nerd was a turd," he said. She could do better.

So — I don't know just when, maybe I was two — she moved in with Billy.

Now I want to tell you about Billy.

He's not good looking and he's not flashy. He's something Jeanine will never be, though. He's cheerful. And when you're with him, it's hard to get too discouraged. I don't know how he does it. Maybe it's that he's seen so much. He's been a social worker for years, specializing in helping the unemployed. He's got more stories about bums on the dole than you'd need to hear in a lifetime.

So Jeanine moved in with Billy, and when he was transferred north she went with him.

Moscow, Idaho, is not a big town, twenty thouand maybe, not counting university students. It sits in the middle of what they call Palouse country. Hard to describe . . . rolling treeless hills, spare in winter, snow-covered tops and fields of green winter wheat, then when spring comes and plowing starts, ridges of deep brown earth make patterns all over those hills. It's beautiful. Anyhow, Billy and Jeanine moved there and that's the place I remember best. A small town. Friendly. When I came here to Carmel, the girls were stuck-up and the guys wanted only one thing. I'm not about to give it.

Billy taught for the state, part time. Jeanine, she's always had ambition, I'll say that. It's hard to put together the pieces of her life. Sometime or other, in between or during Earl and me and the Nerd and Billy, she got a degree in nutrition and went on full time at the hospital. Doing diets for patients, a big job.

She was out every day, so Billy took care of me — taught me how to ride a bike, roller skate, handle a bat and ball, all the rest of it. I never stopped to think I was the only kid on the block that had a daddy when all the rest had mommies. Though he wasn't my daddy, technically, and we were open about that. We'd talk about it now and then.

"Tell me about Earl," I'd say.

"Earl was not a pearl," he'd say. "Earl had a girl who was a pearl."

"Tell me more."

"Earl went away from the girl too early to see how pearly she was, and curly."

He loved my dark curls. Billy's dark, with a black beard. He does a great imitation of King Kong. I pretended to be scared long after I'd really stopped.

I did okay in school. On my reports and all I always put Billy as my dad. Mr. William Hammer. And nobody ever asked about why his name was different from mine. Math was my best subject and Billy liked that. A math whiz himself, he'd play math games with me on the way to the pool or Brownies or wherever I was going after school that year. "If five men can hoe three rows in half an hour, how long will it take three men to hoe seven rows?" I'd stare at the cracks in the sidewalk, counting, figuring. "Ho, ho, ho," he'd say, urging me on. After a while, I got less scared of those problems.

When I finally got my period, in seventh grade, I was relieved After fifth grade the girls all kept tabs on each other. Jeanine was away a lot in those days. Whether she was with someone else, I'm not sure. She'd always be home for breakfast. Anyhow, Billy helped me out. He was calm about it. "You're a woman now, Grace," he said. "An achievement. Don't take it lightly." To that he added, "Babies are hostages to fortune." I didn't have a clue.

Then, at the end of seventh grade, Jeanine announced she was moving out.

I was upset. Who would I live with? I wanted to stay with Billy, but I knew there'd be a problem. In those days, children went with their mothers. Jeanine was staying in Moscow, moving to a different neighborhood. No explanations given — just like that.

So I had to go with her.

I'd already seen plenty of Kevin the Weirdo and hoped he'd limit his visiting hours. How a woman so smart could be so dumb baffled me.

Billy, he stayed on in the same house, and he'd come round two or three times a week. We were in a two-bedroom apartment up over the Army Navy Store on Main Street. His regular day was Tuesday. I was going out for gymnastics and he took me there, waited at the Y through the workout, then walked home with me.

Then, in September of eighth grade, the letter came.

I didn't know what to do. Didn't say much when Jeanine handed it to me. I waited till Tuesday, Billy's day.

After we left the gym I asked if we could walk the long way home.

That meant an extra twenty minutes and, if I was lucky, an ice cream at Baskin Robbins.

Billy looked at me. "Sure," he said.

I had the letter in my pocket. Jeanine had given it to me with barely a word. "This is from your father."

At first I thought she meant Billy. I took the plain white envelope with her name typed on the front and wondered why Billy would be writing her a letter. Then, when I opened it, I saw it was from Earl.

"I've had a letter from Earl," I said to Billy.

He was quiet. I think now he was trying to hear what was bothering me, didn't want to respond too soon. He'd had all those years of training as a social worker.

"What's he say?"

"He says if I'd like to meet him, he'd like to meet me."

Billy said nothing. It was almost five o'clock and the shops were getting out. Cars raced by us on Sixth Street and I was grateful for noise. I felt anxious, uncertain what to say next. Billy was offering nothing.

Finally, "Want some ice cream?" he asked.

I nodded. We walked the rest of the way in silence.

Over a double scoop of rum raisin, he looked directly at me. "This bothers you, right?"

I nodded. I hadn't expected to feel this tongue-tied, with Billy of all people.

"Why?"

We were sitting outside at a round cement table. I worked my tongue around the dripping ice cream, it was a warm day, and tried to think why I felt so anxious about the whole thing. Who was Earl? Why should I want to see him? What was he to me? A sperm of his, one of those wiggly little microscopic tadpoley things they show you magnified a million times in sixth grade sex education, had found its way inside Jeanine and produced me. I was clear on all that, but what had he to do with me, really? Here was Billy. Even though he no longer lived with us, he was always around. *He* was my father.

"Because . . ." The truth was I was dying to meet Earl.

"Because you're afraid I'll mind?"

"What if I like him better than you?" There, it was out. It made no sense. Earl had deserted my mother and me.

Billy licked carefully, then wiped his dark beard and mustache with a small napkin.

"Not to worry, child," he said. Ordinarily I'd have resented the "child," but that day it felt good to hear. "There's room in your heart to love more than one daddy, isn't there?"

It did seem to make sense. After all, look at Jeanine. But daddies were somehow different.

So I said yes. And wrote the letter back to Earl.

❖

A week later I met him. We had agreed to meet at the mall. I could walk there from our apartment, and it would be easy for me to disappear if I changed my mind at the last minute. Jeanine wanted nothing to do with him. And Billy obviously shouldn't be anywhere around. He called me the night before, though, to wish me luck.

When I think about Billy now, it surprises me how much he knew right along. Like where Earl lived. Billy knew it was just over in Pullman, that Earl was married and had a family. Now how did he know all this? Jeanine never told me a thing, just "Earl got in early" — and left early, too. For all I'd known, he was already six feet under.

I wasn't prepared to like him. I was pushing thirteen, as I said. And here was this guy, he couldn't of been more than thirty, thirty-one, waiting for me outside J.C. Penney, across from the Orange Julius, standing there staring at a display of fall sports clothes, sweatshirts, and jeans, trying to look nonchalant. I stood a few stores away for a while, near the theater, just trying to decide if it was him. Finally I got up my nerve and approached. He had on jeans and Nikes and a long-sleeved polo shirt. I'd talked to him once on the phone, just to say I'd be there, and he said he was blond with short hair and a mustache. When this guy turned around, I saw he had short blond hair and a mustache. I nearly puked.

We went across the way and had an Orange Julius, or tried to. He fidgeted, dropped his change. I kept seeing that gurgling orange juice behind his head. I didn't want to get into something I couldn't get out of. Was this a one-shot deal or did he really want to know me?

"Grace," he said, after he'd paid and picked up the change from Simsy, the fellow behind the counter. Everyone in town knew Simsy.

He'd dropped out of high school and picked up odd jobs around. He had that kind of personality people remember, bouncy. He must have wondered where I'd found this good-looking older man. For Earl was better looking than Billy, or Kevin the Weirdo. He had a smooth face, no lines, clear blue eyes, light blue like water, and his mustache grew thick and blond. He had a square jaw, and when he talked he used his hands a lot. His smile was great. He didn't show it much that first day.

"I'm glad you wanted to meet me," he said, stirring his Julius with an orange plastic stirrer. He bit his nails. It didn't go with the rest of him. His hands were clean, so I figured he must have some office job. Then he lit a cigarette. Billy doesn't smoke. Jeanine does now and then, mostly grass. Later I learned that Earl only smokes when he's nervous. "I've thought about you a lot, Grace," he said. "I don't want you to think — "

I knew what he was going to say. *I don't want you to think that because I walked out on your mother and you I didn't care.*

He revved up for it and that's exactly what he did say. Forgiveness, that's what he wanted. I decided to give him the benefit of the doubt. After all, maybe I'd been better off with Billy than I would've been with him. I let him know I didn't want to discuss the past. Not then, anyhow, sitting in the corner of the Orange Julius, with Simsy watching us.

So he told me about his family.

"I've got three kids," he said, "all younger than you. Clara's the closest to you. She's ten, in fifth grade. What grade are you in?"

When I told him, he was impressed.

"Then there's Jake, he's five and motorized, never stops. And the baby Eleanore, with an e."

It wasn't as bad as I expected. He was no monster. Not a weirdo, either. Just an ordinary dude. I was glad I'd met him. He conveyed that he'd got thinking it might matter to me. At the end of the visit (maybe it was half an hour, all told) we agreed to meet again.

Jeanine didn't ask one question. She was busy those days. A whole new kitchen was going in at the hospital, and besides, she had her new man. He kept her occupied off-hours.

I saw Billy that night. We went for a long walk over toward the mountain, past all those low row houses they were building. It was beautiful, I remember it well, that time of evening when the sky grows dusky pink and it gets hard to catch a ball. I was worried about Billy's reaction.

"Well?" he said, as we pushed up Sixth Street and went toward the outskirts of town. "How'd it go?"

Openness. That's what I like about Billy. I knew if I said I'd rather not talk about it, he would have respected that. On the other hand, he wanted to give me the chance.

"He was kinda neat," I said. "Not at all what I expected. I thought he'd suck."

Billy laughed. "Maybe he's been wanting to get in touch with you for years and waited till he thought you were old enough. He has a family, doesn't he?"

"Yes. And I'm gonna meet them. And they're gonna know who I am." I thought that was the most important part.

My friend Renée hasn't been so lucky. She found out last year that her little brother was the product of artificial insemination. Doesn't even know who his daddy is and never will. He's only two now, but someday he'll wonder. She found the record in her mother's top drawer beneath her jewel case. Now she doesn't know what to do. Would it do her brother any good to know? Especially since he can never find out who the guy was. Meanwhile, her mother treats it like a non-question.

So I was glad to have Billy listen. He was having his own troubles then, I knew. His teaching job was over and he had no relief from the social work. Still, he was pretty cheerful. I didn't know how he felt about Jeanine. I'd never been able to fathom that.

"I'm going over to Earl's next week, on Monday," I said.

Billy let on he was glad and would listen more, if I wanted.

⚘

So that's how I came to know Earl and Earl's family.

They lived in a big ramshackle house just outside Pullman where you could see hills for miles around and at night the lights of Moscow. They lived at the top of the hill. To get there that first day Billy had to put the car in first and climb. He'd talked to Earl on the phone and they worked it out that Billy would bring me and pick me up. They'd never met, but somehow Billy knew about Earl. Maybe because of his social work. It's a small community and Billy knew all the people who were on the skids.

Not that Earl was. I saw that the moment I arrived. Not rich, maybe, but it was clear Earl and his wife May and their three kids had more than we did. Seemed to me Jake had every electronic toy going. You could hardly peel him off the computer, a real whiz. As for Clara — ten and already sneaking on the eye shadow. Fifth grade! It took us a while that day to get acquainted, sniffing each other like dogs, and I was sorry at first that I'd said I'd stay for supper. But May said she'd make us waffles and at that all the kids perked up.

May was a surprise. She was a dumpling. Now one thing about Jeanine: she never gains weight. I've seen her stuff herself at Dunkin' Donuts, four glazed numbers at one sitting, and she doesn't put on an ounce. When she's not at work she can wear those tight jeans and look good. Not me. But May, you would've thought *she* was my mom. She bulged all over, a regular roly-poly mommy, and good natured. When she smiled she had dimples, deep ones, and when she laughed it was like someone had turned on a giggle faucet and left it running. I never knew anyone so giggly. The kids all seemed happy. Course, that's never true. It was clear that Clara knew in some dim way that I was her half sister. We didn't make much of that. I played with her a while, but she was into Barbie and Ken, and I hate that stuff. On the whole, the visit went amazingly well. When I left that night, the baby cried.

After that I got to go there at least once every couple of weeks. We became friends, especially May and me. I liked her even better than Earl, and I could see why he'd like her. Nothing ever seemed to get May down. When the baby would drool all over the carpet it was like nothing to her. She'd say, "Don't worry. It'll wash out." If the laundry was piled high, she just took it in stride. Not that she didn't keep house. She did, a lot better than Jeanine. That's one thing I used to hear Jeanine and Billy fight about a lot: why wasn't anything done. No dishes washed up. No laundry folded. Always running out of socks. Maybe that's why Billy hung around so much — besides for me, I mean. I remember him at the stove more than I remember her. But May, that was another story. She'd made a nest around Earl and he loved it. And I loved going there.

Only one thing I remember clearly about that first night. When we went to the table (it was at one end of the kitchen, a big square table with a green plastic cover) and May was just about to serve up waffles, she said: "Now, Grace, where would you like to sit?" No one had ever asked me that before. At home we just grabbed a bite and sat in front of the TV. This was different. I got to pick, and I picked to sit next to Earl. After all, he was my father. Though he didn't feel like it. And I was already dying to tell Billy every last detail about the evening: how the baby was getting spoiled, how Clara was too old for her age, how Jake was a whiz with computers, how they seemed not at all what I'd expected, but . . . happy.

That's why I liked to go there.

꙼

We stayed in Moscow four more years.

I got used to Earl. He never moved in real close, but I began to see the truth of what Billy had tried to tell me. There was room in my heart for more than one daddy. And I liked the new one I'd found. I was missing Billy a bit those years, though. He'd had to take on a heavier caseload once the teaching stopped, and Jeanine was seeing a lot of this Kevin dude. I didn't like Kevin. He just didn't seem good enough for her. As far as I could tell, he didn't have a steady job. Did something in the health food co-op. He'd come waltzing in at meal-time, park himself in the living room in front of the TV, and roll himself a joint. By then I was getting most of the meals. If Billy knew Kevin was around, he'd steer clear. But he never interfered. Jeanine had told him "Hands Off" and he stuck to it. I don't know anything about Billy's love life. Odd, now that I think of it, he knows so much about me.

One day, when I was thirteen, Billy took me out to a movie and afterward we went to the A&W to get a teenburger. As I was munching, he said to me all of a sudden, "Well, Gracie, you've seen Earl and survived that. How'd you like to see the other guy who was your father?"

"You mean the Nerd?"

That's what we'd always called him. The Nerd. As I said, Billy had come along when I was around two. Between Earl and Billy I knew there'd been someone else. The Nerd. He'd adopted me, even, as part of Jeanine. But when he sashayed off, we'd never heard from him again. I thought a little about him — it's no fun having a hole in your sense of history — but I hadn't a clue where or who he was, except for the picture of the man with low ears.

I looked at Billy. He was getting gray around the temples. His beard, right down the middle, showed a streak of white. "Papa Skunk," I'd tease him. I wasn't sure he really liked it, but he was a good sport.

"You mean he's around here?"

"It'd mean a trip, but maybe it matters to you to have the whole picture?"

Billy was always worrying about that with me. I knew it. It's because he's seen these kids who haven't a clue where they've come from, never mind where they're going. Take Renée, for instance. She knows who her father was, his last name at least, but doesn't know where he is now. And her little brother . . . but her mom doesn't think this is important, as I said. Once, Renée tried to ask her something about it, but her mom shut her up, just like that. "Pig," she said. Renée knew she meant her father.

Billy has bright green eyes. They're striking. I've never seen eyes just like them, and they're fringed with dark lashes. His heavy black eyebrows almost grow together over his nose. He's not exactly handsome, but I can see why someone would go for him. For a long time after Jeanine, as far as I know, no one did. Things have changed now. He's got a girl . . .

"It might bother you when you're older if you don't know us all," Billy grinned, wiping mayo from his beard.

I wasn't sure I wanted to take it on. Two seemed enough. Did I want to go for a third, really?

I thought about it for a couple of weeks. Here was my chance. I might never have it again. What if Jeanine really shacked up with this dude Kevin? We'd probably move. I knew Kevin had kids, but I never imagined Jeanine and me saddled with them. Even so, I was beginning to suspect we wouldn't be around northern Idaho forever. This might be my one and only chance to see my third father. I'll never think of Kevin as a father — with his kinky hair, his earring, his silky shirts and high-heeled boots. Kevin scares me. So far, though, he's never touched me.

So I finally told Billy, "Yes. I think I'd better. But I don't want to go alone."

35

I'd survived Earl. Somehow I'd had the courage for that. My instincts had told me if a guy tried to make contact with his lost daughter twelve years later and put no pressure on her, he couldn't be all bad. And I'd been right.

The Nerd was a different matter. I'd never heard his real name, even. I certainly had no recollection of him. He'd been just a presence when I was in diapers. Who knows? Maybe he'd even changed them. Far as I could make out, he hadn't been with Jeanine longer than eleven or twelve months. As for what happened between them, I haven't a clue.

"Don't worry," said Billy. I could tell he thought I was doing the right thing, but he'd never have forced me. "I'll stay with you. We'll make the trip together."

-⊰⊱-

The little trip was back to southern Idaho, Boise, in fact. To the big Sears store there.

"How'd you know where he was?" I asked Billy as we sat in the dinky Pullman airport waiting for our flight. We had to fly. It's a ten-hour drive through mountains and this was early December. A storm could blow up any time.

"I keep tabs for you," he said. "I've known right along but waited till the right moment."

"They call these things 'flying cigars,'" he told me as we bent over to climb into the small plane. It was eight in the morning and the plane was full. We sat opposite each other, one on each side of the narrow aisle, and didn't talk much the whole way. We were flying back that night. Billy didn't seem to think I'd want to stay longer than the day, and besides, he'd taken me out of school.

The flight down was bumpy and I felt kind of green by the time we hit Boise airport. He rented a car there and drove into town, parked it, and we walked around. I wasn't prepared to take much in except the big capitol building, some restaurants, and the mountains all around the outside of town. A different look from Moscow: these hills were higher, pointed, more rugged. The sky above them that morning was shining blue.

"Tell me whenever you're ready," Billy said as we walked around.

"I'll take you there. You don't even have to say hello if you don't want to. But at least your curiosity will have been satisfied."

The truth was I'd never had much curiosity about the Nerd. About Earl, yes. After all, he was my blood daddy. And Billy . . . well, Billy's always been around, it seems to me, except until we moved here to California last year. Now he's too far away.

So we went to this little Italian restaurant and I tried to slip noodles down my throat. Hopeless. The most I could stomach was garlic bread. I still wasn't sure I wanted to go through with it.

I made a trip to the ladies' room, checked myself in the mirror, and decided: yes, I would do it. As soon as we finished lunch. That way, if something awful happened, we'd have the afternoon to walk around, maybe take in a movie or something.

"Okay," I said when I came out.

I'd worn my usual: jeans and a sweater. I love sweaters and there's this neat shop in Moscow that sells them cheap — and unusual. This one had a nubby weave and lots of colors. You could see me coming: red, green, yellow, and a blue background.

"It's not far," he said.

We set out down the street.

⊶⊷

The minute we got inside Sears I was overwhelmed by the smell of perfume, lotion, powder. It smelled like the bathroom just before Jeanine would go out at night.

"You wait here and sniff," said Billy. Without another word, he took off.

I figured he was checking out the location of the Nerd.

I stood there at the makeup counter fiddling with eye shadows and eyeliners. People tell me I have good eyes. Jeanine's the one showed me what to do with them. "It's amazing how people let good eyes go to waste," she told me. So it's the one thing I try to keep special. Your eyes don't change, like your weight does. I keep on just enough eyeliner and shadow to make them glow. They're blue-green, a deep color, and my lashes are dark. It's a good combination. You'd think I got it from Billy.

Here he was, coming back, his face calm and careful like he was holding in a big worry and didn't want me to catch it. That was hope-less. I had this wormy feeling in the pit of my stomach. Did I really want to do it? Why had Billy even suggested it? Wouldn't I have been better off to go on in ignorance? But what if someday . . .

"He's over on the men's side," said Billy. "Come on. I'll show you."

I followed his quick determined step down the aisles between Christmas bells and tinsel, miniature fake evergreens all decorated, brightly colored umbrellas all opened up like rainbows.

Then we left bright colors behind and moved into dark blues and browns, the men's side. He headed toward a deserted counter, men's wallets. Here, he stopped and stood by the glass case.

I stood alongside him. "He's here?"

"No. Just listen. If you look past me to my left, two counters down, you'll see a guy selling shirts. That's the Nerd. Just look, for the mo-ment. Maybe that's all you want to do. Remember, he doesn't really have anything to do with your life."

Maybe he had changed my diapers.

I spotted him, this guy half turned away, showing a customer a bright green shirt. Then he turned back to fold up the shirt again and I got a good look. I recognized the ears. He had a long neck, wire-rimmed glasses. The Nerd. His shirtsleeves looked too short. I could see his wrists. That was all I took in.

Nothing.

I felt nothing. Just a bit wormy. But this wasn't enough.

"Want to meet him or not?" asked Billy, studying brown leather wallets inside the glass case.

A man appeared behind the counter. "Can I help you, sir?"

"No. No, thanks," said Billy smoothly. "Just looking for a mo-ment."

The man disappeared around the other side of the counter.

"I'll meet him if you come with me," I whispered.

"So who'd you think is gonna introduce you?" said Billy, looking at me with those eyes of his. "C'mon."

We sauntered down toward the next counter, stalled there while the customer turned away.

The Nerd leaned over to straighten the shirts in the glass case.

Billy went ahead of me.

"Hi, Drake," he said.

Drake!

The Nerd looked up, stared a moment at Billy. Then, as if this might be a former customer, "Well, hi there . . ."

"I'm William Hammer, remember? Met you years ago. Here in Boise."

"William . . ." He looked puzzled.

"I lived with Jeanine. Remember now?"

The Nerd slammed the glass door shut and set his hands on top of the counter, pale hands, with a ring on the pinkie that could have been a diamond. I was standing behind Billy.

"Yes. Yes, certainly . . . you wanted?"

His voice was too high. His lips twitched, thin lips, nothing like Billy's full, funny mouth opened half the time, laughing or talking. Billy is what they call gregarious.

"I've brought someone to meet you. You must remember Grace."

He looked blank. Positively blank. Now it's something to see one of your daddies look nervous, like Earl had, or wanting the best for you but holding back, like Billy, or even wishing he could kick you out, like Kevin. But this guy looked like someone took the fifth grade eraser and rubbed out the blackboard in his head. Permanently. Nothing. Zilch. Zero.

"Grace is Jeanine's little girl. Only, as you can see, she's no longer little."

He looked at me. That is to say, half looked. Eyes still erased. My God, how did she stand him eleven months, or whatever it was? It was like being looked at by a zombie. An ice cube. How could this guy ever sell a shirt?

"Grace, this is Drake."

"How do you do." Idiotic. But I couldn't think of anything else to say. Did you change my diapers? Why'd you walk out? Whatcha been doing with yourself, big boy? How are you, Nerd?

He didn't put out his hand. He didn't do a damned thing. "So . . . Grace."

He said it as if he were saying, So . . . this is another shirt I could show you. Did you care for stripes?

Only with less interest than that.

I wanted out.

I pushed Billy's elbow. He got my signal. He always does.

That's why I want to write to him this summer. He'll have something to say to me about this virgin business. It's really on my mind. Who wants to get stuck with a Nerd? Or salt something out that could grow up to be a knockout like me? I don't trust the Pill. Why should I fool around with my body chemistry just so I can give up being a virgin?

Billy took me by the arm. "Bye now, Drake. Good luck with the shirts."

We turned and headed out. Just like that.

God, he was the definition of a Nerd. I never even knew what the word meant until Billy brought me a full-page ad from some magazine one day. He loves to make fun of himself.

"Look, Grace," he said. "Wanna see what I was like when I was your age?"

There was this picture of the Nerd: a boy in flat oxfords, glasses, hair plastered down, slide rule in his pocket, pencils sticking out of another pocket, briefcase in his hand. It sucked.

I laughed. Because I knew Billy never looked like that at all. He was tall and dark and probably started to shave early. He laughed easily and probably fooled around a lot in school. He was smart, though. And a good listener. The girls liked him. And some of the teachers. He wasn't sly. That was the thing about him. If he was gonna do something bad, you'd know it. Not that he'd flaunt it, but he wasn't sly. You always knew where you stood with him. He had a good sense of humor and liked a joke, but he didn't play them on people. He tried not to hurt feelings. If he did, he knew how to apologize. He wasn't your perfect student, but people liked him. And he knew how to take care of himself.

If I could find someone like that, this virgin business wouldn't be such a problem. It might even seem a good thing to give it up. I'm still looking. When I hear Renée and the others talking about it in a panic, worrying they'll end up single if they don't want to be, or double if they don't want to be, I think about Billy and tell myself to calm down.

There's still lots of time.

Getting the Picture

I SHOULD HAVE EXPECTED IT. By the time I'd hung up their raincoats and set newspapers on the closet floor, the two of them had already grabbed the best seats in the living room. Milly had sunk into her favorite — the wing chair with the Rose of Sharon slipcovers. She wouldn't last long, I knew. Put her in front of the TV these days and in ten minutes she's out cold. Alice, all decked out in her gold jewelry for the occasion, had pulled the Hitchcock chair over closer to the set and was fiddling with the knobs.

The minute I came in, she pushed back.

"Here, Edith," she said. "You take over. Reception's poor." She moved her chair back a couple of feet and made room for me to pull over the needlepoint footstool. "Pity you don't have one of those gadgets you can operate from a distance. Helen gave me one last Christmas."

I pretended not to hear.

"Yes, but do they really work?" asked Milly. "I was at Mabel Sullivan's for bridge the other day and afterward we tried to tune in the five o'clock news. Can you turn it up a little, Edith?"

She had left her hearing aid home again: predictable. So I pretended to turn it up and went on trying to focus. This was my day and they knew it. Nothing was going to spoil it, if I could just get the picture.

"It's almost time," said Alice

She started that gentle foot tapping she does when she's impatient. But I couldn't get the darn thing right. Squiggles and lines — just blurred images — then collapse. I could feel her beginning to sizzle.

Suddenly, it worked. "There!" A picture: clear, focussed. I pushed back to enjoy, praying we wouldn't miss him. How could I be sure he'd even show? It wasn't as if the cameras were interested in Tim.

"Milly!" Alice shook Milly's knee. "Don't go to sleep yet! It's too early! Come on! It's about to start!"

"Uh. Uh. Oh, what? *Oh!*" Milly opened her eyes, blinked a bit, and picked up her glasses from her lap. "Oh, Edith! What a day! What a day! Isn't it grand we can all be together for it?"

Together, I'm thinking, *when three seconds ago you were out cold.* Sometimes a heart of gold is hard to take.

Then the motorcade started to edge onto the screen. And there was that great athletic-looking figure all in white poked through the top of the limousine.

"Isn't he wonderful?" breathed Milly.

"Did you see him in Chicago?" asked Alice.

"Missed it. Novena night. I'm making it for little Carol. Rita's so worried about whether to keep her in first grade . . ."

"Tim said he'd be right next to the Pope when he goes up on the platform for Mass," I told them. That shut them up.

I *had* to butt in. On a day like this, who cared about "little Carol"? Milly never knows when to stop. Acute grandmother-itis: she bends the ear of poor Father Scanlon so hard it's a wonder it hasn't fallen off.

Then the three of us were watching all those fluttering white surplices, trying to find *the one.* A regular sea of priests. In the background you could see the dome of the Capitol. Every now and then the camera focussed in on a few faces in the crowd. They looked cold. A bitter day for October in Washington.

I was glad right then I hadn't gone, even though he urged me to. What would I have done out there all alone? Frozen, for one thing, and probably missed him completely. Then come home and heard from Milly and Alice what a great view they'd had. This way, I figured, we'd all see the same thing. And I'd have my comfort.

The Pope's robes billowed as he walked around the platform blessing everyone. I don't have color, so you couldn't get the full effect, but at least the picture was clear.

Then the two of them started talking about his performance in Madison Square Garden.

"Imagine giving the Pope a T-shirt!" said Alice.

"I think it's marvelous, in this day and age, that young people can relate to him," said Milly.

Then I spotted him.

"Look!" My finger hit the screen I was so excited, trying to show them exactly where. At least I *thought* it was Tim — about his size, same shape head. "He's right where he said he'd be!"

Well, then Alice really *was* impressed. She poked Milly's knee.

"Edith's right, Milly. Look, off to the right there. Tim!"

The Pope was center screen. He just kept moving about that platform, raising his arms, blessing everyone. I couldn't help thinking how tired he must be — traveling all around the country, no time out for jet lag. Why, when Tim flew me over to Rome for his degree it took me a week to get over it. By then it was time to come home. We had fun just the same, visiting all those churches and eating out. And he's so fluent — he'd carry on and make jokes with the waitresses and all. The biggest thrill was the papal blessing at St. Peter's. Alice's been a lot of places, but I've that one up on her. Paul VI, of course. A cold potato compared to this one. But still a thrill.

"Want me to adjust the picture?" asked Alice.

We were getting a little snow.

"No, I'll just fiddle with it a bit," I said. If you let her, she'd run your life.

Every now and then, when the Pope's arm came down or the camera shifted, I saw Tim right behind him. I didn't want to lose him. I've had the set fifteen years and it takes pampering.

"Maybe if you adjust the light and dark," she suggested.

There. It was coming clearer.

"I expect Lily Jackson is watching," said Alice. "She stopped me at the hairdresser's on Friday and said she'd heard. She's retired now, you know. Seems impossible she had Helen and Tim in fifth grade."

The year Tim's average was higher than Helen's. Alice will never let me forget it. She still feels Lily favored the boys.

"Father Scanlon announced about Tim from the altar at the eleven this morning," said Milly. "Did you tell him, Edith?"

"I told him after the four-ten yesterday," I said. "He'd wanted to go down himself, he said, but he couldn't't."

"Why didn't *you* go down for it, Edith?"

43

The question I'd been waiting for. I knew they'd never understand.

"Tim asked me, way back, as soon as he learned he'd be helping the Pope."

And then the darn thing collapsed. All zigzags. No picture at all.

I twirled and coaxed, hoping I'd get him back before Mass started. After that, the cameras would want only the Pope.

I knew they wondered why I didn't go. Even Tim did in the beginning. But when I told him I'd rather watch it from my own living room with the girls he grinned and said, "Okay, Mom. I get you. Have one on me, you and the girls."

I didn't let on even to him how leery I am of crowds lately. Even in the crowd watching the Pope you could get trampled. Just like the other day on the bus. It was awful. Jammed in like sardines. I could hardly hold onto the pole. And two teenagers sitting right there chewing their gum, radios glued to their ears. I had all I could do to reach the buzzer, then nearly fell getting off.

Suddenly I got it in focus again, just like that.

Milly had begun to snore quietly. The Pope was already into his homily. I couldn't spot Tim anywhere on the screen. Probably somewhere in that row of white behind the Pope, off to one side.

"Did Irene say where she'd be standing?" asked Alice.

I knew then what her mind was really on. Irene is our fourth at bridge, a terrible bidder.

"She didn't say, " I answered. "They got places fairly near the altar, I think. Chuck got the tickets through some old friend at Fordham."

"It pays to have connections," said Alice.

"It's the farthest from home she's been in years," I said, reminding her of what she already knew.

The Pope's script flapped in the wind as he sat there pronouncing into the microphone in that emphatic way of his — *fa-mi-lee . . . mar-ria-age . . . hu-man dig-ni-tee* — many of the same things we'd been hearing all week. Marvelous, really, how he can make himself understood. They say he has a gift for languages. Just like Tim. How well I remember his first word at fourteen months as he was watching me from his playpen in the corner of the kitchen. I was snipping fresh beans. "See-zores," he said suddenly, pointing. "See-zores." The kitchen scissors were by my hand. I knew right then he'd be a verbal child.

While the Pope is talking, Alice starts in on her youngest grand-daughter, Louise, a freshman at college this year.

"Really, Edith, you wouldn't believe what they take for granted these days. Louise actually told her mother she thought she'd live off campus, move in with her boyfriend next year. Can you imagine?"

Yes, I can imagine. What do they think I am? Just because I had only one son and he's a priest. As if he sailed in from heaven on a balloon. The way the three of them carry on you'd think there was nothing else in the world but grandchildren. But I've learned to tune out.

He's always been so good about coming home when he could, flying in over Christmas or during the summer, especially since Clyde went. Of course, it's different being an order priest. They don't seem to realize that, telling me I should let Tim know about every little ache and pain. It's not like being able to call up your daughter, just a few miles away. When you're in an order you can't just up and go home anytime you want.

When he first told me, all I could think was how far away he'd be. I mean, at least with a parish priest there's always the chance he'll be stationed near home. But in an order, I thought, he'll be away with his community all the time. I felt shut out.

But now I can see it's better, what with the upheaval in the Church in the past few years. He's safer.

Even Milly was glad to hear the Pope speak out on celibacy. She called me after the evening news Friday night. "Somebody had to do it," she said, "don't you agree, Edith?" I did. "And he's so masculine-looking. No one can say . . . well, you know." I did know. I felt the same way.

That's why I got so nervous when Tim called to say they were stationing him at Catholic University. What would he be exposed to?

"It's an *honor*, Mother," he said. "You should be pleased. It'll give you something to brag about to the girls. Besides, I'll be able to study with two of the greatest biblical scholars in America."

"But where will you live?"

"I'll find an apartment near campus." Then he laughed. "Come on, Mother. I'm a grown man. You don't have to worry. Maybe at last I'll learn how to fry an egg. You always said I wasn't very practical."

True enough. He wasn't very practical. Not very athletic, either. Not like this Pope, from the looks of him. But sensitive.

"Maybe you're raising a poet or a genius," Alice used to tease. "With a father as ambitious as Clyde, he's bound to go somewhere. And Helen says there's no getting ahead of him in school."

I knew what was in her mind. And they did date a bit. I never told her I knew it was futile. His mind was made up.

We would sit at the kitchen table those afternoons after school and talk about all sorts of things — his ambitions, his friends, his classes. Clyde was away so much. And when he first told me, all I could think and say was, "Wait. Wait until you're sure. You're only fourteen." But I promised to keep his secret. And I started a Rosary Novena for him right then. I knew how upset Clyde would be.

"How do you think they'll manage all those people?" asked Alice.

It was time for distribution of Holy Communion.

"There he is again!" I felt sure it was Tim, right at the head of the line of priests beginning to distribute. "I wonder if he's cold. The wind is up. I hope he has something heavy on underneath."

"Just like you, Edith," Alice laughed. "He's a grown man. Once a mother, always a mother."

"I haven't noticed *you* turning it off," I retorted. "Seems to me you're pretty concerned about Helen and Louise."

Then I felt bad. On a day like this. But you can't let all these things pass.

"Maybe Irene will receive from Tim," said Alice, conciliating.

I was thinking the same thing. I'd forgotten about his hands until the other night when he was having his last cup of tea before he left for Washington. Long slender fingers, like an artist.

"How did they happen to pick Tim, did you say?"

As if I hadn't told them all at least three times! Par for the course. It never sinks in. But let me forget one detail about Carol-the-problem-child or Milly's daughter-in-law out there in — is it Idaho? One of those western states. A thorn in Milly's side, though she'd never admit it. Just let me mention Tim, though, and they close up like clams. I can see it happening, the look in their eyes that says, *Here she goes again, the mother of the priest.*

46

"They wanted all the orders represented," I began to explain, "and he was right down there in Washington — "

"Wasn't there something about languages?"

Well, so she wasn't a total loss after all.

"Yes. You know he's always had a gift for languages, Al. Remember Dolores Cutsky, that great big Polish woman who used to clean for me way back when? He used to sit at the kitchen table with her when she finished vacuuming. 'Please, Mrs. Cutsky,' he'd say. 'Just a few more words? I've learned all the ones you gave me last week.' She was crazy about him. He couldn't have been more than nine or ten — "

"Look! Isn't that Tim — on the far right? What do you think, Edith? *You* ought to be able to tell!"

Her gold bracelets were jangling. She was terribly excited. But to tell the truth, *I didn't know.* Not that I admitted it. The walk certainly looked like his. He's getting heavy. It was hard to tell about the shape. The angle of the head . . . well, yes, it could have been.

"Wake up, Milly." Alice poked Milly again, then shook her knee, hard. "It's almost over."

"Shhh," I said. "Let her be. She'll wake up for the happy hour. She's already seen him once."

Milly let out a great snort and her head dropped back down on her chest.

"Sleeps like a baby," said Alice. "Wish I could." She turned back to the screen.

You have to feel for Milly, though. She may have Rita but she's lost her boys. And she knows it. One day she'd been going on about them and suddenly she stopped and looked at me. "You don't know how lucky you are," she said.

But I do. Isn't that what they're always rubbing in? How I still have him?

It's true, in a way. He comes in now and then overnight. He sits in the living room and notices what I've done to it since the last time he was home. The girls stop in to say hello and he chats with them about their grandchildren and changes in the Church. He sends me copies of his articles and books. His latest book was even reviewed in *The Catholic World.* Milly read the review. Every now and then Alice says

47

something like, "Isn't he gifted, Edith? He's always been so gifted. Helen used to think she'd like to write. Of course, she hasn't any time for it now."

I've been to the weddings of all their children and helped them get started on china and silver. We even sent sterling diaper pins for Helen's first, she and Tim were always such good friends. But Clyde and I had to go alone to the novitiate when Tim made his first vows. No gifts allowed. Then later, in the basilica . . . I never told them what it was really like at his ordination, though they asked. Next to me a man reeking of garlic, and on the other side a family of four whose toddlers crawled around under the pew the whole time. Meanwhile, my only son ordained a priest forever. And Clyde no longer even here to see it. I always felt he would have been reconciled.

"There he goes, Edith," said Alice.

They were getting ready for the final blessing. Such a clean-cut, masculine-looking Pope. I was floored when I heard he was Polish. But he doesn't seem a bit thick. Tim was pleased . . .

There he was, right beside the Pope, now, holding back that — what do you call that cape affair, anyhow? Looking so serious, so competent.

"Wake up, Milly," Alice fairly shouted. "Tim's leaving with the Pope. It's almost over. Wake up!"

Milly gave a deep shiver and opened her eyes. She blinked a few times, then stared hard at the screen.

"Why, Edith," she said. "He has such a marvelous bearing. To think that's Tim. Maybe someday he'll be a bishop. He certainly looks the part!" Then she straightened her glasses a bit.

I've told them at least three times his order doesn't permit it! But she was right. Even I could see that. He did carry himself magnificently. I kept quiet and watched. In a minute the picture would fade. He was moving around up there while the Pope raised his hand again for the blessing. He looked almost like someone else, like the time he came out after his vows, so glowing, so counting on me to understand. I tried, God knows, and never let on. I could understand why Clyde felt so cheated. But he wasn't tactful, and it hurt Tim. I could see that, too.

Suddenly now, up there on the screen, it didn't look like Tim at all.

Not one bit. I hadn't realized he'd grown so stout. And he looked balder than he had the other night. Or maybe it was the angle of the camera.

Maybe it wasn't Tim at all. Just for an instant that flashed through my mind. *What if we were looking at the wrong priest?* Both Alice and Milly seemed so sure.

Except for the Pope, all their outfits were the same. It's hard to spot your own in a setting like that. Hard to connect that dignified figure handing around his Pope with a fat baby staring through the bars of his playpen. Hard to believe I'd sat right here in this room with that shape two nights before. He played with the knobs on the TV while I watched him, trying to memorize his directions for focussing.

"Don't force it," he said. "Just wait and you'll probably get a clear enough picture."

The stout balding figure was climbing into the car behind the Pope. Milly was saying something, but I paid no attention. I *couldn't* have paid attention, even if I'd wanted to. Because I had the feeling, this terrible sense that maybe we had all missed him. It isn't the kind of thing you can say out loud at a moment like that. *Maybe we'd had our eyes on the wrong figure.* Alice would have objected, insisted. Milly would have agreed with her. *Maybe he was someone else. Maybe there was a resemblance, but it wasn't actually Tim.*

I could just hear them laugh, looking at me in disbelief if I said it out loud.

Besides, you just can't. But even if we'd been watching the *right* figure all along, I couldn't feel certain of it any longer, not the way I had in the beginning, when my finger tapped the screen, almost as if I could touch him. That mature, serious priest bending to climb into the long black car. Was he the one who would read prayers over my grave? Where was the Tim I knew? *Where had he gone?*

"Anyone thirsty?" asked Milly.

She never misses.

"I'll fix the ice, Edith," said Alice, jumping up. She'd been fidgeting for the past five minutes. "It's easier for me to reach the trays."

True enough. The ice tray fights me. I need a new fridge, among other things.

So I just sat there and held the last of the picture steady. The mo-

torcade moved off the screen. The camera shifted to an overview —
the Capitol, the Washington Monument, the White House, the Poto-
mac. Geometric dots . . . then . . . blank.

"Tim brought me some Chivas Regal," I said to Milly, who was still
blinking. "He said for us all to have one on him when the show was
over."

I switched off the set.

Parting

"HE'S GROWN SO STOUT," whispered Milly Burke.

And because she'd left her hearing aid home as usual, her voice was too loud.

He stood by his mother's corpse and tried not to show he'd heard.

Milly, with her daughter Rita, was two people away in line. No one was saying much. There wasn't much to say.

"I'm sorry . . . Tim."

The pause before his name, embarrassment at what they had to leave out.

"Your mother was a wonderful woman."

"She thought the world of you."

Edith Morrison lay in her best maroon print dress, cushioned by white satin, hands crossed, clasping her rosary.

And Tim was home to stand by her.

Only it was all wrong. He knew that was what they were thinking, what she would think, if she could. How many times had she given him instructions, smiling always, but with the underlying seriousness, trust, that said, I know you'll be there, Tim. How many mothers can count on having their only son say their funeral Mass? St. Peter will have the pearly gates wide open, waiting.

He shifted his weight and tried to stifle gas. It had been a long hot ride from New Jersey, four hours, and they'd barely made it. Just time to go to the house, drop their things, freshen up, and find the funeral parlor. The worst lay ahead. It was beginning now.

"How are you, Milly? You were good to come." He bent toward the permed white hair.

"Wouldn't miss it, Tim. Edith was my closest friend for over fifty years." Standing on tiptoe, Milly reached her short, freckled, eighty-seven-year-old arms around his shoulders and kissed him, a dry whiskery kiss, on the cheek.

She couldn't have come alone. Milly was past driving. At eighty-five they took her license away. Edith had told him, worried sick she'd also lose hers in a year.

"Thanks for bringing her, Rita." He shook Rita's hand. He had known her for decades, like a comfortable shoe. Faithful daughter, the one who stayed near home. She must be fifty-five or so now.

"Hi, Tim." Rita squeezed his hand. "It's great to see you, even" — she glanced around and whispered — "under these circumstances. How are you?"

"Fine. I'd like you both to meet my wife, Judith."

This was the crucial line, the line he'd practiced silently as they sped up the Garden State, crossed the shining Hudson, and nosed out past lurching transports on Route 84. Judith, asleep on the seat beside him, shoes off, jaw slack, had looked untroubled. Hers, after all, was only a minor role.

This is my wife, Judith.

Except for Alice Callahan, none of the "girls" in Edith's bridge group had met Judith. Tim's wife had been Edith Morrison's best-kept secret for the past three years.

Judith grasped Rita's hand and bent toward Milly. "How do you do, Mrs. Burke? I've heard a lot about you from Tim and Edith."

Milly said nothing, her small, sharp eyes surveying Tim's wife, the other woman, the one who'd taken him away from God, destroyed his manly commitment to his vocation. The Scarlet Woman. That was how Milly would see it.

Who gave a hoot about how Milly would see it?

"You're teaching, also, Judith?" As she asked, Rita was steadying her mother's elbow and gently pushing her forward so the line could move. On the other side of the casket, ladies sat in a row on straight chairs — murmuring, saying their beads, or simply staring ahead as if sheer space might unlock the secret they all faced before long, as if air itself could answer the tremulous murmuring of their hearts.

"Yes, I teach classics," said Judith. "At Princeton. So we live — "

Rita nodded. No time for more. Move on. Make way for the next mourner.

How many times had he thought of this day, then pushed the thought away? Now it was happening, with the inevitability of a movie reel turning, flashing one slide, then another, across the screen. Only it wasn't a screen. It was real. He was back home. He had gone public. Perforce. What better place? he thought grimly, stealing a look at Edith against her satin.

Thinner. She'd always been a full, heavy woman. Thinner now, and immobile. Stone. Remains. A corpse. She looked it. They'd tried — O'Brien's Funeral Home was proud of its reputation — but Edith Morrison still looked dead.

In front of the yellow rose spray Tim stood erect, shaking hands, accepting words of comfort and the occasional kiss, waiting for Father Scanlon.

They'd met only once, three years before, when Tim had been home overnight and gone to early morning Mass with Edith. For the first time in twenty-nine years he knelt with her on this side of the altar. Seeing Tim in the pew with his mother, the pastor of St. Mark's had come out afterward and shaken hands, a real man, making no reference to what Edith must have poured out to him week after week, in and out of the confessional. "Why did he leave? What did I do wrong? Do you think he's happy, Father?"

Father Scanlon was a dedicated pastor, shrewd, compassionate, and smart. He ran a bus around the parish to collect senior citizens and the infirm for Saturday evening Mass. He visited the sick. He offered special English lessons for the large influx of Hispanics over the past ten years. At Christmas some Spanish carols were sung now, and last year at midnight Mass the first reading had been in Spanish. The next day Milly called Tim to complain. "I don't mind a hymn or two, Tim, though to tell the truth it bothered me at first. But the readings! One reading was in Spanish with no translation. Don't you agree that's going too far? Your own grandfather came over from County Kerry and he had to speak English!" Tim didn't point out the obvious. He respected Father Scanlon. This priest dealt with realities. His handshake was warm and definite. None of this, "Do you know what you're doing, man?"

Surely, at fifty one ought to know what one was doing!

"Here he comes," whispered Judith.

She'd never met Father Scanlon. She was leery of priests. Besides, this was her first trip home.

"Well, Tim," said the pastor, grasping one hand and pumping it as he clapped Tim on the shoulder. "It was sudden, but then maybe it's better that way. Don't know who's ready if your mother wasn't."

Judith had left his side.

Tim looked into the bright blue eyes of the pastor. Did he hit the bottle? Didn't look burned out. A mixture of calculating and cherubic. Didn't miss a trick, though, had probably already counted the members of his parish sitting in this very room. He was kind. Not the shrewd self-protectiveness of some priests, or the desperate enthusiasm of others. He'd weathered the storm. Devoted pastor, seventy this year. Due for retirement and resisting it. "I don't know what we'll do when he leaves," Edith had been saying for the past five years.

"We came up as fast as we could," said Tim. "I had class this morning and had to see my dean. I'd just talked to Mom on the phone day before yesterday."

She called mornings before eight, when the rates changed. Every other day, that was their compromise. Before, it had been every day — except when he was in the novitiate, and, later, in Rome. "Insane," Judith said. "Whoever heard of a mother calling her fifty-year-old son every day?" "But how can I change her at this age?" he replied, knowing it was ridiculous. It had perhaps always been ridiculous. So they compromised. Every other day. It couldn't last forever.

"Yes, I know. I saw her at noon Mass that day, Monday." Father Scanlon was rubbing his hands together. Tim saw the scrubbed fingers, clean nails of a priest. "She looked fine. Then" — he gestured toward the casket — "this. When did you get the call?"

"Monday night. Rita Burke called me the next morning to tell me what she could."

"Hmmm. Well . . . " Father Scanlon looked around, saw no one was behind him, and took Tim's arm. "Perhaps we should discuss arrangements. If there's anything you'd specially like?"

He wanted no part of deciding hymns and readings. It had been hard enough to deal over the phone with O'Brien's, to insist on only one day for the wake. He wanted Mass arrangements taken care of by someone else. Judith agreed. "Why torture yourself?" she said, always practical. She was sitting by Milly and Rita now, glad, no doubt, of a break.

"Anything you plan is fine with me, Father."

"But surely, special hymns . . . she must have talked it over with you?"

"Well, yes. But that was before — "

"Ah," said Father Scanlon, clapping him on the shoulder again. "Yes, I see. Well, don't worry about it, Tim. I'm sure everything will be fine. We've a good choir and they'll be on duty tomorrow. Pallbearers?"

"O'Brien's said they'd take care of that."

"Fine."

Damned pastoral innuendos.

"Got a place to stay tonight?"

"We thought we'd stay at the house."

"Yes. Of course." Father Scanlon stepped back and glanced around. A dozen or so of his parishioners lined the side of the room. In front of the casket knelt a large man, head bowed.

"I'll be saying the rosary for the next ten minutes," said the priest. "You can stay and join in or" — he nodded toward Judith — "if you and your wife need a break, here's the time. It's hard when there's only one of you to hold the fort."

Decent. The man was downright decent.

Tim caught Judith's eye and nodded.

The praying man made the sign of the cross slowly and vacated the kneeler. Father Scanlon knelt in front of Edith, fished his beads from his jacket pocket, and began. "In the name of the Father, and of the Son, and of the Holy Spirit."

Judith followed Tim out to the hall where they stood by a low table displaying the opened guest book. Gold letters spelled her name: Edith Morrison. Resting in the Lord. May 15, 1982.

"How're you doing?"

Her eyes were tired. She'd been correcting exams all week.

She smiled. "Hard to tell if your mother's the star of this, or you," she said, touching his forearm. "The question is, how're you doing? They'll never see me again. This is a one-time appearance. But you've got the whole past to face."

"I'll get through it." Her light touch soothed him. "Father Scanlon is okay. But these things are barbaric. Don't do it for me." He grinned. "Cremate me and sprinkle the ashes over Princeton, New Jersey, place of sin."

"Pardon me!" A heavyset woman in a pink cotton dress beneath a dark jacket had just come in. She stopped and studied the three doorways, each leading to a different corpse. "I wonder . . ." She read the small printed notices outside each room, identifying occupants. "I'm looking for Mrs. Edith Morrison."

The heels of her sensible black shoes were run over and she carried a string bag full of parcels.

"I'm Tim Morrison," said Tim, stepping forward. "Were you looking for my mother?"

"Tim!"

As the fat arms inside the scratchy jacket went round his neck, he smelled onions.

"It's me, Tim, Mrs. Cutsky. You don't remember?"

Behind Mrs. Cutsky, Judith nodded to him and headed for the door.

"Of course I remember." He did . . . the years of watching her clean their house, whizzing the Hoover around, scrubbing and waxing the stairs, dusting between rungs, working the mangle in the kitchen. She'd stayed on through the war, rare devotion, the envy of Edith's friends Milly and Alice, who'd lost their help to the factories.

"How could I forget our years in the kitchen, Mrs. Cutsky?"

He took her arm and led her to the doorway of Edith's room. Father Scanlon was still at the rosary. They stood there quietly, Mrs. Cutsky hanging onto him, watching those gathered to pray. A few knelt, most sat.

"I didn't know — " began Mrs. Cutsky. "No one told me. I read it in this morning's paper. Otherwise, I'd never have known."

He felt her warm, thick arm in his, the dry, wrinkled fingers against his palm. Mrs. Cutsky must be — seventy? She couldn't have been more than thirty in those days, coming in mornings, cleaning until tabletops shone and smelled of lemon, making Scotch pudding for Clyde, always asking before she went out to the back hall to put on her walking shoes (for she walked the two miles to their place), "Was there anything more you wanted done today, Mrs. Morrison?" She came three days a week. And during the school year he'd race home

56

after school to see her, for they did something special together. She taught him words, special words, Polish words. *Dzien dobry! Jak sie masz?* Hello. How are you today? Each week he learned them and said them back to her. After a while they could make a little conversation in Polish. It thrilled him to roll the secret words on his tongue when Edith came into the kitchen.

She even dusted his altar, the special wooden miniature Edith had presented to him for his ninth birthday, so beautifully made, with its own tabernacle, its miniature candles, the small pieces of cloth Mrs. Cutsky herself hemmed to fit. She brought him two tiny gold vases and replaced the candles after he'd burned them down playing priest of a quiet evening in his room.

Now Mrs. Cutsky clutched the arm of this lapsed priest as if he were God. Because underneath it all he was Tim, her boy.

"She looks beautiful," she whispered.

Tim squeezed her arm. What was there to say to such idiocy?

"How've you been?" he whispered, wondering where Judith had gone.

"Fine, Tim. Just fine. Children all grown. I've eight grandchildren." When she smiled the flab on her cheeks shook, and small lines showed near her eyes. Her flesh looked pale and soft, like dough.

"In the name of the Father, and of the Son, and of the Holy Spirit." Father Scanlon stood. He went over to say a few words to Milly, his star parishioner, still teaching CCD to the little ones.

"Was she sick long?" asked Mrs. Cutsky.

Where was Judith?

"She'd been suffering from angina for years." He saw the tiny white pills Edith kept on her kitchen counter in the pink plastic container. "But this wasn't heart, Mrs. Cutsky. She had a stroke. No warning. Her blood pressure had always been fine."

Never knew what hit her, said the nurse — was it a nurse? — on the telephone. Then they'd put on Father Darcy, the curate, who'd been called in to administer the last rites. She'd fallen in the bathroom. Tim imagined the scene: heavy body, partly clothed, falling, striking the sink, lying there . . . if Milly hadn't called, got no answer, then sent Rita to check, they might not have known for days. These old ladies had a point with their telephone round robins.

"I'll see her for a few moments now, Tim," said Mrs. Cutsky, disengaging her arm. "Maybe we can visit for a while afterward."

She lumbered across the dark blue patterned carpet and knelt before the casket.

Father Scanlon nodded to a couple near the doorway. Then he approached Tim.

"See you tomorrow, Tim. I don't think I'll get here tonight. We're in the middle of the annual mission. But the Mass will be at ten o'clock. Don't you worry about a thing."

"Fine, Father, and thanks."

Where was Judith?

She was sitting in the car eating chips.

"Couldn't help it," she apologized when he approached. "I was famished, and I spotted this little store at the corner."

The heat and dirt of upper Wildwood Street hit him in the face like a blow after the perfumed airlessness of O'Brien's. Blue sky stung his eyes.

Only then did he realize they'd gone all day without eating, setting out for home as soon as he got in from his morning class at Rutgers. Judith had cancelled her classes for today and tomorrow morning and thrown a few things into a bag.

He slipped in beside her now, blinking at sun glare on the windshield, the soft seatcovers hot against his trousers.

"Want one?"

He took a large curled chip and savored the sting of salt on his tongue. Two small children sat on the curb ahead, watching them.

"What's going on inside?"

"Mrs. Cutsky wants to talk a little afterward. And Father Scanlon's left."

"I saw him go."

"The funeral's at ten tomorrow."

"Then I'll make it back for my five o'clock class?"

"I'd think so. I'll stay on here and see to details. I settled it with the dean. I'm not due back until Monday. There's the house . . ." .

The house. It would be easier if they were going somewhere else tonight, a motel, a rented room. Someplace flat and neutral. But this had to be faced.

"I've got to call Chris around suppertime," she said, munching. "He expected an answer from me today about the Bermuda trip."

"Look, Judith." He turned to her, aching to hold her, to smell the musty sweetness of her dark hair and touch the small of her naked back. "I've got to stay here. Why don't you go on to the house? I'll call you if I need a ride. I'm sure someone from here will drive me up."

"Well . . ." She laid a hand on his knee, hot through his light gray trousers. He wasn't complaining. A hand anywhere. Something that spoke of life. Love. The pursuit of happiness.

He stood a moment on the curb watching the car move down the street, stop at the light, pass Lyons Drug, where he'd guzzled sodas after school until he was eighteen, sipping the sweet coolness, wondering how he looked to the girls in the booth opposite. Odd to think of Judith, his wife of three years, driving down streets for her devoid of depth, holding no memories. She looked at a storefront and saw nothing more. He looked at it and read part of his life. Always, it seemed, O'Brien's had been here. As kids, after school, they'd race by it chanting: "The worms crawl in, the worms crawl out, they crawl all over your gizzard and snout."

He stopped in the doorway of the parlor. Should he go sit near Milly and Rita, or should he stand again by the casket? Sole bereaved. Son, former priest, renegade, married now they say, to a lovely girl but — no one knew if he was still in the Church.

Should he stand there?

He crossed the room and felt himself a stolid, balding, middle-aged man. It would have been easier if she'd died ten years ago.

❈

At six, Rita drove him home. They dropped Milly at the large house on Chestnut Street that she continued to inhabit, though her three children had been gone for years and she'd long ago been widowed.

Then they drove on up Elm past the row of funeral homes — Pulassi, DeVito, Denaro — with their green plastic portes-cochères and carefully trimmed hedges.

"My God," said Tim, struck by the array. "Do they do anything else here but die?"

"Colossal, isn't it? My brother calls it Death Valley when he comes home."

Rita was okay. Better than that. She'd helped him over the phone, telling him what restaurant to call to arrange for the meal after the funeral, advising him on other details. Practical. What, he wondered, was the weight of her burden with Milly? Did the brothers help out?

They parked for a moment in the drive. He saw that the veins on her hands looked blue and swollen.

"Would you come in?"

"No. I've got to get back to Mom. She's really upset about Edith, you know. Each death throws these old ladies for a loop. Who'll be next?" She'd left the motor running. "It's rough. But Edith was the strong one. Somehow I think they all expected her to go last." She paused and looked at him, brushing a strand of faded blond hair from her eyes. "She never told anyone about you, Tim. For months. Years. It was incredible. Alice was the one who let the cat out of the bag after she met you and Judith by chance in Manhattan."

What to say? He remembered Alice Callahan in her gold jewelry and overdone makeup accosting the two of them at the entrance to the Guggenheim one hot June day.

He opened the car door. "Well, we're past secrets now," he said, and thought, strangely, of Mrs. Cutsky and the smell of starch.

"If I can do anything tonight or tomorrow, let me know. I think Monahan's Restaurant is all set. I checked earlier this afternoon."

"You're a sport, Rita. Thanks."

She waved and backed out of the drive.

Inside, Judith had been busy. She'd found lettuce and tomato, made a salad, set places at the small kitchen table in what was once the breakfast nook.

She was sitting at the table.

"I made myself a drink. Your mother kept a pretty full liquor closet."

He laughed. "She and the girls never gave up on the scotch. Bridge went by the boards first. But even when they didn't have a foursome left, after Irene died, they'd still get together some evenings and have a scotch or two. Especially in summer."

"Want one?"

"Thanks."

He sat down and watched her move about, her small-boned wrists twisting the ice tray, the red glints in her hair shining as she looked inside the fridge for cherries. He loved the way she moved, graceful yet efficient. He'd never been well coordinated himself and was still embarrassed at his appearance in a bathing suit, overweight and pale. Beside him Judith was delicate and slender. Her laughter sprang from unknown depths and bubbled up slowly, spilling over in a rush. This was not an evening for laughs.

"One jigger?"

"One and a half. On the rocks. Don't bother with a cherry."

"I ordered a pizza," she said. "Couldn't find much that would appeal around here and I thought you'd like one." She set the glass before him on the table. "It'll be delivered in half an hour."

The scotch cooled his throat. He loosened his tie.

"How was it?"

"More of the same. Barbaric. What ancient rite demands that we display our dead?"

"Maybe it's a comfort to her friends."

"In some perverse way. Anyhow, I've got to get through it. And she wanted an open casket. She told me."

"Your poor mother." Judith sighed.

The sympathy surprised him, though she wasn't mean-spirited and had certainly suffered loss. But she saw Edith's devotion to him as obsessive. And she could never fathom the Catholicism part. Contentedly agnostic, she tolerated his qualms and anxieties with good humor and the occasional shot of irony.

"I've got to call Chris in a couple of minutes. I don't know what to say." She rubbed a spot of water against the plastic placemat. "I left a note that I'd call around six to settle things."

Summons from another world. Her son was a senior at Lawrenceville Prep. "A world I've never known," Tim had tried to explain to her, puzzled over how much to advise, when to shut up. When Chris came home weekends, the atmosphere in the house shifted. A healthy eighteen-year-old looked at this middle-aged ex-priest now sleeping, legally, in his mother's bed. What did he feel? On the surface, they got along well. Christ was a reader. He'd inherited his mother's gift for languages. He loved facts, games, puzzles of all kinds. A whiz at Trivial Pursuit, he creamed Tim regularly. "Where've you been for the past thirty years?" he'd kid. "I'd hate to tell you," Tim would reply. After a while the joke wore thin.

"He really wants to go, Tim," said Judith. As she pushed down an ice cube in her glass, light struck her simple gold ring.

She wanted another perspective.

"Look, Judith." He set down the scotch. "I just can't put my mind on it. How much money is involved?"

"Oh, heavens. It's not the money. Besides — " she hesitated, then didn't say it. The will. Already they knew what was in the will. After the stipulated Masses and perpetual enrollments had been seen to, at least $300,000. Edith had gone over it all with him, haunted by the worry that hospital and nursing home expenses might ultimately leave her on Title 19.

He sipped again and looked past Judith's dark hair at the spice rack on the wall. Neat jars, freshly labeled, all of a size. They seemed eternal. A pain was starting in the back of his head.

"It's just" — she rubbed a pattern in the cloudiness on her glass — "well, you know. There'll be booze by the truckload, girls, certainly pot, maybe even coke. Who knows? It's hard to know what he could get into in a week in Bermuda. Even though he's a good kid. I've resisted the pressure to let him go, right up to this point."

A good kid. This overgrown good kid named Tim sat at the kitchen table sipping his drink. Good kid. A week in Bermuda. How could he comment rationally? He'd watched these tanned preppies in their alligator shirts invade the kitchen, stare into the opened refrigerator, compare muscles, go swinging off with their tennis rackets. What a waste. They owned the world. Youth wasted on the young. Besides, Chris wasn't even his son. "Tim." Suddenly she was quiet and soft. "It's nothing to put on you. You just stay here and I'll call him from upstairs. Pay for the pizza, okay?"

He was left staring at his mother's cupboards, freshly painted pale yellow, and the small-patterned paper she'd been so eager to show him three years before. When he came home without the collar, the wallpaper became an excuse to talk about something. A way of saying nothing.

He thought of Dolores Cutsky, the sad, clumsy woman of an hour before, a young girl in this kitchen, sprinkling laundry, ironing, talking non-stop to him as he sat in this very spot after school.

At that sink, after dinner, he helped his mother do dishes while Clyde went into the living room and read the paper. He seldom thought of Clyde, an ineffective ghost. Disappointed in his son. Was it that Tim didn't have muscles, didn't play ball? He had a mind, as

Edith constantly reminded her husband, waving each report card beneath his nose. Clyde was a shadow, often away. Hard to connect a
dynamic criminal lawyer with the man who'd occupied the easy chair
and read the paper, then tuned in Fulton Lewis, Junior on the radio
and did not want to be interrupted. Maybe, thought Tim, he'd figured
out how to survive with Edith.

Over dishes, Tim and Edith would talk. Afterward they sometimes
went for walks. She didn't laugh at him, ever. She humored him. She
got Mrs. Cutsky's husband to make the altar, then helped Tim decide
where to put it, moving the bed and the desk. It was important to
situate it just right. In high school, when he wanted the altar out of
the room, she understood. It was babyish. By that time he cherished
the desire for the real thing. He told her when he was fourteen, right
here at this very table, and though he saw her tremble for a moment,
she just said, "I'll keep your secret." But he knew she began to pray.

Judith was back.

"I said yes. Chris is going."

He should rise to the occasion. This was her son, her deep concern. But it was *his mother*. And they were sitting in his mother's
kitchen. Judith had met Edith only once, a brief encounter heavy
with silence and willed politeness. Later, as if to find one redeeming
element in the whole regrettable episode, Edith said to Tim: "At least
you have your brains in common." Judith excelled at languages. Starting her PhD at the University of Chicago late, after Chris was finally
in school, she'd persevered through years of stress with Ron, her first
husband, who saw playing the market and investing in real estate as
infinitely more fascinating than attempting to master Greek forms.

She sat opposite Tim now, her breasts rising in soft curves beneath
the navy dress. He longed to touch them.

"I know I'll worry, Tim."

When she worried, the blue in her eyes darkened. Her skin tonight
looked almost golden.

He heard the bell first, paid the fellow, and carried back the steaming pizza in its cardboard box. They set out plates, separated pieces,
and attacked. He wrestled with mozzarella and pepperoni, grateful for
distraction from Chris, Bermuda, O'Brien's, and the dead look of his
mother's face.

"Will he be gone when I get back?" he asked.

63

"Probably. When do you expect to get in?"

"I'll call you Saturday night. There should be a late train from New Haven on Sunday."

He wanted Judith there alone when he returned.

He watched her lift a pizza slice, fold it in half lengthwise, maneuver mushrooms, peppers, cheese, onions, and sausage without making a mess. Even managing pizza she was dainty! She was forty-five. Her dark hair was already turning. In a few years she'd be entirely gray. Lines of fatigue showed in her forehead.

"Don't wait up for me tonight," he said. "You'll need to be rested for the trip back alone tomorrow."

She wanted nothing more of children. She'd had it, she said. Chris was almost on his own.

He wanted a child.

Futile longing.

He lifted another slice.

❈

That evening there were few callers at O'Brien's, only eight or ten None of Edith's friends could drive at night.

Tim took a seat alone near the casket. The backs of his legs had begun to ache.

He should be *feeling* something. Instead, he was floating in a static gray limbo where no one ever shouted, where flowers bloomed forever, stale and sweet. Their heavy scent drugged him. His mind was stalled in a felt-lined maze, no sharp edges, no bright light.

Edith had been good to him. Always there. She understood, or at least she didn't criticize. Above all (he thought of this as he glanced over at the sunken cheeks, the gray flesh poorly disguised by the undertaker's makeup), she honored his dreams.

It is something to be allowed to dream, to have your dreams accepted, treated as worthy, not scorned as so much airy fantasy, so much waste of time in a world bent on more important things.

She honored his dreams.

And fostered them.

And when it came time, at eighteen, to tell both parents (acting as if she hadn't known all along) his decision: "I want to become a priest," he could count on her to talk late, after he'd gone to bed, say what had to be said to Clyde. Who could argue with a priestly vocation? It was her dearest wish.

Longing swept him like a dark pain — to be away from this close dead room, to be with Judith, lying in her embrace, stroking her fair warm flesh.

Judith was capable of distance. Was it because she was older, had long since come to terms with the ambiguities of belief? Or disbelief? Which was it? He was glad he hadn't fallen (as he'd seen several priests do) for some young thing in her twenties who'd expect a lot. Judith expected some things, but she wanted her own life now. "I've worked hard to get here, Tim. Ron could never understand. You can. I'm at a different stage."

He understood about stages.

He stood to shake hands with a tall square-jawed woman whose powdered cheeks and dyed red hair seemed faintly familiar.

"Is it you, Tim?"

Who was she?

"I'll never forget your class, Tim. You and Helen Callahan were two of the best students I had in thirty years of teaching."

"How are you, Mrs. Jackson?" Mrs. Lily Jackson. Fifth grade. A devil on grammar. Adored spelling bees. He and Helen Callahan standing at the last, on opposite sides of the room, eyeing one another, vying to win. Their mothers would compare notes that night.

Lily Jackson's husband, a shrunken pale man with a cast in one eye, stood back a few inches after they shook hands to let Lily do the talking.

"I learned about your mother from Milly Burke, Tim. Rita brought Milly in to have her hair done this morning and I was there at the same time." Lily slipped her arm through her husband's arm.

He saw them — a row of aged ladies waiting their turn, leafing through *People* magazine as they compared notes on Edith Morrison's sudden death.

"At least she didn't suffer," said Lily.

How do you know? he longed to shout into the powdered face. "I hope not," he said.

"You've been away a long time, haven't you?" Her smile uncovered large dark teeth. He remembered them. "But I hear about you from Alice and Milly."

"Thank you for coming, Mrs. Jackson," he managed.

He wanted to bolt, let the dead bury the dead, run out the front door past the golden guest book, down the street with its decaying three-storey houses, fly, take off, float high above the dingy smoke-stacks of this dying factory town, higher, above the ocean with its surging whitecaps, look down at the world in all its pain and contra-diction, move into a new ether that spoke only and always of life . . .

Eight-forty-five. Fifteen minutes to go. He pulled himself together. He'd go out for a breath of air, clear his head.

At the far end of the almost empty room he nodded to Lily and her husband.

At the outside door he was stopped by a tall woman and a dark-haired young man coming in.

"Oh, pardon me!"

The woman looked straight at him. She carried the scent of some-thing piney.

"I was just coming in to see Mrs. Morrison — "

Tim stepped back inside. The fellow beside her was half a head taller, with dark brown eyes, dark curly hair, and a way of standing that suggested shyness.

"I — I wonder if you know where — "

She looked at him carefully. "It's you, Tim?"

It had to be Helen, though the face was older, the hair white. He hadn't seen her in over twenty-five years. Still beautiful, still capable of smiling in such a way that something mysterious and wonderful happened to her eyes.

"Helen?"

Her arms went around him. He felt the softness of her breasts as she pulled him to her.

"I want you to meet my son, Tim. This is Robert."

They shook hands.

"Robert, this is my oldest boyfriend and" — she smiled — "my ear-liest competitor. Long before your father."

She looked about. "Where is she, Tim?"

He gestured toward the parlor he'd just left.

"I'm sorry, Tim. It must have been a shock. It's *always* a shock. Except that — " she paused, as if uncertain whether to go on —

66

"they're all on the verge. It's awful, like cut trees about to fall. They watch one another like hawks."

He glanced at his watch. "Better go in, I think," he said apologetically. "It's almost time."

She nodded. "You're alone?"

He knew what she meant. "Judith's back at the house getting things in order for tomorrow." Probably out cold.

"Oh." Helen turned to enter the parlor, then looked back for a moment. "If there's anything I can do, let me know."

From the doorway, he watched them approach the casket. She still had good legs. Judith's weren't so hot. And small hips. Amazingly good shape for fifty.

Helen blessed herself as she knelt. Beside her, Robert blessed himself also, and bowed his head. Tim thought of Chris, untroubled by religion. A good kid. Off to Bermuda. Fun on the beach. Fun in bed. Who knew what else? Chris wouldn't have a clue about blessing himself.

⚜

When he reached the house at nine-thirty, Judith had already gone to bed.

He changed quietly in the bathroom and examined the contents of the medicine chest over the sink. Dry skin cream. Eyebrow pencil. Blusher. A razor. Shampoo. Toothpaste. Detritus of life. Edith dead. Four nights ago she'd stood here fingering these vanities. All remained in order, ready — as if at any moment she would return, open the mirrored door, take out the denture cleaner, run a glassful of water, and drop in her bridge.

Pain cut his heart.

When he climbed in on the other side of Judith, she turned toward him and mumbled, "How'd it go?"

"Few people. It's over. Just tomorrow."

"Ummm."

She put her arms around him, pulling him close. "You're okay?"

He smelled something new. Sweet. Had she explored the medicine chest also? Was this Edith's perfume?

67

"I'm okay. Go to sleep. You'll need to be rested tomorrow. You've got to drive home."

She mumbled something he couldn't make out and rolled over.

They were in his parents' bed. It was dark out, but the streetlight filtered through the window shade. He could discern objects and shapes: the low, freshly slipcovered lady's chair in the corner, the dresser, the framed pictures on the wall — Clyde, Tim. There used to be more. She'd removed the ones of Tim as a priest, replacing them with baby and childhood pictures. A small shelf near the dresser still held the books he'd written. He'd noticed them earlier. He imagined her of an evening sitting here reading, trying to plow through his prose from some odd conviction that this was what a worthy mother must do.

A sense of remoteness stung him. He connected with nothing in this room, this house, not even with the woman by his side. Judith. Faithful companion. Lover. Sensible, practical, passionate, agnostic Judith. She'd had a child, raised it, put in her years. She was "out from under" — her phrase. Chris was almost on his own.

Now, Edith Morrison's money might help educate the other woman's son. What irony. Was it right? What was *right*? There was no one else to leave it to.

Tomorrow night he'd be here alone, Judith back home coping with Chris. He'd go through closets, handling print dresses and coats, sorting shoes, underwear, jewelry. Maybe Rita would help.

As Judith breathed evenly beside him, he shut his eyes and tried to blot out images from the evening — casket, corpse, the strangely pink and powdered look of his mother's hands clasping the rosary, the blue nails, the silver crucifix gleaming against her dead flesh.

⚜

Next morning, the church was not crowded. Maybe a hundred people. Not bad, he thought, for a woman of eighty-four.

Judith was beside him in the pew.

It wasn't the church of his childhood. Years of raffles and bingos and bazaars had finally canceled the parish debt and accrued enough capital to build this new St. Mark's. The old plaster statues were gone, and the gold-leafed tabernacle, replaced now by the mandatory altar facing the people.

Father Scanlon was celebrant, assisted by Father Darcy.

"The Lord be with you."

"And with your spirit."

The casket, covered in white to symbolize the completion of baptism, rested in the center aisle, beside Tim. Tall beeswax tapers flickered near it. Where was Edith? Watching this? From what height did she now survey it all? Tim looked at the altar and wondered what lingering childishness of imagination made him even think this way — Edith flying around, disembodied, still there.

The priests moved slowly, eyes down, attended by two solemn altar boys. Beneath the surplice of the smaller, towheaded boy, scuffed blue and white Nikes showed.

Tim watched the ritual unfold. He could feel the sharp edge of the altar, the cool clean linen, the smooth gold rim of the chalice.

"Lord have mercy, Christ have mercy."

It was as if a button had been pressed down deep within him and a voice — his, yet not his — had begun to echo the words murmured at the altar. He had to watch this tendency. He knew the danger of continuing to act priestly, pastoral, in perfectly ordinary human circumstances, turning on the confessional ear or the pulpit voice when all people wanted was normal chit-chat. Judith had warned him. "Watch out, Tim. Don't play the priest or you'll really be in trouble." He'd scarcely been aware at the time, then began to catch himself slipping over into the expected — only no longer expected — gestures and words. He'd learned to control it. But this was different. No one here could know. It was secret and silent, this response . . . simply language . . . words so new, so old, so . . . *his.*

They stood for the gospel.

Father Scanlon ascended the pulpit and turned on the small light. He smoothed the page in the book.

"The kingdom of heaven," he began slowly, "is like a man on his way abroad who summoned his servants and entrusted his property to them. To one he gave five talents, to another two, to a third, one: each in proportion to his ability. Then he set out . . ."

Judith nudged him. "Perfect," she whispered.

He knew what she was thinking. She'd alway been puzzled by the two sides of Edith as he described them: manic about religion and money. Maybe not manic, but absorbed. He'd tried to explain the contradiction away but was himself puzzled. Edith had followed the Dow Jones as religiously as she said her daily rosary. For his part, initiated late into the material pressures of life, he sympathized more than Judith with his mother's concern to live comfortably but not extravagantly, keeping up, as she said, her standard of living, not squandering. She chose her forms of thrift. She saved used aluminum foil but drank Chivas Regal.

"Well done, good and faithful servant," Father Scanlon read, "you have shown you can be faithful in small things. I will trust you with greater; come and join in your master's happiness."

Had she been faithful in small? Yes. What were the small? Were writing weekly, calling daily, having Masses said, remaining faithful to Clyde and after that faithful to Tim? How could one measure small or large, after a certain point? Would not rejoicing in Tim's late but evident happiness, and embracing Judith, the cause of it, have been truly large? Had Edith now been called to join in her master's happiness?

Undoubtedly . . . whatever it meant. Hard to imagine her surrounded by flames. Yet what could the words really mean? Judith was content to imagine herself eventually returning to the elements — "A mist in some future being's face," she'd laugh. He wasn't ready to accept such a prospect. He kidded her — "You might become acid rain" — and freely admitted he wanted to live on as more than anonymous drizzle. Would he ever relinquish such a hope? Unlikely.

"You wicked and lazy servant!" read Father Scanlon. "So you knew that I reap where I have not sown and gather where I have not scattered? Well, then, you should have deposited my money with the bankers, and on my return I would have recovered my capital with interest. So now, take the talent from him and give it to the man who has the five talents. For to everyone who has, will be given more, and he will have more than enough; but from the man who has not, even what he has will be taken away. As for this good-for-nothing servant, throw him out into the dark, where there will be weeping and grinding of teeth."

"Isn't it gnashing?" whispered Judith.

"New translation," he whispered back, touched at her attentiveness. Hideous translation. One candle by the casket seemed in danger of going out.

She settled back to hear Father Scanlon's words.

Tim couldn't listen. He was seeing Edith lead him to the bank at the age of nine, showing him how to deposit his weekly allowance, advising him on how to withdraw when he bought his first good bike, bringing him brownies in the seminary . . . small things . . .

She'd met him for a week in Ireland once, after he'd finished a year of study at University College, Dublin. On the road outside Cork the car broke down. He'd lifted the hood and figured out the problem. To her that healing act was almost as mystical as transubstantiation.

Soon it would be Communion time. Would he receive? The old ladies behind him would be watching. How much did they know? Did they think he had a dispensation, or that he'd married outside the Church?

Father Scanlon bent low over the altar. Tim knelt upright and bowed his head, aware of Judith's knee beside him as she sat through the consecration.

The church had grown still, attention focussed on the act about to take place on the altar. He knew this moment as a familiar place in which he'd stood day after day, year after year, gathering energy, concentrating, feeling time split to admit eternity as he bent low over the altar holding this thin dry host, his tongue forming the ancient transforming sounds: "On the night before he suffered, he took bread into his hands . . ."

Tim shut his eyes and saw, as on an intimate inner screen years could not erase, his mother opening her mouth, extending her tongue to receive her God from the hands of her son at his first Mass. *She was gone. For what had she lived?*

Pain seized his shoulders, his head, spidering through his whole body. Something was tearing him with a force he could sustain only by kneeling upright, head in his hands. Her nails were blue, her cheeks gray, and against her dead flesh the silver crucifix gleamed. Once, those dead eyes had looked at him with pride that grew oppressive, wanting from him a certitude he could not guarantee. Could she even imagine the terrifying slippage he felt occurring day after day as he genuflected and, holding aloft the consecrated bread, announced to the faithful: "Behold him who takes away the sins of the world"? Did any mother really know her son? *Could she?*

Judith was poking him. They stood.

At the Agnus Dei he leaned toward her and kissed her. Father Scanlon came down from the altar and shook his hand, then Judith's. "Peace of Christ."

Behind their pew, feet shuffled and kneelers scraped. A hand tapped Tim's shoulder. Turning, he faced Milly Burke leaning on Rita's arm. Milly extended a trembling freckled hand. "Peace of Christ, Tim."

Then came the moment. A tremor of anticipation ran through the congregation as everyone knelt. Father Scanlon raised the host high. "This is the lamb of God who takes away the sins of the world. Happy are those who are called to his supper."

As Tim looked at the white disc in the priest's hands, a new hardness gathered within him. *No.* This time he would not be called to that supper. He would sit here by Judith, by the casket, as others moved forward, accepting their God from their pastor.

He sat back. Judith reached for his hand and held it, her palm warm and a bit damp. What was she feeling, sitting in this alien church by the side of her husband, enduring a rite that for her had, at most, the meaning of a magic show?

Many of the older ones, he saw, still took Communion on their tongues. It is hard to change a whole way of life.

He thought of his mother. "Don't forget all those Masses for me, Tim. I'm counting on it." Playful, but meaning it. Beaming at him as they stopped at a pub on the road to Killarney and had a Guinness stout. "Not everyone has such insurance," she told the genial bartender. Tim was her talent. Capital investment. To be returned, plus interest. There would be no interest.

At the altar rail, in front of Father Scanlon, stood a young man in a dark suit, and behind him a white-haired woman in gray linen. Helen and her son.

That was the other life. The one not to be. At sixteen he'd been tempted by Helen's smoldering innocence. When she turned to look at him with eyes that could laugh like no others he'd known, he dissolved inside. He'd taken her to his senior prom, gone dancing and drinking afterward, the last fling before leaving for the sem. They'd talked late in the car that night, sitting outside her house beneath the streetlight, dreaming their futures. He'd trembled with desire to chuck it all and stay home. They kissed again and again, long and hard. *What would that life have been?*

Here, in the cool pew of new St. Mark's, he can imagine its contours: the firm daily habits of a faith grounded in and supported by place, the certitude that no sin was final, no fall unredeemable. They might have lived in this parish, Robert serving on the altar, Tim licking the weekly envelopes and making his Easter duty, Helen teaching CCD and playing bridge with friends. A secure world, embraced by the comforts of belief. He would have known the Church less intimately, been spared the acid touch of her monstrous beauty that ate through him until he sought relief in distance and the seductions of ordinary life. He would have known less . . . or at least known something different.

Helen turned to follow her strapping son back down the aisle. She blessed herself slowly, eyes down, and moved discreetly around Edith Morrison's bier.

Tim squeezed Judith's hand until she loosened her fingers. "You're hurting," she whispered.

One taper beside the casket sent a thin stream of dark smoke heavenward.

With a quick glance around the congregation to be sure that all had been served, Father Scanlon turned and ascended the steps to the altar.

Crossing the Border

BEN ZORINSKY STRETCHED HIS ARMS across the motel bed, pulled out the drawer on the side table, and extracted a dog-eared Gideon Bible. Propping the book open against his stomach he read: Jeremiah 34. Across the top of the page in wavy, faded blue letters someone had written *the hat check girl fucks*.

No date, though.

He smiled and, too tired to get up and turn on the TV, he lay back, Bible heavy on his belt buckle, Jeremiah pressed against his empty stomach. He'd been traveling fifteen hours, three to the boat and then the long ferry ride across the bay. Now, just half an hour to himself. He'd meet Steve at seven.

He lay there drifting, the sharp blue ocean sky still pressing behind his eyeballs, the heaving boat still fluttering his guts. A rough crossing. Not enough to make him actually vomit, just enough to make him feel, as Caroline would have said, *woozy*. That was one of her words.

Forget Caroline.

⸘⸘

Crossing the border into Canada always made him anxious, even when customs officials were benign. He hated the self-justifying: passport, please. Carrying plants? Meats? Presents? Worth how much? Fill in the blank and sign. Though he never cheated, he always felt uneasy. He lacked the courage to cheat. Around him, middle-aged women

74

with shopping bags from Filene's, L.L. Bean, the Dexter Shoe Outlet propped against their weary ankles would be kibitzing — wondering aloud what to declare, what not. Anxious, smug, careful, they cheerfully bore the anxiety of cheating for the triumph of bringing home a bargain. Visibly refreshed by their foray into foreign markets, they figured, erased, refigured, and calculated the exchange rate, until the sum was less than their yearly allotment.

He did none of this. He was merely a visitor for a few day. He brought nothing but himself and a fifth of Bacardi light from the Duty-Free for Steve, who wanted, needed, nothing else.

For up here in Canada, contrary to all predictions, Steve had made good.

Ben snapped the Bible shut, reached down and dropped it on the floor, rolled over, pushed his face into the pillow, and dozed.

-ᢳᢰᢴ-

The brothers met by the front desk at seven sharp and headed into the dining room, Steve first. No one would have guessed they were twins — one blond, short, compact, moving with the confidence of a cat, the other paunchier, darker, less full of spring, looking tonight as tired as he felt from his trip. Ben was, in fact, older than Steve by two full minutes.

The dining room was small and low-ceilinged, with pictures of lobsters and fishing dories displayed against yellow and brown patterned wallpaper. A large stone fireplace occupied the inner wall, where three artificial logs burned purple and blue.

They found a table beside the fire.

"What's with the phony logs?" said Ben. "Hardly a come-on for tourists." He pulled out the captain's chair nearest the chemical flames. "Isn't this bad PR for the land of Christmas trees and clean living?"

Steve had made a small fortune through the unlikely venture of growing Christmas trees and shipping them to northern New England each November. When spruce budworm had become a threat, he'd switched to real estate. Now he was converting apartment houses to condominiums in Halifax and had offered Ben the chance to go in with him.

"Tourist season's over," said Steve. "The American money's gone.

Besides, these things are great. Ninety-nine cents at your local super-
market. Called 'Romance without the Heartache.' They burn for
three hours. Maybe you should take a couple home."

A waitress in a brown ruffled apron over a yellow uniform stood
before them.

"Drink?" Steve raised an eyebrow at Ben.

"Scotch on the rocks. I'll nurse it." His stomach still swooshed, but
he'd need a stiff drink. The first night here was always hardest.

Steve looked at the waitress. She was thin, with overlarge wrists
and a hesitant smile. The hand holding the order pad bore a wedding
ring.

"Any Keith's Ale?"

She nodded.

"One for me."

As she left, he leaned over the table toward his brother. "The new
highway patrol has cracked down on Breathalyzer tests. They can stop
you anywhere, anytime. I'll stick to one beer, for now."

Ben watched Steve strike a match, hold the small uncertain flame
steady to the end of his cigarette. Still the same deft movements that
said what he was: a decisive man who didn't suffer fools gladly. Ener-
getic. Shrewd. Finding chances for profit where others saw nothing.
The scar on his cheek looked angry tonight, redder, gathering the
flesh near the corner of his mouth to make his smile crooked. A fascination to women, he claimed.

"So?" Steve sat back, relaxing. "What's new?"

The ritual opener. It drove Ben crazy.

"So . . . Caroline's happy, she says." In a day or two he might begin
to enjoy himself. Then it would be time to go back. "My ninth graders
continue to drive me nuts. And Karen's come to live with me this
year."

"Hmmm. Complicating?"

"Not in the ways you might think. Pantyhose in the bathroom.
Never enough hot water. But . . . she's okay. A good kid."

She invaded his bachelor quarters with her nail polish and records,
her eye shadow and bath oil. She bought yogurt by the huge carton
and drank only skimmed milk. She wanted special water-decaffei-
nated coffee, and when he was about to watch *60 Minutes* she put on
the Jane Fonda workout tapes. Still, his own tolerance surprised him.

76

As a rule he found her disruptions novel, refreshing. When occasionally they went to town together, he felt himself seen in a new way. Or an old way, enfranchised again as a parent.

None of this had he expected when Caroline had proposed with undeniable logic: "She's young to start college, Ben, only seventeen. She's been through a lot. Why have her board her first year when her father lives twenty minutes from campus? Doesn't make sense." He agreed.

"How's her love life? Is she into boys?"

"Don't know yet. She's only been with me six weeks. She's still scared about starting college, and she's never been talkative. You may recall that her mother did all the talking."

The waitress brought their drinks and took their orders: two Fisherman's Platters.

A lot of things he didn't know. Some he no longer cared to. He'd watched her grow by installments, a month each summer to rediscover the intricacies of dawning womanhood, the strains of parenting. One month to work out a friendly balance of silence and talk. He felt her watching him, noticing his hesitancies, sizing up his limits. She never spoke of life with her mother. They kept busy for that month, gorging themselves with lobster, prowling through antique shops along the coast, sailing together off Camden. One summer they'd taken a cottage at the Cape. Still, there's no substitute for day-to-day living with your own child. He'd known that as he stood in the white light of pain that hot August day and waved good-bye. She wore braces then, and almost no makeup. She'd run back from the car for a last quick hug, then whispered, "Take care." "Don't worry, hon," he said. She pressed so close he could feel her soft small breasts and the beat of her heart through her light summer shirt. "You'll see plenty of me."

Now she would. Was it too late? What did too late mean? Too late for what?

"She gonna come up here next summer?" asked Steve. "Bike around the Island with me?"

"She's talked about it. Bought herself a Raleigh with the money she's made waitressing. You're the only one in the family who could challenge her."

"Why don't you come with her?" Steve took a swallow of beer.

"You might get a surprise, enjoy it."

True. Maybe. There was a pull — back to the simpler way of life, rural Nova Scotia where people grew their veggies and still went to church. Not America, though. And try to explain that to a brother who'd found refuge here from Vietnam and continued to chant the blessings of peaceful, angelic Canada. It had given him a home. And money.

"Maybe I will. On the other hand, by June she might be dying to escape."

"Caroline bring her up to Lewiston?"

"No. Greyhound. Lugging a ton of gear."

She'd been at the bus station when he arrived, twenty minutes after final dismissal. He'd wanted to be there first, but Mr. Dalmar delayed him. Urgent business. This principal's business was always urgent. So he'd been late. She was standing there perfectly calm, centered in an island of duffel bags, stuffed nylon pouches, cross-country skis, rackets, and the one hard-sided green suitcase Caroline must have lent her. For a split second he thought of a poem he'd taught the day before about a single jar on a hill in Tennessee, a jar that by its presence composed about itself (he tried to persuade the yawning tenth graders) a whole world. Seeing her there — young, quietly beautiful — he felt awkward. And afraid.

"Hi, Dad."

When he hugged her he smelled perfume and felt the body of a woman. She'd let her hair grow. It was almost like welcoming a stranger, except that when the wrist turned a certain way, the eyes glanced at him over dinner (deep blue, almost purple eyes), or when at night she left a bedroom door slightly ajar and he could see her dark hair against the pillow and hear her light breathing — in these and a dozen other daily movements he saw Caroline. A nearly neutral seeing, now. Once, such recognitions would have caused pain, spelled threat. But these echoes were like a gentle touch whose resonance he had yet to plumb, whose danger — if indeed they held any — he had yet to test.

Attention to such nuances was out of place when one was savoring Bay of Fundy scallops in Yarmouth, Nova Scotia, with a brother who prided himself on being a free spirit. They worked their way through clams, lobster tail, halibut. Steve appeared to be in no hurry.

"Night life in Halifax is picking up, Ben," he said, squeezing lemon onto a scallop. "Used to be pretty quiet. But now . . ."

The usual. A review of Steve's conquests, sexual and financial. Annoying prick. Ben fed his responses in slowly, timing them with the quiet irony of one who knows his conquests are hardly news: coaching the debating team to first place in state competition, conveying the treachery of misplaced modifiers to a comatose afternoon class.

Finally, they were done. Steve picked up the check.

"I'll get it, Steve."

"You get the next one."

They left a healthy tip for the undernourished waitress, got their coats, and headed past the huge stuffed moosehead over the cash register at the entrance to the dining room. Steve paid and picked up a toothpick.

⊣⊩

Outside, though it was only nine o'clock, the streets were deserted.

"Gonna have a treat," said Steve. "Cheer you up."

When had he said he needed cheering?

"It's over in Pointe de l'Église."

"Good God, what's that?"

"Spot on the highway between here and Digby." Steve dropped his toothpick onto a frozen puddle and stooped to open the car door on the driver's side. "You can get in. It's not locked."

Ben opened the door, threw his small bag in back, and settled himself.

"Buckle up," said Steve. "The law here now."

Ben obeyed, then released his bucket seat as far back as he could. His back had begun to ache. At least the meal had settled his stomach. His mind was awash with vague impressions. Steve seemed more aggressive than ever, or was it simply, once again, the hard edge of reality pressing in? Distance softens. Outlines blur. Here was Steve himself, turning on the heater, easing the car onto the winding two-lane highway — that assured profile, that sexy scar. Ben closed his eyes.

He dozed. He was somewhere back on the ferry from Portland. Too cold to stay on deck, he'd sat up front in the lounge watching the marbled blue of the bay from behind huge windows, waiting for the whales you could sight if you were lucky. He hadn't been lucky. No whales. No porpoises. Just frothing waves that crested high toward

79

the center of the crossing, then leveled off toward shore. He'd found himself thinking of Karen, remembering her grin as he left. "Tell Uncle Steve to keep a couple of weeks open for me this summer."

High above them hung the round orange moon. Halloween moon. Beyond the dark treetops lining the road, he could make out a few stars silvering the sky.

Someone on the radio was singing in a nasalized twangy voice. "Stompin' Tom," chuckled Steve. "He stands on a board and beats time while he sings and strums. By the end of a performance he's stomped clear through the board. Caught on for a bit in Toronto, but now he's dropped out of sight. Came from the Island."

Ben grunted. He was trying to find the Little Dipper. Never very good at this, he remembered frosty nights in the backyard in Lewiston straining to identify the heavenly configurations with Karen, small and anxious, by his side. She wanted her homework done properly, the names accurate. His daughter.

They passed small darkened houses set back from the road, a village in which everything appeared closed except one roadside Fish and Chips stand and the Club d'Age d'Or.

"What's Rapee Pie?" asked Ben, noticing a sign.

"Big Acadian dish."

A motorcycle zoomed toward them out of nowhere, tipping crazily.

"Bastard," muttered Steve.

He turned off the highway and headed up a narrow dirt road bordered by dense trees. Despite the high moon, Ben could make out nothing but walls of black.

"Where are we going?" asked Ben.

"You'll see."

Ben had his suspicions. Every year, when he made the trip to Nova Scotia, they had an adventure together. Once, it had been snowmobiling on Prince Edward Island. Another time, a flight to Newfoundland, where Steve had taken him ice fishing. Always the push was to try something new. Always, at some point, women were involved. At the end of the visit, Ben went home convinced again of his own incorrigible conventionality. His longing for simple domestic comfort seemed tame, pale, suspect. He enjoyed sex, God knows, had sought it in various ways through the past three years. But he wasn't made for singles bars. He could not slip into the role of the forty-year-old looking for a quick fix. "Your problem," Steve told him, "is you just fell too early for the old monogamy model."

Maybe. In any case, beside Steve he turned out to be the wimp. Even though he'd fought — and Steve hadn't. Somehow, that bravery or cowardice (depending on how you saw it) seemed no longer to count. He'd shot men at close range, seen their faces split. He'd caught the severed legs of a friend.

Steve was pulling into a small clearing crowded with battered cars and half-ton trucks. Beside the small, one-storey dull red building, a mud-spattered green and white van was parked. Dark brown shutters covered the front windows of the building.

Steve switched off the motor. "We're here." He got out of the car. "Better lock it," he said in a low voice.

Ben followed his brother along the dirt path to the front door.

The small outer hallway reeked of mud and tobacco. Jackets and parkas crowded the hooks along the wall. Ben shed his coat as Steve spoke to the swarthy man with a sagging jaw and one crossed eye who stood by the inner door.

"Been here before?"

Steve opened his wallet and showed something. The man opened the door.

Steaminess and sweat — that was the first impression, a dense smoky atmosphere of bodies at close range suffused with a strange, dim orange light. Men filled the room. They sat crowded around small tables, smoking, drinking, talking. Against the back wall, to the right, stood a bar with one bartender. Three men were hunched over the counter watching a TV set high on the wall behind the counter, above stacked bottles and glasses. Hockey. To the left of the bar, on a small crude stage, sat five women. For an instant Ben thought them naked; then he saw that each wore a scanty bra and bikini panties. They sat quietly on high stools. Three of them looked out at the men, expressionless, as if their minds had been completely turned off. The other two kept their eyes down.

"He said there was one table left," said Steve as they stood for a moment adjusting to the half light.

Ben saw now that the orange glow came from a fluorescent light above the bar. In front of the stage three orange spotlights beamed down on the girls. Except for dim light from a few wall brackets, the rest of the room was dark.

Music came from speakers hung in each corner, soft French singing.

"C'mon," said Steve.

They pushed between crowded tables toward the empty one over near the bar. Immediately, a man in jeans and a black T-shirt approached.

"Something to drink?" Already he'd sized them up as English.

"Two Schooners," said Steve.

In the center of the table stood a folded white notice with something printed on both sides. Ben brought it closer to read. He flipped to the English side and finally made it out. *For $5.00 the female of your choice will dance on your table for the length of one record.*

He should have known.

He looked carefully at the girls. Four were blond. The one on the far right, dark-haired, appeared heavier than the others. Impossible to guess their ages beneath the glaring lights. How impassive, almost lifeless, they seemed. Perhaps they were drugged. Hardly likely. Perhaps they had instructions to sit quietly. Now and then the dark-haired one swung her crossed leg slightly. Were they bored?

"Where do they come from?" he asked Steve, who was smiling as he lit another cigarette. He allowed himself three a day, stoutly defending his right to this, for he jogged, exercised, was fit.

"Bring 'em in from Quebec. Ever see anything like it?"

Yes. What point in saying so? More aggressive, too. In San Francisco — where the women weren't as good looking and taunted you to tuck a dollar bill, or more, into their G-strings. In Saigon, where they kowtowed to you in a way that had finally made him sick.

He sipped his beer.

The music was lovely — a soft female voice now, singing an unfamiliar song in French. Simple guitar accompaniment. Occasionally her voice was lost beneath talk and laughter, the clink of metal and glass.

At the table nearest them a thickset man in a dark threadbare flannel shirt kept rubbing and twisting one end of his rather theatrical black mustache. He called the waiter over and with a broad hairy hand motioned toward the stage. Nodding, the waiter left him and approached a man standing in the shadows to the left of the stage. He wore a dark jacket and trousers and a bow tie, and his black hair was slicked back flat against a head that was itself somewhat flat.

The man listened to the waiter, nodded, turned, and walked to the third girl from the left. Leaning forward over the edge of the low stage, he whispered to her. The other women paid no attention. The girl looked down at her high-heeled shoes and swung her leg. After a few seconds she uncrossed her legs, stood, and moved slowly toward the stairs. She walked like a cat. Accompanied by the man in the dark jacket she threaded her way past tables of men in jeans, work pants, steel-toed boots, padded vests, open-necked flannel shirts. A few still wore their orange hunting vests. Eyes trailed her. She approached the table near Ben.

He could have reached out and stroked her thigh. The cold metal of his beer can grew damp against his pressing fingers.

She raised a shining slender leg and, with the help of her escort, pulled herself up onto the empty chair. The man with the mustache said something to her in French. She ignored him and, still holding her escort's hand, stepped onto the table.

Someone put on a new record.

She began to move, rotating softly to the rhythm of the high sweet French singing. Ben wondered if her movements connected with the words of the song. Her knees, hips, shoulders undulated, pulsing faster and faster. She moved with incredible grace, her whole body singing a sinuous invitation, the thrust of her breasts, her hips, calling to them, calling. She arched her body proudly, exuberantly, as if she wished its every muscle, its hidden nerves and secret pores, the shining of its radiant flesh to be seen by everyone, not one detail overlooked. This was not coyness but pure and lavish display.

Ben looked at the face of the man who had hired her. He leaned back in his chair, his eyes traveling slowly up and down the vision gyrating before him. The small red silk bra dropped to the table. The man leaned forward to pick it up, then stopped.

"Rules of the house," whispered Steve. "No touching."

They sat about five feet from the dancing girl. She moved her shoulders back and forth, swaying, her hips rotating, her smoothly curved buttocks back, then forward, her elbows flickering first in

83

front, then behind. She glanced at her client and then away, past him, toward the others held in the circle of orange light now trained upon her. Her flesh glowed. Every few seconds she'd stop, hold her polished body immobile. Then she'd start again, slowly, languorously, her long silver fingernails catching spears of light.

Desire licked Ben, flaming every nerve. She looked almost sweet, almost soft, the full pointed tanned breasts (difficult to tell in this light, but she did look tanned) swinging slowly as she rippled and revolved before them.

And then she was naked.

Not everyone seemed to notice. Some went on talking and laughing. One man at the bar swung his stool away from hockey and stared at her, his cap pushed back on his dark hair. He looked about nineteen.

Suddenly the girl raised her arms high above her head. In her armpits Ben saw tufts of gold. Then, as if she knew time was almost up, she reduced her movements to a subtle sway. The music stopped. The man at the table clapped, joined by those nearest him. Boots pounded the floor. As Steve clapped, he looked over at Ben for his reaction.

She ignored it all and leaned toward the man in the dark jacket, who had approached the table quickly as soon as the record stopped.

He handed her a short blue covering which she slipped on. Her golden breasts disappeared. Then, with his help, she stepped down, scooped up bra and panties, and, holding these, she disappeared somewhere behind the stage.

As though a curtain had parted briefly before them and then been pulled shut, the men folded back into themselves, bending toward their beer. The young man at the bar swung his stool around toward the TV.

⊰⊱

"What d'ya think?" Steve's eyes were on Ben. "Wanna get one?"

"Are you driving all the way to Halifax tonight?"

"Not on your life. Got reservations in Digby. We won't stay here long, but I wanted you to see it."

Plus ça change . . .

But who else was there? And when the chips were down, three

years ago, who'd come through? Agreeing even (though he'd sworn he never would, amnesty notwithstanding) to come over the border, all the way to Springfield, testify in court, fight for his brother, certify that he lived clean and worked hard and didn't abuse his wife and deserved the best he could get in privileges connected with his daughter Karen, then fourteen and vulnerable.

"So?"

Ben nodded. Why not? He couldn't analyze his feelings. Didn't want to. The beer and Scotch had begun to work. He felt half in a dream. There was some strange chemistry in this godforsaken place, something rough but . . . well, honest, maybe. None of the phony glamor or heavy sleaze he'd felt elsewhere. Or maybe it was just the orange light. Men here drank their beer, watched their women, went home to their Catholic wives, begot more children, took them all to Mass next morning. The church was just down the road, Steve had said. Provincial landmark. Baptized brutality. Or maybe it was something more complex, the sense of time passing and nowhere to go. On the other hand, maybe it was quite simple. Lust. Mixed with voyeurism. He was tired of thinking.

"It's up to you," he said.

Apparently Steve had made up his mind long before. He called over the waiter and whispered in his ear. The man nodded, offered Ben a sly grin, then headed toward the keeper. After a nod from her boss, the dark-haired girl on the far right stood up, left the stage, and came toward them.

There were only two chairs at their table. Steve stood as she approached. He offered a hand, then retracted it as the escort helped her onto the table. She wore a thin gold chain about one ankle, like the ID bracelets they'd worn years ago, in high school. Ben couldn't decipher the engraved lettering.

Someone put on a new disk. A man and a woman began to sing in low sweet harmony.

Her underwear glowed green and silky. When the bra dropped, Ben stared at the soft shining pile. He longed to finger it, stretch it, rub his hand against its smoothness, sink his face into it. Instead, he trained his eyes on the flickering gold ankle bracelet inches away, then slowly looked upward — up the slender legs, past the green bikini panties held in back by one narrow band, up farther, past the slender waist, the ribs which moved like keys someone was playing beneath the taut shiny skin, up farther past the full and slightly sagging breasts, their pink nipples, up farther . . . to the face.

He stopped.

The face was Karen's. Same small upturned nose with the bump in the middle. Same high cheekbones and dark full eyebrows. Same hair, a bit shorter, lying against her bare shoulders with just a hint of wave, parted in the middle, unchecked, so that when she bent her face downward her hair fell into her eyes, and then she'd snap her head back and the hair would fall against her shoulders, down her back . . .

She gazed off into space as though no one existed, as though around her were no gaping men in lumberjack shirts, no steel-toed workboots tapping to the music, no eyes devouring her, longing to touch but forbidden, no smell of dust and whiskey, but only an empty uninhabited place in the center of which she danced, her smooth and shining limbs singing of pleasures they would never know.

Karen had the same way of staring, the same way of tossing her hair back, the same —

Ben stood up. He'd spotted the sign for the john when they'd ordered drinks, over between the bar and the stage. *Garçons*.

He pushed between men toying with their cigarettes, downing their Schooners. The young man at the bar, again turned sideways on his stool, eyed Ben as he passed.

⊰⊱

He pushed open the door into the small cold bathroom. One lightbulb hung suspended from the ceiling. To its short chain someone had tied a black shoelace from which dangled a small naked pink plastic doll. The room held one toilet, a copper-stained sink, a small high window.

He stood quietly for a moment. Then he used the toilet and rinsed his hands. No hot water. No soap. Above the sink hung a small cracked pocket mirror. He glanced in it. Same face.

Outside, the music continued. Same melody. Same voices. Surely Steve hadn't paid another five dollars so his brother wouldn't miss anything! Be just like him.

Ben leaned back against the door, trying to steady himself, trying to blot out the picture of Karen at the boat that morning. She'd driven him there (was it really this same day?), waved good-bye as he steamed off into the blue yonder. Glad, probably, to be left alone. She was going to study, she'd assured him. Had two term papers to work through in rough draft. Wanted to get off to a good start. She wouldn't be fooling around. She'd watch the house, feed the dog, put out the garbage.

Same house where she'd been born. She knew the routine. Same house where he and Caroline had raised her to the age of fourteen. The house he'd got when Caroline got the child.

The rough hard surface of the door pressed against his shoulders, flattening the nap of the fisherman-knit sweater Caroline had made for him during her pregnancy. "Honeycomb stitch," she'd called it. He dredged up the word absentmindedly, only vaguely aware of memory's dangerous flick. What other treacheries lay there, waiting to ambush him?

He was seeing, again and again, the dancer. Her slim buttocks, her moving muscles, the play of her singing hips. Her soft breasts, her emptied face, the lazy fall of her shining black hair. Her vacant eyes looked somewhere far beyond them. Where was it? Was it anywhere? She'd be covering herself now, walking back with her keeper. Where would she be by tomorrow evening? Back over the border into Quebec? Did she come here every week, or did they rotate?

What feeling burned behind her luscious breasts? He *wanted* feeling there — lust to lick her in a slow yellow fire, passion to flare silver and crimson and blue, torching flames to sear the insides of that radiant body, transform her glowing shell to a husk of spent life, ashes that could speak. He wanted her to *live*.

"Ben?"

Steve, his voice low and controlled.

"Ben, you still in there?"

Water gurgled in the toilet tank. The small high window rattled. The wind must be coming up outside.

"Anything the matter, Ben? You okay?"

He stared at the stupid plastic doll with her straw-colored hair. His tongue grew dry, a thick slice of felt filling his mouth. Through the center of his chest shot a sharp burning pain. It would pass. All of it would pass.

Steve hated to wait. He would have to. No other way.

In a moment, just a moment, when he could find the words to answer, Ben would open the door.

Sin

BY EIGHT O'CLOCK ON MOST Saturday evenings the air in the confessional was absolutely putrid, an ammoniac mix of cabbage, garlic, beer, perfume, hair tonic, halitosis, and innumerable body odors that no simple hose-down could aerate or sanitize. The seemingly endless procession of penitents all afternoon and evening (two hours out for Mass and supper) deposited on Father O'Connor's forty-five-year-old shoulders not only its burden of guilt and sin, but left as well a lingering memento of corruption and filth, the heavy odor of mankind at its worst. Not twenty feet from the immaculate sanctuary with its linen-covered marble altar lay this dense penetrating residue of life's ongoing decay.

He'd sometimes think, as he finally shut the heavy door of his middle compartment (usually at ten after eight), "When people tell me sin is passé, a mere relic of a time when humans actually believed in such medieval, simplistic notions, I should lead them to the confessional. Give 'em a good sniff of the stench of sin. It's real."

⚓

This particular Saturday evening the smell was especially bad. It was the end of a hot August day and his lines had been extra long all afternoon. His one assistant, Father Greg Donovan, was on holiday. "Great time to pick, Greg," his pastor had complained mildly when Greg requested these two weeks off. "August. Tourists. The Regatta . . ."

"It's my mother's eighty-fifth birthday," said Greg, well aware of his pastor's soft spot. "Whole family'll be there."

"Oh, for God's sake, Greg. Go ahead. I'll manage. And give the sweet ol' gal a kiss for me."

So Greg was off.

But the sinners still came.

⚜

He'd lingered over the supper — corned beef and cabbage — ready for him at six-fifteen when he finally made it to the table after five o'clock Mass. For these two weeks he was eating in the kitchen on Saturday night.

"Kept you a bit late tonight, Father," said Dora Blake, who'd wanted to be done by seven to take her nephew to the show.

"Epidemic of sin, Dora," said he, gearing himself up for the challenge of corned beef and cabbage after an afternoon of equally devastating odors.

"Go on, Father," said she, pouring him a tall glass of milk.

No beer between confessions on Saturday nights.

"Don't hang around after, Dora," he said. She looked weary tonight, somehow. "I can wipe up the dishes later."

That's what people liked about Father O'Connor. Regular. They'd had him as pastor at St. Michael's only a few months now, but it didn't take long to see that he was regular, didn't put on airs like his predecessor, Father Tooley, now on his way, it was said, to becoming a Monsignor. Very Reverend.

Father O'Connor knew how to wash and dry a dish. He was a decent pastor in a time when they could be hard to find.

⚜

Back in church, Pete O'Connor saw penitents already kneeling near his box. Women, mostly. He'd never get out early tonight. He glanced at them absentmindedly. No point in trying *not* to identify them. In a community this small, this Catholic, you knew the voices, the weekly sins, the smell of each one. Turnips. Beer. Cabbage — yes, cabbage. (Well, they'd have to put up with his smell tonight, though

90

he *had* used mouthwash.) Perfume. He'd like to personally annihilate the makers of those sweet musky perfumes which so often permeated his Saturday afternoon box as he listened to whispered narratives of petting, illicit or kinky sex, delicious but anxiety-producing pleasures stolen from lives he saw as otherwise drab, monotonous, and often downright crushing.

He settled his cassock on his knees. It still seemed necessary in this rather conservative small parish to wear the cassock as he walked through the church heading for the box. He knew that, like so many things, priestly garb was somewhat out of fashion these days. Younger folk, who knew nothing about the old Church, often sought him out in the rectory or in the sacristy after Mass on Thursday nights, when they'd sit down and tell him their sins, eye to eye. Sex didn't seem to trouble them so much. Unless accompanied by promiscuity. Or if one party was married. They still saw that as wrong, thank God. But the straightforward pleasures of the body — these seemed to them normal, God-given to be enjoyed, not a source of worry. Except for AIDS of course — but that was a whole other story. And there the question of sin became so distorted in the minds and mouths of biblemongers, even among his own people, that it didn't bear thinking about. Though he'd had to preach on it.

He heard the first penitent settling on the other side.

He took a breath, inhaled deeply through his mouth into which he popped a Cert, and slid open his window.

The figure (instantly he knew it was a woman) knelt with her head against the screen, eyes down.

Ah, blessed illusion of anonymity! Still something to be said for the old-style confession.

"Bless me, Father, for I have sinned — "

Mrs. Rafferty.

Without turning his head, he saw her — the narrow crafty eyes, the sloping face, the mouth that always looked as if it had just, to its surprise, bit an onion. She was one of those parishioners they said had a heart of gold. And no doubt about it — she worked hard for the church. For the annual bake sale she produced half an acre of baklava. Who else could do that? For the Altar Guild she took up or let down servers' surplices, as the case might be. At Easter and Christmas she knocked herself out cleaning and decorating the church. She seemed to be related to everyone in town. 'Twas said she'd had a firm hand with her children, now grown and gone, and he didn't doubt it. Nothing soft about Mrs. Rafferty.

"I have come very close to losing my temper, Father."

In the dim light, he polished a faded button on the lap of his cassock and wondered at Mrs. Rafferty in a temper. Would she throw something? Swear?

"And I have lied several times."

They all lied. Who, he wondered, told the truth? What was truth? Christ himself had shown how complex that one was.

"For these and all the sins of my past life I am sorry."

She rustled a bit and started on her Act of Contrtion.

"O my God, I am heartily sorry. . ."

A lot of them didn't know that prayer any more. When he had tried to explain contrition to his Youth Group in their unit on sin, they had been puzzled.

"You must have a purpose of amendment," he told them. "A firm purpose."

They'd never heard of such a thing.

"You mean otherwise you're not forgiven, Father?"

"What's the point?" he'd replied. "This is not a game. God sees your heart. Why ask forgiveness if you fully intend to go out and do it again?"

"But what if you don't intend and you just go out and do it?"

"Every case is unique," he said.

"And what about Magdalen? Didn't she go out and do it again?"

"Who knows?" he replied. "We're not told." (Personally, he thought she did.)

"And what about 'Let him who is without sin cast the first stone'?"

He'd felt a tiny thrill of satisfaction. They knew their gospel, at least.

"We're not talking about judgment. We're talking about sorrow and what it means. And forgiveness."

They wanted forgiveness. No doubt about that. Oceans of it. Sometimes they weren't even sure for what. But they wanted it available.

". . . I firmly resolve, with the help of thy grace, to confess my sins, do penance, and to amend my life, Amen."

She would know about a firm purpose of amendment.

Trying to suppress threatening flatulence, he lifted his hand to absolve her. It was the corned beef. He'd try to control it. He didn't want to sit trapped in his own smell!

"*I absolve you, in the name of the Father and the Son and the Holy Spirit,*" he said, sitting tight. "Go now, my daughter, and for your penance make the Way of the Cross once. Ask God for the grace of forgiveness in your own daily life."

You couldn't give this penance to everyone. Mrs. Rafferty would like making the Stations.

"Father — "

He took his fingers off the handle of the sliding window he'd been about to close.

"Yes."

"Father, I want to talk to you about something."

"Yes."

He leaned his head against the screen, his ear closer to her mouth. Odd, but often they talked about *real* sins after confession was over. As if the ritual opened up some possibility for them.

"It's my son."

"Yes."

She'd had three. Which one? Something pulled at him . . .

"He was home from the mainland last weekend, Father."

Ah. Jeremy.

"And he was very upset, Father. He's been working over there for over ten years now. He usually only gets home for a week or so in September."

Mrs. Rafferty always carried a faint pine odor, like bathroom spray. Clean. Refreshing. It came upon him now, as he felt his hands clasping one another too tightly.

"He's been following the . . . the scandals in the papers, Father." Her voice dropped. He barely heard her.

He saw Jeremy — Jerry as they called him. A slight boy with an angelic face, sky-blue eyes, a way of ducking you if he saw you coming. As if he was afraid. He'd been at their school only one year, 1974. The year of Mrs. Rafferty's breakdown or whatever it was. "She took a long bad spell," Dora had told him once. "Hallucinations. The works. Had to put her away for a whole year, Father."

He knew it from Jeremy.

"My mother doesn't *want* me!" the boy sobbed, night after night, pounding his pillow, soaking it. High strung. "My two brothers went to Uncle Jim. Kate's with the sisters. They sent me here."

"It's only until your Mum gets better, Jerry," he'd say. Wincing inwardly. Because he knew something about mother loss. His own had died when he was fifteen, a young fifteen. "My son Peter has a gift for languages," she'd say to anyone who'd listen. "He wants to be a philosopher and a priest." Doted upon, that's what he'd been. Tenderly doted upon. Thereafter he'd been delivered into the hands of pseudo-maternity in a figure not unlike Mrs. Rafferty herself. A distant aunt. After Auntie Bea's ravings, the rigid decorum of seminary training had come as a relief. For he had a mind. That at least they addressed. If not the body.

Mrs. Rafferty sighed.

Had he missed something?

"Jeremy came home to talk to me, Father."

He heard the pride. He'd observed that before. How mothers like to be sought out. Confided in. But now, in his heart, ice.

"He waited until the final afternoon. I knew he must have come for something, Father, made the whole long trip. He couldn't afford to fly so he came over on the ferry — "

"Yes," he heard himself say quietly. "Better not to pry into a soul. It's God's business."

"Exactly."

He'd almost slipped and said "Mrs. Rafferty." Surely she knew he knew. Was she counting on that? He saw her sly eyes, downcast now. She gave him the creeps, heart of gold or not. "Have 'em in every parish," said the Bishop once just a few months ago when they were trading notes on his new assignment. "Just be glad she doesn't cause you any real trouble, Pete."

"Well, Father," her voice caught.

Was she crying?

He heard the sharp intake of breath, as if she were willing, struggling, to hold herself together.

"I . . . I . . ."

"It's all right," he said quietly. "Take your time." Better pine than garlic. Who knew what might come next? Besides, she was obviously troubled.

94

"Then, the last day, he took me for a drive, Father, and when we were high on the bluff overlooking the ocean he — "

She caught a sob.

He bowed his head lower. His foot had a cramp. This was minor compared to the wave of dread sweeping through him, in every pore, engulfing him. An overwhelming nausea. He'd forgotten about Jeremy. It had been only once —

"He — "

Sniffs.

"It's all right, now. Take a deep breath. We have time."

It was very important not to convey a sense of hurry. They'd been drilled on this in the seminary. Allow time. *Be patient.* He was not a patient man.

"He told me, Father, that he" — here, another gulp — "he, too, had had . . . that . . . well, he was away from us only one year, Father. I was . . . sick . . . He would have been thirteen . . ."

Surely she knew he knew her! He kept his eyes down. His heart pounded and he felt a tic starting in one cheek.

"He . . . one priest there, Father . . ."

One. Was it only one? He'd suspected others. Had asked immediately for a transfer. And the bishop (what a man, Bishop Clancy, moldering now in the grave) had said, "Yes, yes. Of course. Where to? That's the question. You do have a mind. You were miscast at St. Alban's. We should never have sent you there after those years of teaching philosophy. But we had a need . . . it's all God's work, you know. I'll put you in town. Lots to do. Work, Pete. It's a great distraction. Better get a hold of yourself or you could get us all into real trouble." The bishop leaned back in his chair and looked at him with those smoldering blue eyes. "Believe me, there's more joy in heaven over one sinner returned than ninety-nine never lost. How's your golf game coming?"

That was all. Neat. Swift. No ravelly edges.

Except, of course, for the boy. Jeremy. Whose surprised and terrified pale blue eyes returned to haunt him in sleepless nights for months afterward.

"He said it happened only once, Father — "

She stopped. He heard her beads rattle against the wood. She was shifting her position, rummaging in the dark through her purse. He heard it unsnap. After Kleenex probably.

"He . . . he . . . didn't give me details."

She honked.

He *saw* the details . . . the dusky summer evening, the head boy running into his office, it must have been ten o'clock or after, it stayed light very late in midsummer. "Father, we can't get to sleep. Jerry Rafferty is making too much noise. He's crying. He keeps it up. We've told him to shut up and he just gets worse."

"Tell Jeremy to come here."

Then — the slight figure of the pale golden-haired boy standing in the doorway of the office. The light from the corridor behind shone through his thin seersucker pajamas, outlining the slim legs, the narrow chest, the darker wedge near the crotch, the shoulders still quivering.

"Come here, Jeremy. What's the matter?"

He stood before the easy chair. Only one light on in the office, sufficient for reading the breviary. Its words that night had fallen like chalk dust in his mouth, his mind. It had been a long, hard day, week.

She unsnapped her purse again.

"And I didn't want to pry, Father. Like you said. But" — she caught her breath tremulously — "he cried, Father. A grown man, crying. Right there on the bluff above the ocean. 'It wasn't right,' he said. 'I knew it. It scared me. But I didn't dare tell anyone.'"

It wasn't right.

Now, in the fetid closeness of the narrow confessional fifteen years later, he can feel it again, the light fragile warmth of the boy as he took him in his arms, sat with him there in the rocker, turned out the light finally so the only light in the small office came from evening gathering slowly outside.

"Tell me about it, Jeremy," he said softly.

And the boy, hesitant at first, then in a rush as strong arms did not give way but continued to hold him, rocking, in the dark — he told about the father found dead in a gutter, choked on his own vomit, about the mother who pinched him when he wouldn't obey, whose whole personality had shifted so drastically three years before, who seemed no longer able to tolerate this youngest, unexpected son, who'd grown thin and pale and tight-lipped until finally she was called "very sick" and he was told the priests would take him until she got better.

Sitting there in the quiet gloom, warmed by an intimacy wondrous and new, Pete O'Connor had been overcome by a surge of desire. "Lust" he'd call it later when he told his bishop — eye to eye, for in those days he sought perfect contrition. "I went too far," he said.

"And now, Father" — Mrs. Rafferty sounded more together, as if the Kleenex had done its job, she was mopped up, she could get on with life — "here's what really troubled my Jeremy. 'A matter of conscience,' he called it. He came over here, he said, because he felt he should have some input into the Inquiry."

It had been going on for weeks, would continue for months. The island was rocked. He strove to be direct with his people, to allay their sense of betrayal.

What was this church he served?

"But he didn't know whether he should, Father. He'd tried to forget it, he said. And he almost did. And after he came back to us, life went on, he graduated from high school, valedictorian, Father, at seventeen, and went off to the mainland to get himself a job. We felt bad, but — "

Here, one long emphatic sniff.

"He's made good, Father. And we're proud of him."

What did she expect him to say?

He waited.

" — but I don't know, Father, that he should get into this whole mess. He has his career, his family to think of. 'Why not let sleeping dogs lie?' I said to him. 'It's a matter of conscience,' he said, staring at the waves. 'A matter of conscience. The truth has to come to light. And if I can help — ' He always was a sensitive boy, Father."

She rattled her beads again.

"What do you think, Father?"

There it was. The question.

This was what she wanted.

What did he think?

A layer of dread had crept through his body and soul as she spoke. He saw it: the courtroom, the faces of the men he'd taught with during those three miserable years when, for reasons he couldn't fathom (he should have known better than to try), he found himself stuck in a country boarding school for poor boys aged seven to fourteen. Teaching spelling and arithmetic, monitoring play yard and dormitory. When he longed instead to argue with Kierkegaard, take on Karl Barth, unravel the intricacies of Wittgenstein. On the shelf now, after successfully teaching philosophy to their own seminarians. He saw the face of the judge, a man about his own age perhaps, attentive, inscrutable, possibly someone he knew. He saw the headlines, the talk shows, the microphone stuck in the face of a casual passerby on the street, "Tell us, what do you think of — " A spasm of disgust choked him.

So much for the secular arm.

What did he think?

He saw the other arm, ecclesiastical, equally revolting: the office, the large desk, the weary bishop behind it — a man these days bowed down with iniquities — the dialogues, private interviews, interrogations, innuendoes, the cynicism, hope, faith, faithlessness, corruption and idealism, he'd come to recognize as life in the church. Life, period.

What was sin?

Was it wanting the truth *not* brought to light? Was sin wanting to let it lie?

Jeremy had gone off and made a life.

He, Pete O'Connor, a priest who for one dusky summer evening fifteen years ago had thrilled to hold in celibate arms the warm, responsive, quivering body of a thirteen-year-old boy — he was now to come forward as the sinner?

What is truth?

He turned to look at Mrs. Rafferty. Through the mesh screen he saw her small sly eyes. Surely she was baiting him. But what if she was not? What if Jeremy Rafferty, from of old a boy who kept his counsel, what if Jeremy Rafferty, now the husband of a comely woman and father of three, what if he had needed only to utter it, to tell his mother, what if that was as far as it would go?

And what if she, inscrutable as she was, needed only in this very moment to hear a word from her confessor — a word of counsel, forgiveness, reassurance. What if that was all?

"I do not know, Mrs. Rafferty," he said. A lump the size and weight of a stone grew in his aging throat. "I do not know, Mrs. Rafferty. It's a matter of conscience. Jeremy's conscience. And conscience is always a private matter. I'm afraid I do not know. You must pray, pray hard, and it will come to you. God bless you, now. And pray for me."

With a quick decisive movement, he slid the door shut.

—❧❧—

That night, after confessions, Father Pete O'Connor knelt half an hour on the prie dieu in the sanctuary of the emptied church. Except for the red vigil light hanging high above the main altar, all was darkness. The wind was coming up outside, a north wind. It rattled the back door, the windows. Branches of the large elm on the north side of St. Michael's brushed against ancient stained glass. He heard all this but vaguely, as from afar. Eyes shut, head in his hands, he was praying, searching within himself, he hardly knew for what, for something needed, nameless, elusive. Something that would answer his question, something, someone, that would answer him.

At length, rising stiffly, he cast a sharp eye about the large church, then headed out through the sacristy and locked its door behind him. Stars were coming out and the wind already held more than a touch of fall. He walked slowly across the small neat yard toward the back door of the rectory, climbed the steps and opened the door.

Once inside, he carefully wiped his shoes on the mat, snapped off the porch light behind him, and turned into the kitchen, toward the sink, unbuttoning his cassock as he went.

I Only Teach Comp

IT ISN'T MUCH. Some in the department carry a heavier load, three courses a semester. That's considered "full." I carry three, but I'm paid for a two-thirds load. It's the way they figure it over in administration — three courses, thirty-five in a class, regular conferences, papers graded on time: give her two-thirds of one salary at the Instructor level.

But I understand.

Because I haven't put in all those years getting ready. One argument. Because I don't have all those different preparations each semester. Another argument. Because really, when you think of it, I only have to do the same thing over and over — teach them how to punctuate, subordinate, rearrange, write. Help them resurrect the I they've buried in paragraphs of prose that defy analysis because you can't find the speaker.

Some days I feel eaten alive. I long for food, peanut butter spread on a thick slice of whole wheat bread, to keep up energy for those big guys who stand outside my office door waiting to get at me. Meeting so many students hungry for their I's leaves me oddly empty, ravenous. Worse yet: my officemate (whom I rarely see) favors sandwiches with pickles, onion, tuna, and peanut butter. The leftover smell of her lunches haunts this office. A peanut butter-holic, I salivate over her remains.

The office next door houses a full professor: Reginald D. Fulkins, noted scholar in his field. He inhabits his endowed chair with weight and stature and navigates the halls like the QEII. Actually, he's handsome in a craggy, whiskery way. The goatee is just so, the strands of gray hair are arranged across his pate. He is extremely vain and has one habit I detest — he pollutes our end of the hall with chain-smoked cigarillos. Occasionally, he sees me.

Just last Wednesday, he stopped me in the hall.

"Don't you live on F Street?" he said, as if decoding some obscure symbol.

"Yes," I said, "right behind you. I — "

"That's what I thought," he said, and sailed on down the hall.

I didn't tell him I knew his wife wore red underpants. She hangs laundry on this old-fashioned circular clothesline in her backyard before she goes out to work each morning. I'm usually up, wrestling with breakfast or feeding the dog. Often I catch sight of her bending over her laundry basket. Fire-engine red underpants have given me a whole new perspective on the chaired professor of linguistics.

I couldn't have chatted that day, even if he'd wanted to. Wednesdays are hectic: class at eight-thirty, conferences every fifteen minutes from nine-thirty to noon, then a bite (if I'm lucky), twelve-thirty and one-thirty classes, home just in time for the kids. They're still pretty little. Bubby's twelve, Jennifer nine. Once in a while, when I have to stay late, they go to Mother's. That particular Wednesday morning it was only nine thirty-five but already the hallway was crowded with the sea of jeans and backpacks and muscle and eyeliner I must navigate to reach my office door.

"Mornin', Ms. Henderson." "Mornin', Ms. Henderson."

Everything from jocks to dolls to budding scholars to kids so vague you wonder they ever found their way to school. Most of them I like, though less when they call me at home over misplaced modifiers, persistent run-ons, and other grammatical defects.

There I'll be, at the stove, trying to remember if I'm on the noodle or mozzarella layer of lasagna, say, and some light sweet voice will call for Ms. Henderson. I balance the phone on my shoulder and continue separating sticky noodles.

"I'm awfully sorry to bother you at home, Ms. Henderson, but about that paper . . ."

I survey the lasagna operation, shift gears, mimic the voice of the Comp 104 teacher. "Yes?"

Afterward, the paragraph may be better but our lasagna is a mess — one big run-on of cheese, noodles, meat sauce.

Season of Apples

Last Monday I missed lunch. That afternoon I was in the middle of a conference with Harley Richardson, a fourth-year business major. Without my course he cannot graduate. That lends a certain seriousness to the process. Harley's a cool one. Sits in the back row and taps his cowboy boots all through class. I could strangle him, but I try to smile. At the beginning of the semester I dismissed him mentally (a hazard when you teach comp), but Harley is not dumb. So there he was, sprawled out by my desk in his jeans and cowboy boots, waiting to hear my comments on his failed efforts at subordination.

The telephone rang.

I picked it up reluctantly.

"Gladys"

Mother. She lives ten blocks from campus. A widow of fifteen years and lonely, she's tediously good, determined not to be a burden. She saves up problems until something explodes. This was my lucky day.

"He absolutely refused to take them off," she nearly panted into the receiver.

I could guess what was coming. Bubby lives plugged in.

Harley began swinging his boot. I pointed to a trouble spot on his paper. He nodded, grinned, and looked down.

"Mother, it's just a stage. He'll grow out of it. The less attention you pay the better." He'd refused to take off his earphones, the ultimate insult.

Harley was writing something on his paper.

"But Gladys, if I let him get away with it now . . ."

"But Mother, he's always wired for sound. Don't be fooled. He knew every word you were saying. He can read lips, I swear — " How could I say maybe he had the right idea? You just cannot do that to your sevenry-five-year-old mother, not when she lives in the same town and takes care of your kids *gratis*.

So while I'm figuring out what to say doesn't Harley grin and pull out a peanut butter sandwich. At one-thirty in the afternoon! Hadn't he eaten lunch? I tried not to drool.

Finally she said, "I can see you're not listening, Gladys," and hung up.

"Troubles, huh?" he said, with the most extraordinary understanding, as he chewed.

We chatted a moment about subordination, compression, and he went off reconciled to his C, or at least mollified. Had he but known, I could have been bribed into a B: one taste of that peanut butter.

⊰⧓⊱

The quality of conferences varies with the student. Some are shy, some aggressive, convinced they already command the arsenal of grammatical nuance. The modest ones are often smartest. They know how much there is to worry about when you put a word on a page.

I have one rule: they leave their gum outside the door. It's difficult to be serious about a comma when someone is exploding a pink bubble against his face.

Ralph Lynch is a tall, dark-haired, soft-spoken student, quite literate and he knows it. He's just fulfilling a requirement. Occasionally, he gets carried away with adjectives. I was showing him how to cut and compress one paragraph that same week, just two days later, when the phone rang again. You can guess.

"Gladys, I know you may have a student right there, don't say a word, dear, just answer yes or no and that will tell me what to do. Cinders is loose."

Our dog. A Heinz 57 with lots of golden lab and a little collie. Gentle as a lamb, but wayward. We tie her up out back when we leave in the morning.

"She's arrived at my front door, Gladys, and she's carrying something. Guess what? Bright red underpants. Nice ones, Gladys. Silk, I think. Real silk. In fact, I didn't know you could get anything like that in town."

My mother has this thing about synthetics. Won't carry a vinyl purse.

Ralph, supposedly cutting adjectives, didn't move an inch.

"I mean, Gladys, someone paid a lot for these. Do you think I should try to find out whose they are?"

"No, Mother."

I reached over to his paper and pointed to a clot of adjectives. He nodded.

"But I just hate to take them," she said. "I wouldn't feel right."

I heard the longing. In a flash I saw my mother trying on red silk panties in the soft afternoon light of her tidy, empty house. Upstairs, so no one would see. Except God. She's convinced He's always looking.

"So you think I should forget about it?"

"Yes, Mother."

"You don't have any idea whose they are, then?"

"Yes, I mean no, Mother."

I had another flash vision, this time of me requesting an audience with Professor Fulkins. "Pardon me, distinguished man, but could we go somewhere and discuss an intimate matter . . ."

"No, Mother. Just forget it."

"Very well, dear. If you say so. But I certainly won't throw them away."

I never supposed she would.

"What about the dog?"

"Bubby will take care of her when he comes home."

I turned back to Ralph. We dealt with a misplaced modifier: *Running down the street my pants grew wet and wrinkled.* We straightened that one out. He left, grinning.

❈

Usually I do the first assignment with them, just to show that I too can sweat over prose. It seems to help their morale. They must write a simple narrative about taking a trip. Anywhere. Corny, but it works. With this assignment I first discovered their penchant for metaphor. For me, at that age, taking a trip would have meant something literal: you get in a car or on a train and go somewhere. These days, the smartest ones in Comp 104 often talk about some other kind of trip — hallucinogens, Jesus, the bottle, sex.

Last year I wrote my paper telling of our trip to the Redwoods: how Granny loved it but wanted to rest every two minutes as we wound our way through the Trees of Mystery; how Cinders ran away and had to be extracted from the women's bathroom; how Bubby wanted only to pick up idiotic souvenirs in the gift shop; how Jenny spent the whole time standing outside the shop calling dumb questions up to the huge Paul Bunyan guarding the entrance. I tried to work my little piece up to a climax, telling them how the end of the guided tour brought us to the "Cathedral Tree" which oozed piped-in music and Nelson Eddy singing "I think that I shall never see A poem lovely as a tree." I wanted them to see the absurd uses to which we put both nature and language. It fell flat. A-Number-One Dud.

I don't think I'll do even the first assignment next year. Perhaps I'm in no position to judge what climaxes can be shared.

⚜

Our office walls are thin in this old building. Now and then I can hear Fulkins on the phone. He has a low deep voice that resonates.

The other day he was talking to someone about his dream. I'm an expert on dreams. Once, I joined a dream group. A week was all I could stand: ten women in a room revealing their secrets. I'm no longer sure this is healthy. It was enlightening, though.

Talking of dreams loosens up students, too. After their trip narrative, I have them write out a dream, or make one up. (What's the difference?) Then we talk about the nature of metaphor and transitions. The last can be especially tricky. Do you always need to state transitions? How much can you count on your reader to follow your leaps?

The day of Fulkins' phone explosion, Darlene French was sitting in front of me with her journey narrative. Darlene is a case: always the too-low neckline, the swinging hips, the ironed-on jeans. When she bends over to pull on her boots in the morning you'd think something would split. Underneath, though, Darlene is intelligent. Sloppy, but intelligent. We were discussing the function of the semicolon and the use of adjectives. She's convinced that heaping on adjectives makes an image more "vivid" — a word I loathe. I restrained myself from the obvious comment: "You, Darlene, know intimately what only one layer can do. Why use two?" It would have been too sharp, too snide. Darlene would look puzzled, be puzzled. We were in the middle of the semicolon when Fulkins started.

". . . and then this huge diesel was coming at me," he shouted, "chug-a, chug-a, chug-a — "

"Now you understand that the semicolon is stronger than a comma and by many considered more formal?" I said.

Darlene looked distracted. "Yes," she said, batting her mascara.

"Then this huge train was coming from the opposite direction," he yelled, "and I could hear its wheels ringing on the track, the whistle screaming — "

.Was his wife on the other end, minus underpants?

"So how would you recast this?" I asked.

"Oh . . . oh, you mean the sentence?" Darlene looked as if her paper had just been delivered from the sea in a bottle.

"Yes, the sentence."

"Whammooo!" he yelled.

She jumped in the chair.

"Oh, oh, Ms. Henderson. I'm sorry — "

She looked at me with violet eyes. She circles them with something black and thick.

"That's okay. Suppose you take this home and recast the whole thing for next week, eliminating semicolons."

I was left with thoughts on the semicolon. Stronger than a comma. Needs a *however*, a *moreover*, after it. Use sparingly in modern prose. I've known a lot of relationships hanging on a semicolon. Perhaps that would be a way to teach it. If only a semicolon joins you, separate and recast. Seems too oblique an approach. Some people have trouble identifying independent clauses. For my part, I'm fascinated by the nature of conjunctions.

These kids are addicted to comma splices. I was trained to call them run-ons: two independent clauses run together. There are a number of run-ons in the department, but that's another story.

My mother returned the underpants. She worried about it. Dick, my husband, was full of suggestions. Special Delivery. COD Or maybe a singing telegram just to let her know they're at the PO in the unclaimed articles box? Or put it in the classifieds: *Found, one red silk pair of you-know-whats.* Better yet: have the deejay on KORX mention it in prime time.

I Only Teach Comp

My class produces pretty good dream papers, perhaps because I encourage them to forget about grammar, punctuation. Run-ons galore appear, radiant fragments, scintillating misplaced modifiers. Isn't that the relief of dreams? The composition is out of our hands, at last. They always like this assignment.

My own most recent dream I cannot tell them. Or anyone. Because "I only teach comp." That's what my colleagues say. It's the *just*, the *only*, that provokes me to question: What is real life?

Not this? Not in composition? Somewhere else, some other trip? Not the trip to Ms. Gladys Henderson's office to identify comma splices — though that can be fun, man, especially when her mother calls. She must be some bitch. But Ms. Henderson, she's okay. She just teaches comp.

But I know more about real life, the real lives around me, than you might think. That's the way it is here. We live in a town of ten thousand. Hills surround us. Everyone knows everyone, well, almost. Maybe I should say everyone knows something about everyone. Dick isn't with the university, thank God. He works out of town. Even so, paths cross. If it isn't church, it's school. If it isn't school, it's extracurriculars for your kids. Networks intersect.

So we know a lot about Fulkins. I know his wife wears red underpants, but that's just the tip of the iceberg, to use an unfortunate metaphor. I know he dreams. I know he dislikes students. I know he barely sees me. Perhaps to him I'm a bug. Remember Gregor Samsa's feeling about how his employer saw him? Fulkins is not my employer, of course, but he's higher on the scale. What scale? Pay scale, for one thing. About twenty thousand higher, at least. He has his PhD, his sabbaticals, his carefully arranged hours, his grasp of transformational grammar. I'm down here in the trenches uncovering I's, deleting adjectives, squashing semicolons, searching for valid connectives.

Where is real life?

In my trench, I fantasize. I dream. I used to worry about this. No more. Everyone does it. My daylight self goes on looking serious about punctuation. Meanwhile, I support the semicolon of several friendships, survive the comma intervals in a day, endure the ellipses of life, try to penetrate adjectival disguises. I've learned to subordinate a lot. And I retain delight in the vision of an old lady trying on someone else's red silk underwear beneath the forgiving eyes of her creator.

Perhaps real life is in dreams.

When I first came here, I would dream about Fulkins now and then. I hadn't met his kind of snobbery before, you see. I'd just assumed everyone saw how crucial it was to teach comp.

I'd pass him silently in the hallway and suppress various nasty thoughts. Don't dangle your participle at me, Buster. Okay, snob, ignore me. I happen to know your wife misplaced her modifier. Have you ever examined the strength of your connectives?

Of course I said none of these things because I only teach comp.

Then I had my dream, the final dream that put him in his place. That's the climax of this little piece, a climax I believe can be shared.

I captured him first. It wasn't hard. I snared him in metaphor, built him a pen of prepositions, and tossed him poison adjectives to munch while I got busy. I slammed the door shut on him and turned the key with a good solid period. Then I hooked up a hose of paratactically arranged nouns and piped in a steady stream of them to subordinate him.

When he was finally cowering in one corner near the bottom of a paragraph, I stood outside his pen and yelled exactly what I felt: "I question your persona, Mister, chaired or not. Your thesis sentence doesn't interest me one bit. In you I find no climax that can be shared. You'd better watch your verbs because I, for one, wouldn't want to be the predicate adjective to your disgusting copulative. So drop the persona and resurrect your I, literalize yourself back to life. It's out here. We're in it together, Herr Prof, and comp, yes Comp 104, is the ongoing essay that counts. I'm invisible to you. I'm the voice on the other side of the wall examining sentences, eliminating phrases, deleting and reconnecting. So you'd better watch out. I hold the key to your release.

"You stay in there a while and examine your connectives. I am thrilled not to be the object of your preposition. After you've thought over your place in the paragraph of life, perhaps we'll confer. I'll turn off the hose awhile so we can talk.

"I warn you, Herr Doctor, I've one condition for your eventual release. Next time you get a merit raise for navigating your prodigious fictional hulk through the waters of academic life, you are to find yourself a discreet manila envelope. In it you are to place a duplicate copy of the modifier your wife misplaced — pure red silk, please.

Nothing less. You don't have to tell anybody. I can keep a secret. Put my name on the outside — Ms. Gladys Henderson, Comp 104 — and slip it under my door. There's a certain little old lady whose derrière could stand to be modified. One silky red adjective might make her feel more vivid.

"Besides the envelope, I want one more thing. One jar of pure peanut butter. Jumbo size. No additives, oil and crunch intact. That's all. Not much, you must admit. A little something for body and soul.

"So now, just crouch there for a while. Experience the power of parataxis. Feel the confinement of subordination. Meditate on linguistic coherence. Morphologically speaking, you're placed. Masticate your adjectives, rearrange your sentence patterns, transform your grammar. Prepare for the end.

"There's no telling when it may come."

With the Continuing Ed Teacher

YOU WONDER HOW IT HAPPENS? It's easy.

My children understand it well.

You follow your parents around, you go to school, you marry, you follow your husband around, you have children, they follow you around, and then at some point it all begins to add up. You see them go, you figure you have some talents yet to be used, you use them, you make stuffed animals, you sell them, you make pocket money, the tax people take that, you decide to go back to school. What for? No one can take that away from you.

You know what? This is the best thing I've done in thirty years. And my daughter, the flower child still at thirty-eight, she envies me. "Mom," she says when she sees me poring over Augustine's *Confessions,* "Mom, why didn't you make me be a doctor?" She's finally learned how to do therapeutic massage and is busy at that these days. "Debbie," I say, "it was my dearest desire that one of my children would be a doctor. But I've never *made* you do anything. Maybe that was my mistake. But I'm trying not to think about it now. At last we've moved into town and I love this class." My husband says, "Why medieval history?" "Because," I say, "it has absolutely nothing to do with anything. So I want it."

He follows me around when I make beds in the morning. "Why are you making them fresh today?" he asks. "You did it four days ago."

"Because I do it when I feel like it," I reply. That drives him crazy. He's used to his own order.

Or take the grocery store. He follows me about, beside the cart or sometimes pushing it. "Why this?" he says. "Why this?" He scrutinizes my every move with the shopping cart. Yet all those years when the kids were home he was out in the barn painting, always the hope to make it big. He made it big enough to enable us to live out there with one car, which he always needed. Now we're in town and I can walk here. Take your class. Walk home. Move about on my own. And I love every minute of it.

Why did we come back here, thousands of miles from nowhere, when we've lived in the big cities: Boston, New York, Montreal, Toronto? The threads of a life may look tangled in a mess but really one strand hitches to another in amazing ways. From the inside, if you look at it long enough, you can find that strand, even though you can't make out the final pattern. You'll have to pardon my talking this way. For years I cut and stuffed and sewed these darling little calico stuffed animals. Brendan would come in sometimes — I was always working on the dining room table, till now, when I have my tiny sewing room, I made that the condition of my agreeing to move back into town — and he'd say, "Why do you waste your time doing that?" It didn't feel to me like waste of time. It was *my* time, when I was doing something for me, and the shape and feel and final perfection of those forms — people said they were much better than anything you could find in Halifax — satisfied me.

But we ended up here because we'd each gone to college here in this town. It's where we met. And there is a charm about Tantramar. People are friendly. Like you. Maybe in a big university I'd never have got up the nerve to talk to my professor, or maybe even to take a course. But your wife called me that day to see if I was still making my kangaroos with a baby in the pouch and we got talking . . . she said you were teaching medieval history . . . I got thinking.

We came back to retire. But before that we tried the country, out there in Midgic, eleven years of it. The drafty old farmhouse, the wood stove, the heavy winters sans snowblower — because at heart we've always been city folk, even though there was that lure to the country, where Brendan felt he could paint full time and "make it." Anyhow, we lived there eleven years. We bought the place outright. He planned to "fix it up" in the local way. But to do that you need years of experience and contacts here. We had neither. Just a degree from a university and years of moving around while Brendan's graphic design talents took him here and there, never too far from the top. So when he was about fifty he began to get serious about "Let's go back to the Maritimes," and we both knew anyhow that it's a hard place to leave. His father comes from PEI and mine from Halifax and they'd moved away, both of them, his to Calgary and mine to Long Island, but when it came time to send their kids to college they'd sent them both back to the Maritimes. That's where we met.

I'm sorry. I do get off the point. Brendan gets after me for the same thing. I say it's from years of living interrupted. But now he's the only interruption and it's constant. For the first time he's lost his space, his office, so he moves around in my space. And I feel crowded. That's one of the reasons it's so wonderful to get to campus, come to your class, have this chance to talk, and above all be reading something I know he wouldn't touch with a ten-foot pole and cannot ever talk to me about.

⚜

I hope your wife liked the kangaroo. I'm thinking about giving them all up soon. Maybe have a sensational yard sale. Can't you see it? It would have blown Augustine's mind. Acres of gaily colored stuffed animals, acres of multiplying kangaroos. Twin monkey sets that can swing from a branch. Fish you can use as a pillow at night. Puppies that have ears in which you can stuff children's pajamas. I'd just like to see it all spread out like that, my work, my inconsequential work, let the townsfolk wander among the animals, watch Brendan look puzzled. You mean she's been doing this all these years? You mean she's actually produced this much?

⚜

But now I'm not so anxious to produce any more. I used to think that middle age would be hideous. Retirement worse. But the word doesn't mean anything to me. I've already been retired. I've resurrected. I'm back here in town, at last. I'm learning. I'm taking your course and communing with the great minds of the Western world. What do I need with kangaroos any more?

Maybe Brendan could find comfort in a hobby. I'm done with hobbies.

I'm into higher education. Thanks to you.

112

Trick or Treat

"WHAT TIME WILL IT BE OVER, Dolly?" she croaks from the bed.

Scarcely a ripple now beneath the quilt. All year she's been shrinking. Bones, bones, a speaking mound of bones and breath. Soon the breath will stop.

"By nine, Mother."

The *mother* gags me still, a stone in my throat. Is it worth this price, this deception? Is she deceived?

"Who's taking the boys around?"

This much she knows. In such a small, dark room how can she keep track of anything?

"Jeff took Sean out an hour ago. They went in the car."

"What about Freddie?"

"He went out on his own this year, with two friends."

"*Alone?* Haven't you read the papers? There've been warnings on the radio all day. Last year five children were poisoned in California."

"I've heard the radio, but that's California. Besides, you can't keep them in on Halloween. Freddie's twelve, after all. In grade seven. And he's always been reliable."

"Reliable has nothing to do with it."

"He has a flashlight and is to go only to houses where he knows the people. He's Sherlock Holmes. I even put luminous tape on his briefcase and shoes."

"Nonsense, Dolly. Luminous tape can't cure a poisoned child. Your father and I never let you or Willie out on Halloween without an adult."

Tell her. Go ahead. Tell her Willie's long dead, moldering in the grave for five years. That you're not even her daughter. Just the dutiful granddaughter-in-law, lucky you. Give it to her straight for once: Dolly died, dropping in the restaurant a year ago when none of us even knew she had a heart condition. "One of those things," said the emergency room doctor with the easy sympathy of the still living. Tell her now, while Jeff's out. "I've been your Dolly for a year."

I cannot. Her teeth and gums bubble in water beside her bed. A cone of light illumines withered hands.

"Get some sleep now," I say, pull her door to, and go down to welcome the spooks.

❖

It's like this: you get through weeks of being pestered about costumes; you resist pressure (*other* mothers do it, why not you?) to create whole new disguises from scratch; you ransack the house for old sheets, oversized coats, false mustaches, anything; you deal with How late can I stay out this year?; you survive pumpkin scooping and carving; you get it all together and launched; and finally, at seven o'clock on Halloween night, you stop in for a cheery goodnight to Grandmother Mahr, who thinks she's still in Detroit with daughter Dolly, and the dear little old lady calls up chilling visions of razor blades in apples, licorice laced with LSD. Jolly grannies these days.

I try not to hate Halloween, the children love it so.

And I do understand the thrill of disguise — swarming along dark streets in clusters of vampires, ghosts, gypsies, and Indians; giggling as you hold out a trick-or-treat bag to someone who sees you every day of the week but doesn't recognize you tonight; coming home loaded with goodies that may even last two days into November; falling asleep warm in the triumph of having ventured into a world so hidden that no parent, not one snooping well-intentioned adult, could penetrate it.

Even now, as a well-intentioned adult, I savor one part of this night — between their coming home and their going to bed, when lights are out and we all sit on the rug by the blazing fire. Jeff tells ghost stories. First one, then another, escalate in spookiness until the children each beg for a turn, competing for effect, straining to scare us all, to call from the grave and beyond tales that will leave us paralyzed with fright, or stone dead on the gold rug by the smoldering logs.

⚛

Heavy steps pound on the front porch.

"Come in! Come inside!"

Damp, cold air blasts us as I shut the door.

"Trick or treat!"

"Now, what have we here?"

The polka-dotted clown is losing his stomach. Dracula hovers behind two small shivering unidentifiables. "Trick or treat!" Eyeballs blink behind masks. The rouged little mommie tee-hees as tennis ball breasts roll about beneath her yellow sweater. She carries a black patent leather purse daintily.

"You may have one or the other," I say, holding out to them the large wooden salad bowl we filled with bags of chips and small chocolate bars before the boys went out.

The vampire's gloved hand hovers, then invades the bowl.

"Move over, Cheryl," orders the clown. One hand carefully supporting his stomach, he advances with his pillowcase.

"Anyone for UNICEF tickets?" I ask. How we work at it, we adults. *Think of others less fortunate as you're drooling for a Hershey bar, kids . . . remember starving children in Africa . . . bombed out villages in Lebanon . . .*

"Me!"

"Me!"

Clown and vampire reach for orange tickets, insert them in UNICEF boxes slung round their necks. We are proud of the ticket system in our small town that keeps children from having to carry money about on Halloween night.

"Can I please have a candy bar for my baby sister?" asks the mommie, shyly swaying.

They crowd toward the door, craving release.

I open it, usher them out — a giggling, stumbling horde, hurrying down the steps, bumping against one another in the dark, half-blinded by their masks.

"Did you remember to say thank-you, Cheryl?" calls a male voice from the edge of the lawn.

A flashlight beams across leaf-sodden grass, searching for Cheryl.

⋯⊟⋯

I must check the pumpkins on the living room window sill, always a fire hazard.

Sean's flickers conventionally through the three-toothed smile, the triangular eyes. Pumpkins were hard to come by this year. They tended to be small and green. Freddie's — bought late, for until this afternoon he scoffed at the idea — is lopsided. "Exotic bone structure," I told him. The plastic nose with eyeglasses attached hugs the earless head precariously. A most distinguished pumpkin, this, with its bushy black mustache, its rakish captain's hat. By each side of its un-scooped-out head a small green candle burns.

In a steady stream they begin to arrive now: pirates, cowboys, Madonna, Indiana Jones, ghosts, Superman, Rambo, Michael Jackson, Elvis, little ones anxiously anonymous in witches' hats. Most of them politely limit themselves to one candy bar or a small bag of chips. They tote half-filled pillowcases and speak little. "Thank you." "Trick or treat." Occasionally, one adds, "Mrs. Mahr." I try vainly to identify the voice.

It's the older ones who drive you crazy, junior high boys obnoxious in their size twelve Nikes, shoving and pushing and holding out grubby pillowcases for all they can get. Not even the courtesy of a disguise, some of them. Just, Gimme something. They travel in packs with multicolored hair, and some terrorize younger children beneath the streetlights. The police are out tonight. Our one theater is closed.

Here stands a child I should know: penciled eyebrows, wig of string in several tiny braids, gleaming red lips.

"Boy George?" I try to be with it. "Stevie Wonder?" I cannot keep up with their stars.

"Boy Johnson," he grins. "Thanks, Mrs. Mahr."

Our paperboy, Glen Johnson. A small, self-contained fellow who delivers the morning paper before we're up, he collects on Saturdays with the earnestness of a branch bank manager.

The stream continues. Soon the salad bowl will be empty. And

then, our time by the fire. I've turned out the lights in the living
room. Already, sinuous shadows play across the gold rug.

Then I hear them, the loudest group of the evening.

"We wish you a merry Christmas!" they bellow into dark drizzle as
they tromp up the front steps.

The door bursts open.

"My arm's killing me, Mom."

Freddie drops his bulging briefcase on the front hall floor. Tape
hangs from it in strips. Behind him in the doorway lurk a mummy and
a green-haired punk eye me.

"Oh, I'm loaded, too," groans the punk. The bicycle chain around
his shoulders rattles and he drops his bulging garbage bag. Over his
shredded T-shirt he wears a faded Army fatigue jacket splotched with
purple paint. "Wait'll you see how much we got, Mrs. Mahr."

"Can I leave my stuff here?" asks the mummy, setting his pillowcase by the door. Bright blue eyes shine through slits in the cheesecloth
winding sheet.

"Of course. Shut the door, Freddie. And remember, Granny's asleep."

At least I hope she is. Probably up there listening to the chronicle
of Halloween disasters. She tries to be good, holds on by her fingertips, mighty fingertips of steel. Always the six o'clock news, which she
forgets the minute it's over. She never did like Dolly, her youngest.
All three of the girls gone now, she lives on in her only grandson's
house. Makes me into my own mother-in-law. Some trick. "I could always count on you, Jeff," she'll say, conveniently forgetting his betrayal
— marrying wrong, escaping Detroit, his mother's disappointment, and
her own threat that he'd never see a red cent. All is forgiven. She needs
my hands.

"Hey, Pete, want us to unwrap you?"

They race round and round him, howling as strips of gauze, cheesecloth, masking tape fall to the floor.

"Wait'll you guys see all the chips I got," yells Freddie, yanking.

"Old lady MacDonald let us choose three candy bars!" The punk
fairly dances around the mummy, uncovering a strip of bright blue
sweatshirt. "Can I leave my bicycle chain out here, Mrs. Mahr?" It
thuds to the floor near the coat-stand.

"Let's trade," says Freddie, and leads them into the darkened living
room.

Peter follows, trailing bits of gauze from his ankle.

I start after them, then stop.

For a second, just an instant, I seemed to hear something. Upstairs? No. A rustling, a kind of scratching. It wouldn't be Granny. She sleeps well now. A boon. If she needs us, she has a small bell by her bed. When she first came she rang it every night, several times. We were like new young parents, bleary-eyed with sleeplessness.

The kitchen door slams.

"Where are they, Mom? Are they back?" Sean darts by me, his mustache smudged into a dark shadow on one rouged cheek. Spotting the cheesecloth, he heads into the living room.

In the middle of the kitchen stands Jeff, bleached yellow by over-head fluorescence. His dark curly hair, shiny from light rain, lies plastered against his forehead.

"How'd it go? Many kids out in the street?" I ask.

"Murder to drive. I almost ran over two Ninja Turtles. How's Granny?"

"Worried about the kids. Filling my mind with possible disasters." Suddenly I want to leave. Run. Join the spooks, float with them up the dark streets, prowl backyards and alleys, discover that other world, the hidden one. Not this. Oh, not this.

"The older boys back?"

"In the living room counting loot."

"Fire okay?"

"Yes. I poked it up once. I'll go turn off the porch light now. We've had enough visitors. I'm almost out of stuff, anyhow. If the lights are all out, no kids will come to the door."

Whoops and snorts erupt from the living room.

"Better go keep the lid on," he says, and turns away.

This tall serious man with slicked-down curls, this man weary of a dark night with crazy kids: Who is he? We will grow old together.

"I promised John's family I'd have him home early," I call after him.

Did he hear?

<hr/>

Cupboards and countertops comfort. They say life goes on — lettuce gets chopped, bread sliced, dishes washed and put away. I feel it right now, that subtle reassurance, as I set out margarine to soften for the popcorn.

When Jeff's mother, Dolly, the one tough-minded female of that generation, died, Sean wanted every detail from us, in Technicolor. How much did she eat? How did she fall? Did her head go into the dinner on her plate? How many did it take to carry her out? Details, details. He was eight then, in love with facts. He'll never remember her as the grandmother with the money, the hard bargainer, the one who saw marriage as a trap and children a nuisance, the one nonetheless who agreed to take on her mother and care for her after benevolent Willie was gone. For Sean she'll always be the granny who died with her head in the mashed potato, the one who conferred on death the glamor of a public event, the immortality of family anecdote, story. When we got through our explanations to him that night (we were standing right here by this counter) he looked about the kitchen thoughtfully. "Well," he said finally, "at least the furniture goes on."

I turn out the kitchen light, the front hall light, the porch light, and snap the lock on the front door. They are laughing and talking in by the fire, the older boys' cackle drowning out Sean.

I shut the living room door behind me. *Please, God, let her sleep.*

⌗

"Had to turn on the lights, Mom," says Freddie quickly. "Had to see so we could count."

He knows I like the darkened room on Halloween night, the ghost stories. Freddie butters me up, tries to win me. He's good at it. Sean has never learned how. Granny Mahr does not like Freddie.

"How many candy bars didja get?" asks Peter, leaning back on unraveling white ankles.

"Dunno yet." Freddie's pipe lies on the rug. His deerstalker hat dips over one eye. He has dumped out the contents of his briefcase. "Lotsa chips."

"Chips were the best buy in town," I feel compelled to say. It isn't heard. I've become invisible to them. Boring. Just a mother. To Sean

I'm still a body, a warm arm, hugging his soft smallness here on the sofa. On the other side of the coffee table, colossal twelve-year-old feet sprawl.

"Do you know how much Halloween candies cost these days?" I dare. Spoilsport.

"Wait'll you see my chocolate bars," croons Peter.

He is starting to pimple. His muscular shoulders show years of diligent swimming, early morning practice. Intensely competitive, he is not popular.

Between Freddie and Peter, John's green hair hovers above candy kisses, chips, chocolate bars, caramels, gumdrops, popcorn balls, the rare, unwanted apple. John's persistence is of a milder sort.

"What'll you swap for two boxes of Rosebuds?"

"I've got Smarties. Look at all the Smarties!"

"Chips? You got twenty bags! I only got nineteen. Wanna trade any chips for my Rosebuds? I don't like 'em."

"A Cherry Blossom! You got a Cherry Blossom! Lucky!"

The mummy will trade anything for a Hershey.

"How're your teeth?" asks Jeff sardonically of no one in particular. He's poking up the fire. Holding in irritation. I can tell by the set of the shoulders.

Suddenly they remember.

"Sean!" shouts Freddie. "Show us what *you* got!"

Sean eases away from my arm, slips from the edge of the sofa to stand upright behind the coffee table, facing them. He so seldom gets the stage.

He opens his bag, leans over it, looks inside. "Hmmmm."

"Come on, Sean. What've ya got?"

He reaches inside the bag. One by one he lifts them out — gumdrops, caramel, chips, suckers — sets each on the table.

"Look!" squeals John. "Three Hersheys. No fair." He grabs one.

Holster and gun on one hip, cowboy hat pushed back on his dark curls, Sean holds himself composed. He lifts up one Hershey bar.

"Let's see. . ." He eyes John's rainbow of suckers. "Well . . ."

This could go on all night.

Thump. Thump. Thump.

Jeff looks at me.

Thump.

120

I part the drapes behind the sofa and look out on the porch. Nothing. Freddie pauses in his counting. "Did you hear that?"

The doorknob rattles. Someone is in the hallway outside the living room door.

"Granny?" says Jeff.

"I left her listening to the radio," I murmur. I cannot move. The house doors are locked. Nothing can happen. The knob is turning.

The living room door swings open into the hall.

"Yes, children. It's me. Your mother."

She stands there, sparse fine white hair sticking out wildly, her long white flannel gown reaching the floor. Wraith from nowhere. From upstairs. How did she get down? She needs help to get to the bathroom. She grasps the door frame, eyes us, each in turn. Without her glasses she looks dazed, pained by the sudden bright light. The blue veins of her feet, her hands, trace intricate trails beneath papery white skin. There's something frail, unbeaten about this woman. She has survived all her daughters, grasping the end of her own life with iron claws. I know her body — its smell, its bones, its blemishes. I know the wrinkles of her arms, the withered small breasts, the bumps down her back, the secret crevices. I have fingered her skeleton. She weighs barely ninety pounds. I have bathed and clothed her for almost a year. I know the secrets of her flesh better than I knew my own mother's. This alien blood is my care. She despises me.

"What's going on in here?" she says, vigorously claiming the right of a mother *to know.* She sways, then rights herself, thin fingers clutching the doorjamb. "Noise, noise, all night. Doors opening and closing. Voices. The doorbell again and again. What are you doing? Am I missing something?"

"But I told you — " I begin.

"Yes, yes, told." Her teeth have been left bubbling in the room above. Her caved in mouth whistles. "That's what they all say. Told. Is Willie in?"

Jeff avoids my eye. He knows I've wanted to tell her the truth. Beneath our caring lie the questions: Why prolong the charade? Why protect the near-dead from the fact of death? Wouldn't a mother rather know? But from the day she arrived she's insisted I'm Dolly — despite my dark hair, my shortness, my voice. She'll wrest this comfort from final days: a daughter who cares.

"Now, Granny — " Jeff stands up. "Everyone's in and safe. Not to worry. It's just Halloween."

Freddie sneaks a glance at his friends. Embarrassed, they look away.

Granny's fingers loosen. "And these?" She points at the boys on the rug. "Green hair? Or am I seeing things?"

Sudden confusion clouds her eyes. Her head begins to tremble. "I thought — oh, never mind what I thought. It is green, isn't it? You wouldn't lie to your own mother?"

"These are all friends, Mother. The green — yes, it's green — washes out. It's just a disguise. Do you want some chips?"

"Chips! Caramels, please. All you've got to spare. I'll save 'em for morning when my choppers are in."

Old age is hunger, sucking against the sharp sweet tit of life.

Jeff nods at Freddie, then Sean. *Be good. Generous. Give. She's an old lady. Don't make me have to tell you.*

Freddie looks down.

Without a word, Sean is over to her, putting three fat caramels into her withered hand. He folds shaking fingers around the candy.

"There, Granny. Save 'em till morning."

She looks at us — the boys on the rug, Jeff (moving toward her now, taking her hand), Sean, back behind the coffee table with me. Dolly. For an instant I want to say, *Come on in. Join us.* The words stick in my throat. It is only a fleeting half-thought. I don't want her here. Life holds too many disguises. They grow heavy, rocks on the heart. "Come on, Mother," says Jeff. "I'll help you back upstairs."

She looks at him, trembling. "Jeff?"

"Yes?"

"You're Jeff?"

"I'm Jeff."

"Where's Willie then?"

"Come on. I'll help you upstairs."

She takes his arm and turns away, chortling. "Three caramels. Three whole caramels."

Jeff closes the door behind them.

We can hear them laboring back up the stairs.

⚜

And now, the final negotiating.

Quietly at first, then louder and louder, the boys compete, dicker. They watch Sean, solemn behind the coffee table, master of his Hershey. He surveys them, takes his candy bar and breaks it in two, handing half to Peter, half to John.

"Here. For half of what each of you got."

Who are these children?

"I am the original tourist in my children's lives." A friend said it to me recently, describing her forays of discovery into closets crammed with dolls, scrapbooks, toy instruments, yarn, empty cages, bits of material . . . the colossal random gatherings and scatterings of her daughters' young lives as they nibbled their way through childhood into puberty.

These size twelve feet. These craws lusting for one more Hershey. These loot seekers. They came from somewhere else.

Jeff is back, closing the door carefully behind him.

"She'll be okay now," he says.

She'll be okay. Upstairs in the dark. Dreaming of her caramels. Sinking into sleep. She'll be okay.

"She looked like a witch," says Freddie.

"A ghost," says Peter, pushing around his potato chip bags.

"She's just our Granny," says Sean, matter of fact. "And she doesn't even know who we are."

The punk looks at the cowboy.

The mummy looks at the punk.

Sherlock Holmes takes off his hat.

"Next year I wanna be a Ninja Turtle," says Sean, setting his black water pistol on the table beside his new Hershey.

Next year, I think, I may no longer be Dolly.

"Come on," says Jeff, the stranger who shares my bed. "Time for you guys to break it up. John has to go home."

How reluctantly they stir at his command. Nothing more to trade, nothing more to gain. Mummy unwound, Sherlock Holmes dismantled, the punk looking gloomy, they stand, gather their goodies. Sean runs ahead to the kitchen.

"I'll start the car, John." Jeff is eager to go.

"Want me to take him?"

"Nope. Roads are really slick. I'll be right back." He pulls on his windbreaker as he speaks and is out the back door in a flash. He's had it with Halloween. He'll have a few moments of peace driving the dark, wet country road to John's house, coming back alone beneath the shrouded orange moon.

John slings his bicycle chain over his neck and grasps his garbage bag. He grins at me shyly: "Thanks a lot, Mrs. Mahr. It's boring out in the country. This is the first Halloween my parents have let me spend in town."

And he's gone, slamming out the kitchen door into the dark.

Freddie spots the unopened package of popcorn on the counter. "We never had it, Mom, we never had the popcorn. You forgot!"

Outrage.

"Can we? Please?" Sean turns away from the open fridge door, a can of Coke in his hand.

This kitchen is too bright, too real, after the flickering darkness of the living room, their solemn negotiations. Freddie has dropped his hat, his coat, his briefcase. All that's left is the pipe he left on the kitchen counter the minute he spotted the popcorn, a relic of the great detective adrift on a Formica sea.

Sean, cheek still smudged, has lost his pistol and cowboy hat. "Please, Mom. We always have popcorn on Halloween."

They stand before me, these children of my life, mere remnants of those ghostly selves.

"Don't you think you've had enough for one night?"

Mothers specialize in pointless questions.

"C'mon, Mom. Dad loves it! Sean gave up all his caramels. And Peter gave up half his loot to Sean." Sean is already opening his Coke. "Besides," adds Freddie, "you said Pete could stay over. Remember?"

Of course I remember. "

They've already spread the sleeping bag on the floor upstairs in Freddie's room. They'll talk all night as they munch their treats.

Sean is melting the margarine.

Freddie has the popper out.

An hour at most to go before Jeff and I are alone.

"Okay, okay," I say, "but only if" — our children teach us such maneuvers — "only if you all promise to go to bed in half an hour, that means you and Peter, too, and only if you two don't keep us all awake till dawn." I give Freddie and Peter the kind of look they expect. "Now I've got to go upstairs and check on Granny."

I leave them busy in the kitchen, the three of them, chattering away as they work.

They're right. Jeff will like it. We'll have a round of popcorn. No spook stories. John's gone, the fire is dying. I must remember to snuff out the pumpkin candles.

I climb the stairs. Did she go back to bed? Or did she put her teeth back in and chomp on caramels in the dark, listening to tales of disaster beamed in from afar? *Is she still alive?*

I stop at the landing, halfway up, halfway down. From the kitchen below I hear their voices, the boys, managing the corn popping, arguing, laughing. Just boys now. From above, the steady rasp of a snore. I look out the window. Headlights are coming down the street, high beams parting the sheen of light rain, waking bushes and poles to instant, passing life.

Remembrance Day

"NOT EXILE. TOO PRETENTIOUS."

This he says in his mellower moments.

"By God, it's exile."

This in his harsher moments, usually to himself. Because Camille — blessed with that softer rounder temperament, that way of deflecting, of demurring, that throws into relief his claims as just so much show-off — Camille would understand and she wouldn't. Mostly wouldn't.

This is a harsher moment, right now, as he pushes along beside Pops in freezing rain, down the hill, cheeks stung by November wind, holding Jimmie's hand.

Yes, definitely. Harsher.

Lead on, Ace, toward the cenotaph. New word, *cenotaph*. New ceremony: eleventh hour of the eleventh day of the eleventh month. New and not new. When was it new to remember the war dead? Think of Homer, Thucydides, Tolstoy. But here, in rain about to become snow, in this small Canadian town, with your dwindling father-in-law sporting five polished medals on his old trench coat, with your eleven-year-old son in his Cub hat and uniform (covered with a parka at your predictable insistence) — here, today, it's exile.

"What time's it start?" says Pops for the fifth time in the past half hour.

Camille got him together — pulling the beret just so over the shaggy brows, rubbing her sleeves against the medals, straightening their striped ribbons, jollying him into a good mood, setting them all up. It's the annual parade from Thomason Hall at the edge of the university campus, down the main street, to the cenotaph in the small park near the railway tracks. It's the laying on of wreaths.

God, it's exile.

"Ten sharp," says Ace, hurrying. Jimmie has begun to skip. One of his sneakers is unlaced. "Lace up when you get there, Jim," he says.

Clusters of people now, lining up along the sidewalks, meeting friends, relatives. Then they'll all file in, sing "O Canada," listen to the local VIPs, lament war and death — heavy on religious participation, all the local clergymen sitting solemn in a row on stage.

Sure bet it isn't the USA, where God is not only unfashionable but illegal, the public God, that is. There was Memorial Day of course — the picnics, the parade, kegs of beer, steaks on the grill, kids racing among the tombstones while elders fixed geraniums. . . . The smell of steak assails him now, cuts through the freezing rain. There was Mike.

"You gonna come to the ceremony this year, Dad?" asks Jimmie, pulling him now toward the hall. He's spotted the Cub pack lining up out on the side steps.

"Part of it," says Ace. "I'll see you march for sure, Jim. And I'll be at the cenotaph. Mom said she'll get down for that, once Em's set."

Camille had the better, simpler part, he sometimes thought. Right now, for instance. Home to put the baby in the crib, talk to Cassie from next door, who'd agreed to watch everything for a couple of hours.

"She's bringing the wreath," says Jimmie.

"Remember what I told you," says Pops. "No looking around, James. March straight, set it by the base of the cenotaph, salute, turn, walk back."

Jimmie eyes his grandfather. "Don't worry, Pops. Got it down pat."

And he does, after nights of practice out back, where Pops has drilled his grandson in the apartment they put on after Lena died just two years ago. "Send the boy out," he'd say at the end of supper, pushing back from the table. "We'll have a little practice."

Jimmie, glad to get out of dishes even if it meant this, would slide toward him, escape the kitchen, and drill the cenotaph scene. Because it mattered.

Here's Clem Larsen, bemedalled and grizzly, waving at Pops from the group of veterans assembled on the front steps of the hall. His blue beret tips, positively jaunty.

Is there anyone without a medal? Ace eyes the assembled heroes preparing to remember. Their big day . . . understandable. Lest others forget that these feebling bodies once walked straight, carried rifles, marched steady in heavy boots, took aim, fired. Lest they themselves forget.

Mike came home in a box to full military honors. Bullshit.

"Gotta go, Dad," says Jimmie, loosening his hand. "We're supposed to be in line by the side door. See ya later."

He's off, darting around the side of the hall toward his buddies.

"You gonna stay?" asks Pops. He's nodding toward his cronies, Ed LeBlanc, Pierre Landry, friends of the late afternoon porch, beer time in a pool of spilled sun, remembering what had been . . . Dieppe . . . Ypres . . . God knows what else. Ah, the girls were beautiful then.

"I'll stop over at Gunther's and wait there till the parade starts," says Ace.

Once, Pops would have been insulted. But these days he's receding into tolerance, a vague, benign resignation beneath the unbending sky. He wanders. He forgets. He makes lists with a trembling hand and loses them. He sits by the window in his living room and watches the trees wave. Tonight he must be picked up at the Legion. There was a time, not long ago, when he could navigate home after an evening at the Legion, find his way alone up the hill to his tidy bungalow on Pritchard Street. Before Lena died and he moved into the tacked-on apartment out back of Ace and Camille's. Before he became a live-in grandpa. A worry.

"Father Julien's giving the talk, you know," says Pops.

Not that he'll listen. He long ago tuned out on the Catholic business and shares, with Ace, a kind of distanced humor about it all. Julien is Camille's uncle, Lena's brother, a pious brother too, and a good speaker.

"I know, Pops, but he told me basically what he'll be saying."

Ace can see the eyes glaze. Pops is already with his friends in that other world, back there, moving into a haze of memory.

"You'll be at the cenotaph?"

"Don't worry. Camille will bring the wreath."

Pops turns away without a word and heads toward his comrades.

⧈

Damned wreath, thinks Ace, crossing the street clogged with parked cars and bystanders, people eager to see the lineup but not so eager to hear the speeches inside, parents of Cubs and Girl Guides, daughters and sons of vets, friends . . . for what else is there to do on this morning when everything is closed?

Gunther will be getting ready. Gunther understands.

His restaurant will open officially after the cenotaph, people coming in to warm up over cocoa or coffee and a piece of Sacher torte, Black Forest cake, or whatever rare concoction Gunther's wife has provided for the occasion. She doesn't come into town anymore to run the small restaurant they pioneered here. She does it all at home, Gunther bringing her wonders in each day when he opens their pastry and coffee shop, which, over the past nine years, has become well known in the area. Authentic German pastries, everything pure: real butter, real cream, real homemade bread.

Ace opens the door and the smell of fresh coffee grasps him like a friendly hand. Gunther's there, down in back, whipping cream to the sound of the coffee perking. *Blip. Blip. Blip.*

"*Wie geht's*, Gunther?"

"Hi, Ace. *Mir geht's gut, danke.* And you?"

"Not bad."

"Skipping the ceremony, Ace?"

"Freezing. Besides, I've heard it all before."

It's written deep inside him, the hidden messages of the day. War. Heroism. Nobility. We must remember.

He wants to forget.

He takes a table near the front window, slips off his jacket, and lays it across the empty chair opposite.

When his father called to give him the word, Ace was sitting in his graduate dorm in Chicago contemplating soot, the black soot that filmed curtains, windows, walls, everything in that city of soot. Rain outside, freezing rain like today, the eternal gray. And then the phone.

129

Somehow, the moment he heard his father's voice, he knew — though there was no reason to believe that this brother, the less studious one, the one who'd never got the grades that enabled him to go on and so duck the draft — this brother of wit and rare devastating irony would himself be snapped in two by the jaws of irony and come home in a box. These things happened in movies . . . These things happened in real life.

"Coffee?"

Gunther sets a cup of steaming coffee on the table in front of Ace.

"Thanks."

"Anything else?"

"No thanks. Had a big breakfast. And we'll pig out before the day is over."

Gunther stands beside him staring through the window into the rain that now has people lifting umbrellas, tightening parka hoods. They remain silent a moment. Then Gunther breaks out, "Quite a day, Ace. Quite a day. I'd rather forget . . . Ever been in a war? You too young?"

Ace nods. How old is Gunther anyhow? Fifty, maybe. He has music going, something operatic. Strings galore.

"So where were you for Vietnam?"

Always the question. Were you in it or out of it? Did you resist or did you fight? How come you're in Canada, anyway? Did you run? Though no one asked in the beginning when he saw his way clear to come, PhD fresh in hand, and announced to his parents that he'd decided.

"I came over here, Gunther."

"Smart."

Gunther snaps a towel against his thigh. "Nothing more, then?"

"No, thanks. We'll probably be back here after the cenotaph. Keep some cocoa for us. Camille and Jimmie and me. Pops is off to the Legion."

As Ace speaks, Gunther is already on his way to the back of the restaurant to finish his preparations. The place is small and tidy, patterned cloths on the tables and small bud vases with real flowers. About the walls pictures of Germany and Austria are spaced. Newspapers available for browsing. Fresh cakes daily. Gunther and Katharina started from scratch here. Tried to create a European atmosphere. Hard job at first to win the townsfolk. Now they gobble up the whipped cream. Summer tourists search the restaurant out.

Ace stirs his coffee and stares at the stone building across the street. He can see it all, he doesn't need to be inside. He's sat through five years with his niece Jacqui as a Girl Guide, and this is Jimmie's second year at the service. What new word can be spoken to the squirming respectful mass of assembled veterans, widows, wives, aunts, uncles, nieces, nephews, and post-Sixties children in their tidy uniforms? What comfort can Father Julien offer? Or what defense of remembering? He's not sardonic, Julien. He's patient and gentle. No grim jokes, no lethal reminders. "*Kaboom. Better button up for nuclear winter.*" Just words . . .

To Ace's own words, spoken that day in a restaurant much like this, his father merely replied, "You're sure, Ace? You know what you're doing?"

"Of course I don't know what I'm doing! Who does? Did Mike? But you've lost one. That's enough. I don't intend to sacrifice myself pointlessly. In a corrupt cause. How dumb can you be?" It was 1967. There was talk of a lottery.

"You don't feel the obligation to fight for your country?"

The question smelled musty, syllables from disintegrating pages of an ancient church hymnal. Quaint. Innocent.

"This is an illegal war, Dad."

"You may never be able to come home."

"I'll be just over the border. Not that far."

And so he left.

Went "just over the border" to this small town in eastern Canada, a town of one traffic light, one university, which, mercifully, took him in to teach literature. An alien.

The rest was history.

It plays before him now in quick fragments as he sips coffee and awaits his son and father-in-law, palpable connections to a place never his. They will march past Gunther's establishment down the two blocks of Main Street to the cenotaph. Remembering.

First will come the Mountie, Banter Colsen, only one in town, dashing in his scarlet, his handsome broad-brimmed hat, his polished leather boots, astride his dazzling steed. Just like a postcard. Just like the one image his mother could summon when he told her he'd go to Canada. Mounties plus cold weather. Both were true.

As for the rest . . . how explain that even here, just over the border, America saturated the consciousness daily, was somehow always present, just below, just over the line, "the States" — palpable shadow stalking the clear Canadian sky. Children knew more about American presidents than about their own prime ministers. It was hard, impossible, to explain this to parents and friends who asked. Hard also to explain that America, his own country, even after amnesty and friendly return, felt and looked different to him now. His own, yet not.

If he'd gone to Mexico, the differences would have been easier to spell out, the colors flashier. But this was Canada, a land of pastels, not pizzaz. So he tried to convey little differences to his parents: the Queen's picture in the PO, the bilingual signs, the funny money, but somehow he never could share the felt difference, the ambiguities of soul, his rootedness and non-rootedness even now, married into an old Acadian family, tenured at a university, raising children, undoubtedly destined to spend the rest of his life here. Just over the border.

⟨⟩

Here they come now, slowly spilling out of Thomason Hall, lining up in the street for the march.

Ace pushes back his chair.

"Thanks, Gunther. I'll leave it here." He puts a dollar bill by his cup. "See you later."

Gunther, never voluble, waves his towel at Ace. "*Wieder sehen,* Ace." And now into the still-freezing rain, bits of snow mixed with it. Typical Remembrance Day weather.

⟨⟩

He moves quietly down the street past townsfolk clustered in doorways, greets those he knows as he passes the dress shop, the natural foods store, the cone shop, the corner drugstore. The marchers behind him have begun to move, are catching up with him. Somber lines . . . old men in trench coats, berets tipped, medaled chests out, heads high or backs curved with arthritis, eyes straight ahead. Old Willie Strenson, bent almost halfway. Pops . . . there's Pops . . . leaning into drizzle and snow . . . looking set, distant, unaware of Ace standing on the corner now, waving.

He moves on down the block, fingers numb.

Now it's the women in navy blue with white berets who march by, the Legion Auxiliary . . . Where's Camille? Will she be at the cenotaph already?

"Pardon me." Ace steps carefully around a young woman behind a stroller. A red-cheeked toddler stands beside her, holding her hand.

She smiles briefly.

On to the cenotaph.

Beside him now march the Cubs. He spots Jimmie, fifth row, two in from the end, sneaking a look at him.

Ace waves.

The small park at the bottom of Main Street is already crowded. Ace moves past a group of hatted ladies and a trio of girls in jeans and parkas to a place near the front where he can see Jimmie. The Cubs are filing in behind the Air Cadets. Their faces look determined, pained, against the freezing rain. Jimmie's ears shine almost purple. He stands straight, eyes forward.

Facing the people from the bottom steps of the cenotaph stand the mayor, Father Julien, the Mountie, and some veteran Ace doesn't recognize. The town band, to Ace's left, hold their horns up, plastic-covered sheet music carefully propped

O, Canada, our home and native land . . .

It happens every time. He cannot remember the words. Not that anyone is actually singing out loud. It's too cold, and besides, no one sings when the band plays it on Remembrance Day. But the words, the words . . . he wants to sing along, mentally at least, but he cannot. Until they reach: "O, Canada, we stand on guard for thee."

A rousing finale. He sees Jimmie's lips moving. Is he mouthing the words in French or English? He's in the French Immersion program at school, can now carry on long conversations with Pops that Ace cannot grasp.

The Union Jack to the left of the cenotaph flutters. The Mountie snaps his salute. Snow has begun in earnest, thick wet flakes dotting the veterans' berets. The presiding veteran steps forward at the cenotaph, his strong voice cutting through the miserable rain and snow. "Roll call for World War One: Ernest Gaines, Timothy Blanchard, Harold LeBlanc . . . "

Ace can see only the back of Pops, where his white hair touches the collar of his coat. What is he thinking of . . . blood, bone, bodies falling about him, the dark cold damp of trenches, the horror of gas? Or is he in some vaguer pre-Elysian field visiting heroes, counting himself among them, a survivor, a medal wearer, dignified, heroic, walking the fields of the dead with news from the land of the living?

"Roll call for World War Two . . . "

Closer to home: husbands, fathers, brothers, uncles, sweethearts. A hatless woman in a red windbreaker leans forward beside Ace, listening. She might be in her late sixties. Was it a sweetheart? What pain has she nursed these years? Or does she bend forward out of simple curiosity, anxious not to miss a name? Ace's father went through college on the GI Bill, never spoke of the war. Did he have a medal hidden away in a deep drawer? Did he sometimes pull it out, contemplate it, walking in his own Elysian fields?

A warm hand slips into his parka pocket, grasps his numb fingers. "Hi."

Tiny bits of snow dot the fur that frames her face.

"I brought it. Where's Jimmie?" She holds a wreath of poppies in her other hand.

Ace points to their left, up ahead.

"The Korean campaign . . . " continues the voice from the cenotaph. Fewer names here, only three from the town.

"I'll bring it over to him."

She extracts her hand and slips down the line of erect Cubs to hand Jimmie the wreath. Already the drummer has begun his full minute roll. The silence grows heavy with the weight of all this remembering, this rain, this snow. Camille whispers something in Jimmie's ear and hurries back to Ace. The drum roll goes on and on in the cold and wet amid the gathered rememberers, opening out and holding all in a nameless vacuum — cold, songless, the steady rain of war, of memory.

She slips her hand back into his pocket and smiles up at him. Camille knows how he detests this wreath business.

"Why put it on a kid, a mere eleven-year-old? What purpose does it serve?"

"It matters to Pops, Ace. You know that."

Yes, he knows that.

The drummer stops. People stir. Father Julien steps forward to the cenotaph. Heads are bowed.

". . . Let us pray that these men may not have died in vain," says Julien, his strong voice shaving the rain, urging them.

God. Oh yes, God. Remember the Old Guy. What is "in vain"? Ace would like to ask someone.

Instead, they'll put a wreath on the cenotaph. Camille squeezes his dead fingers. Hers are oddly warm. He is thinking again about this Christian country where, technically at least, God is not dead. Gone now in the States. Christmas handed over to the Grinch. A good thing, perhaps. Who knows?

The horns are pleading for mercy.

One by one, relatives of the deceased, of those lost in war, have begun to come forward carrying their crosses or wreaths of poppies to the cenotaph. Jimmie steps out from his row, carefully not looking their way.

They'd had an ugly scene — late at night, out of Jimmie's hearing. Because it seemed to Ace such a waste, an unnecessary burden. Why should a child bear the burden of their remembering? But Arthur had been Pops's youngest, only twenty. For Pops it mattered. And Pops was on his way out.

Looking neither right nor left, Jimmie Diamond moves to the front of the assembled veterans. The trombone flares. Jimmie walks straight, head up, tall, past the hatted ladies, the Women's Auxiliary, the Air Cadets, forward toward the cenotaph. He stops a moment, faces the stone, then climbs three steps to lay the wreath. He pauses a moment, his back to them. Does he pray? Then he salutes, turns carefully, comes down, and walks quickly back, not even glancing at them.

The snow has started to thicken. Already it is beginning to cover poppies and wreaths and crosses. The Mountie has snow on his scarlet. The last person to lay a wreath, old Mrs. Ward, is coming back down from the cenotaph. Pops is looking around as if he's just awakened.

"Want to go for a cocoa?" whispers Camille.

"Jimmie's counting on it," says Ace.

"Let's stop at Gunther's."

The band begins to play. Flags are raised higher. Caps are doffed. Ace removes his. A solemn, quasi-religious look comes over faces nearby. Even Camille grows quiet.

"God save the Queen."

The trumpet is sour.

Ace has heard this — how many times now? For almost twenty years. Year after year — commencements, movies, formal gatherings, you name it. It means nothing to him. He doesn't find royalty interesting. He cannot connect with the Queen. In some company you cannot say this. The Queen herself was here in this very town, a year ago. She had a walkabout on the football field and took tea at the town inn. He didn't go.

He knows the words of this song. He will always know the words. They sing themselves in his head — fruit of elementary school assemblies, Mr. Dalton, the principal, standing solemn on the stage, Miss Prescenski in her pale print dress leading the children: "My country, 'tis of thee, Sweet land of liberty . . ." His mother would do a takeoff of Kate Smith belting out this very tune.

He sings it now, quietly, without word or voice, somewhere deep within. It can't be helped. The music starts and this is what comes: " . . . Land where my father died, Land of the pilgrims' pride, From every mountainside, Let freedom ring."

The crowd is breaking up.

Pops passes them, in line, marching to the Legion. He looks over and waves. Snow sits on his brows.

Jimmie is jumping up and down in front of them. "Can we go get a hot chocolate, Dad, can we please?" His lashes are white, his ears glow bright red.

Ace takes Jimmie's hand and then Camille's.

They head back up the street, quiet together, nodding to friends, suddenly peaceful, the dying sound of the trumpet, the feel of falling snow all about them. This is a warm place.

The words remain singing within him, no words he can tell them. It can't be helped. He sees his mother whirling around the kitchen, her dark hair flying as she belts it out: "My country, 'tis of thee . . . "

"I'm getting Black Forest cake," says Jimmie.

Camille squeezes Ace's hand. "Half a piece," she says, "or you'll spoil your dinner."

On the Other Side

Two weeks before Easter.

Earth clings to snowskin; heaven refuses blue. Rolling marsh shows bare maples, the rare pine, ridges of stony mud. Here and there a bundled child skates or walks on ice-filled ditches. In the distance transports and cars inch along the treacherous Trans-Canada Highway.

All this one could see from the huge windows siding this overheated room. Someone has arranged chairs to face front: the blank wall, the lectern, the doorway, the piano.

At this I sit, my back to inmates.

Already the room seethes, a coughing sniffing expectant sea of pink and brown and purple-patterned dresses, patient souls. In their midst one man, blind, hunches over in his wheelchair. Along the back row, five nurses, erect in spanking white.

The choir stands ready. They sing of mercy and love and hope to eyes glazed with loss, bodies contorted in pain or numbed to it. I sit by the doorway, angled to see choir and priest. He waits quietly, a man easily unseen, behind the lectern which holds his Bible.

1:50. To set the mood I play hymns quietly, godawful slush extracted for the occasion from a tattered hymnal. *On the other side is a land of wonder, Watered by unfailing streams; There the parted meet, torn by death asunder — Oh, how near it sometimes seems* . . . I've never seen this hymn before. Spontaneous humming arises from bodies scattered throughout the room. *On the other side of the rolling tide, We shall meet and sing with the glorified. We shall see the Lord and be satisfied!*

Everything will be all right on the other side. Quiet, happy sound. Comfort.

Suddenly a form on a bed is wheeled past me. I cannot look up long enough to make out the face. The attendant parks the bed somewhere behind me, near the exit.

2:00. The choir straightens up and moves closer together. Steve, the director, lifts his hands. Dedicated and competent, an ex-seminarian from way back, he bring to his task a pastoral heart, a musical imagination. The sixteen choir members who could make it today watch him, hymnals in hand. They've learned to concentrate on his slightest signal. Most of them cannot read music. Glen Woods, our milk deliveryman and a natural tenor, stands beside Don Cartwright, the ex-chief of police. Fortunately, Beatrice Cormier could come. An untrained singer, she has found in choir the chance to release and share her gift, a rare, pure, soaring soprano that more sophisticated and ambitious singers would kill for.

I play the opening bars of "Now Thank We All Our God."

Behind me — sighs, sniffles, muted groans, one long low "ohhhh." Someone whispers urgently, "I can't help it, I can't help it." From outside, down the long hallway, come buzzes and murmurs: nurses talking, rubber heels pounding, TV static, squeaking wheels, trays, the constant quiet messages of mortality at bay. Why has no one closed the door?

"Now thank we all our God, with hearts and hands and voices," sings the choir.

Today their voices blend. It has taken Steve five years to teach them to listen. In the hot, overcrowded room they sound too loud, almost strident against intimations of mortality. Finger against his lips, he motions them to soften. They reach the cadence, slow down, draw to a finish, stand quiet.

2:05. Father will read words to comfort and inspire.

He has chosen a passage from St. Paul. Something about Christ willing to suffer, about our being part of that suffering. Impossible to listen: the rasp of breathing too raw, too strong. Priestly shoes too shiny. His voice flattens into a straight line, the monotony of certitude.

2:10. Father sits down.

Another hymn. "*I will sweep away your transgressions like a cloud, and your sins will be to me like a mist dissolved, So return to me, and I will heal you, for I love you.*"

Behind me someone starts to cough, ugly rasping sounds, clutching and straining, smothered, then erupting in loud staccato bursts. Is someone choking? Is it the man who sat hunched over?

"*If you say to me: 'I'm in prison, Lord, Imprisoned by my fears,' Then I'll come to you, I will comfort you, Let me wipe away your tears.*"

Father moves again to the lectern. Sweet heavy perfume from someone near engulfs me, hundreds of gardenias browning at the edges.

This time he has chosen a passage about Christ's agony in the garden. "*Father, if you are willing, take this cup from me . . .*"

The cougher has stopped. Did she stuff Kleenex into her shamed mouth, hot with mortification as her neighbors glared at her?

"*Peter followed at a distance, and sat down among some people who had lighted a fire in the middle of the courtyard and were sitting around it.*"

Suddenly a voice cries out in pure terror, "I can't get out, I can't get out!"

"Go on, Father," urges a loud whisper. "I'll take care of her."

I long to turn around. I steel myself to manners.

"I can't help it," sobs the voice.

Father barely blinks. He goes on, his words collapsing and blurring, numbing against the cry of terror. To my left someone is pushing a wheelchair from the room. I catch sight of a bowed head, a pastel robe. The head bobs, hands on the armrests tremble and lift to claw air. The body passes me, muttering. "Now, now," whispers the attendant.

Wheels squeak faintly down the long well-lighted hall.

2:15. "O Sacred Head, Surrounded."

They will know this melody, at least. Balm of Bach.

Behind me, loud breathing. Bodies shift ready themselves for words. Father, seated behind the lectern, wipes his forehead with a perfectly folded white handkerchief. A young priest, he gives the impression of having been neutered. He cannot relax. He communicates tension. Nothing he says will comfort. Perhaps nothing will be heard. He was taken at an early age and sent away to become a priest. The

God he speaks of is an omniscient abstraction devoid of life. He serves up phrases I faintly recall, embalmed in *The Baltimore Catechism*.

I've always felt sorry for St. Peter. Who knows what he felt toward that servant girl by the fire? Was she perhaps a knockout? A certain winsome appeal shone from her in the evening light, her tawny skin burnished by firelight, her bare limbs glowing, her eyes caressing this dark, brawny, awkward fisherman so evidently needy and sad, so ill at ease, so — worried. Her look toward him was soft and curious, not accusing. Others were there, a circle by the fire. How he longed to be part of it, to break his isolation. His bones ached, his brain reeled with images too painful, images he would bury if he could, bury away. The blood. The kiss. The capture. The pain of silence, desolation. The other ten were gone, who knew where? And who could blame any of them for having slept this night? Who in his right mind would have proppped his eyelids up for such an hour?

2:22. Father will speak now, words about words in this season of Easter. Against the breathing, the coughs, the restless sighs, the cramped bodies, the strained muscles, the futility, he begins.

"Dear friends, this is the great season of our year, the time of death and above all of resurrection."

"I'm sorry I ever left my room!" shouts a desperate voice.

"Shhh — " ripples everywhere.

Father is trained to persevere.

Did someone gag her?

He tells them of Easter, of fruitful suffering, of the coming kingdom. His hand shakes. Others cannot see it, hidden behind the music stand. Does he sense his inadequacy, his absurdity? Did his mother tell him he would always succeed? Did that cry penetrate a hollow within him? What are his secrets? His hand shakes.

2:27. Choir again.

"*Amazing grace! How sweet the sound, That saved a wretch like me. I once was lost, but now I'm found, Was blind, but now I see.*"

He stands erect to bless them, raising high the now steady hand. "In the name of the Father and of the Son and of the Holy Spirit . . ."

Most bow but do not bless themselves. This is a largely Protestant congregation, pushed to extremes where distinctions dwindle. A blessing blesses, music soothes.

2:30. Over. Perfect timing.

As I gather my music, ladies come forward — grateful, shy, wanting to shake hands and thank. One totters toward me in a burgundy skirt with a pink silk blouse, a burgundy scarf tied about her neck in a big floppy bow. So carefully thought out it hurts. She takes my hand and pumps it. "Thank you. It was lovely." Her over-rouged cheeks glow. Her brown eyes wear a mucous film. "I'm glad you liked it," I manage.

The doorway beside me is jammed.

Another approaches, wearing the heavy shoes of the cautious old. She toes out and appears confused. Her glasses are thick, and thin yellow fuzz covers her head. To reach the door she must pass me. She takes my hand, her yellow head bobbing gently. "Thank you so much. It was lovely." Her hand is cool and soft.

I know her.

I hadn't expected to know anyone here. It is my old neighbor, Mrs. Grant. Should I tell her? Would she remember me from across the street? That was two houses ago, how many lives? Or would I catch her out in her own forgetfulness? What life is she in now? Her husband, prematurely senile and paralyzed by stroke, sat by the day, the week, on their front porch staring over at my children playing in the yard.

Where does charity lie? Will it mean anything to her to be recognized?

"Mrs. Grant," I try. Uncertain. "Do you remember me? I used to live right across the street from you. Eleanor White."

Rattled, she looks at me more carefully. Small faded blue eyes brighten as they move across my face, my features, searching for clues. *Who is this person? When, where did I know her?*

She seems to survey me from the far end of a telescope, from somewhere I've never been. Alien turf. She squeezes my hand, a dry strong squeeze. Her left eyelid quivers. I am ridiculously aware of her fuzzy halo.

Suddenly she smiles. Delight.

She loosens her grip.

"Yes, yes, of course." Her smile is broad with relief, recognition. "I remember now. Mary Johnson! How could I forget?"

The Day the Grocery Store Fell In

I WAS UNDER THE DRYER at Hazel's. She's put a beauty shop in her base-ment, now the kids are grown and gone — well, almost. Josh still hangs around, says he's looking for work, but that doesn't interfere with Hazel's business, really. People understand. Anyhow, there I was, feeling the heat on my new perm, hoping it wouldn't turn out kinky this time, skimming the mocha recipes in *Family Circle*. I joined Weight Watchers this fall so I was drooling at the thought of what I'd given up, telling myself it'd be worth it. I'm tired of wearing size twenty.

I was just about to ask Hazel if she'd get me a pencil and slip of pa-per so I could jot down the recipe for mocha-mint-chip squares. I looked over at her blow-drying Mrs. Gerta Williamson's hair, a tough job if ever there was one. Hazel caught my eye in the mirror and nod-ded, when in ran Katie Stevenson fairly bursting.

Katie runs the flower shop that backs on the alley entrance to Ha-zel's Cut 'n' Curl. Now that she's got a reliable girl out front, Katie can run out the back door of her shop and into Hazel's kitchen and make herself a cup of tea when business is slack. Folks say there's something goin' between her and Josh but I doubt it. She's too smart. She got through Tantramar High a couple of years after my Packy. Wouldn't have a thing to do with him and his crowd, though they all thought she was some cute. She'd already taken up with Harold Bour-geois's young fella. Sad story. She must be pushing forty now. Pretty young to be running your own business, even in a town this small and friendly. Being friendly don't make money. But her daddy had it, socked it away, mean as a termite, old man Stevenson, and nobody mourned when his Ski-Doo hit that moose in the '75 blizzard. Dead on arrival. Tough moose.

Anyhow, Katie ran in.

It was like watching TV with the sound off. She was waving her hands, talking up a storm, as Hazel blew Mrs. W's freshly dyed coal black hair. Doc Williamson brought most of my generation into this world. Left her a bundle, they say. Finally, Hazel stopped, set down the dryer, and listened. Mrs. W. was talking, Hazel was talking, and it drove me crazy to see their lips moving and not have a clue what it was about. Katie was waving her hands like there was an emergency, but they just stood there so I figured it couldn't be fire or death. I wouldn't of heard the sirens, but if the engine had of been called out I would've seen Josh, for sure. He's one of the town volunteers and would've popped in to tell Hazel. A fire seems to be the one thing gets Josh Erwin off his backside.

I wanted to lift the darn heater off my head, but those things are tricky to manage and what with the bursitis or arthritis or God-knows-what in my right shoulder lately, I didn't dare fool around. They seemed to have forgot me. Went on talking and gesturing, and Hazel did a last quick whip with the dryer, Katie just leaning her weight against the partition. Long as I've known her, Katie Stevenson's never been one to stand on two feet when one would do.

Finally, I couldn't take it any longer.

"Hazel," I called.

Musta been my voice was pretty loud. Hazel jerked around and looked over at me, her red mouth making a round "O" and mouthing, "Sorry, Gloria."

Gloria is my name. They've always called me Glory round here, something you don't even think about after a while, but when I'm introduced as Glory to someone new in town, they kinda blink. After he had a few aboard, Ellard called me Hallelujah.

"Be right over," Hazel mouthed, unsnapping the pink nylon cover from around Mrs. W's neck and shaking it out. Mrs. W. stood up and picked some hair off her suede skirt. She's a dresser. Some in this town do and some don't. You can't tell a thing by it. Mabel Straight goes around looking like the wrath of God but they say she's loaded. Ever since her hubby, Willie, got outta cars and into antiques, they been making a killing off the tourists from Upper Canada looking for pine.

Hazel pushed back the dryer and felt my rollers. "Just about done."

"What's goin' on?"

"Grocery store fell in," said Katie, still leaning. She was biting the skin around her nails.

"The grocery store!"

There's only one in the center of town. Harry Colton's boy took it over about ten years ago and it's been growing ever since. All the Coltons, staunch Baptists, know how to make money. Harry put the other two groceries out of business.

"Fell right in," said Katie, nibbling.

"How could that happen?"

Mrs. Williamson banged out the door and Hazel came back from the cash box. She began to comb me out.

"Looks pretty good, Glory." She pulled one roller out too fast and stung my scalp. I didn't complain. I only had till noon and I wanted to see what was going on. That night I was serving the lobster supper at the Curling Club.

"Don't fuss too much," I said to Hazel.

"I just ran up to Main Street to see for myself," said Katie, "then hurried right over here to tell you, Hazel, and whoever was in the chair. Nobody'll be looking for flowers for a while."

Katie has one shoulder higher than the other and when she walks you'd almost think she had a limp. Some complication when she was born. Her mother was old Doc Williamson's niece, I think that's how it went. He never had much to do with the Stevensons, though. Besides, he was a Liberal. But Katie's done good for herself. That day she was in a mauve slacks and top outfit, not too flattering around the hips, but stylish. I'd seen it in the catalogue but decided it was too youthful. Thirty-nine ninety-five. Her husband sits at the Legion nights and drinks himself stupid. Poor Katie. Can't blame her for taking her fun where she can get it.

"They say there wasn't any warning to speak of," she went on, shifting her weight.

"What about Auntie Bill?" I asked.

"Auntie Bill?" Hazel yanked on the right side.

"Auntie Bill. You know. Old Mrs. Colson's daughter. The one lost everything in the fire last year. Junior" — that's what everyone calls Harry Colton's boy, though he's a grown man with four kids — "put her on in the bakery. What part of the store fell in? Couldn't of been the whole thing."

"The bakery." Katie straightened up and popped her eyes at the thought of all those doughnuts disappearing, to say nothing of Auntie Bill. She stretched too-long mauve arms and said, "Didn't hear a thing about Auntie Bill."

"The footings gave way?" asked Hazel as she fluffed me on top.

"That's what Sam LeBlanc said. He was just coming outta the post office, looking over at the grocery store, and whoosh — whole side just sank. And part of the front. The side toward the hardware store, next to the big hole they've been excavating for the new extension. He said the digger went under too far, loosened the pilings, and they had more water down there than they'd counted on."

They'd been digging all week, day and night. Kids lined up after school to watch the huge machine dig, swing, lay pipe, drop gravel. Fascinating. I live a bit out of town so hadn't seen much of it, but Leonard would stop by nights to give me a report. He'd stand all day watching how they were doing things. If Ellard had been here he'd a been down there too, chewing the fat with Sam. Leonard is Sam's brother, lives just down the way. Once you're retired there's not much to do in this town but chew the fat. And hunt, of course, in fall, but duck season was still three weeks away.

Hazel swung me around to look at the back. She'd put in a nice neat wave just above my neck.

"Fine," I said, "but I'm still wondering about Auntie Bill."

"Maybe you'll go up and have a look."

"How 'bout you?"

"I've a customer at eleven-thirty. Maybe after that — "

"Well, I'd better be off," said Katie. "Told Marilyn I'd be back in ten minutes. That was an hour ago."

I fished out the bills. Hazel's gone up to thirty dollars a perm, but it's still cheaper than going out of town, if you figure in the gas.

"Where's Susie at this morning?" she asked.

Susie's my granddaughter, five. I'm half raising her, you'd have to say. She stays with me days while my Luanne works for Dr. Carlson the dentist. Good job, steady hours, and since they closed down the foundry it's been a godsend. You'd think Chester might take care of Susie, but he's busy looking for work, so he says.

Anyhow, Loraine Beaton, my next-door neighbor, goes in three mornings a week to work at the Sears catalogue office but this was her morning off. And she doesn't mind watching Susie. Since Loraine's mum died, there's no one else in the house. She just turns on the game shows and lets Susie play around on the floor. I'd said I'd be back by noon so she wouldn't have to worry about lunch. Planned to pick up some muffins at the bakery. Fat chance now.

"Thanks, Hazel," I said, pocketing my change. I handed Hazel three dollars. Don't usually tip her, specially for a perm, but Josh had been in trouble lately and if I know Hazel, she'd bailed him out. She's proud, Hazel, and would never ask. It's bad enough to be a widow and starting your own business, without having two lugs of your own hanging around. Men, really. Both past twenty. Josh just eats ice cream all day long, so they say. I've seen the empty containers around the yard but never said anything. Looks a mess. I can imagine him sitting upstairs pigging out on peppermint flake and rum raisin, eyes glued to the boob tube, while his mum works away downstairs. Why should she pick up after him?

I let myself out. Hazel was already gabbing with her next customer.

I headed up the alley, past the back of the florist shop (Katie inside working), the Tea Room. The big SMT bus was parked out back there, where it picks up passengers and delivers packages from Halifax. When Chester was over in Halifax looking for work he'd send home his clothes for Luanne to wash and iron. "Don't be a fool," I tried to tell her. Every Wednesday they'd arrive, every Friday she'd send them back. My Luanne's always been a worker. Got her tubes tied after Susie, though. Must of seen the writing on the wall.

At the top of the alley you come right out on Main Street between the Royal Bank and Stedmans.

Traffic was backed up, bumper to bumper. Took me a moment to realize it wasn't going anywhere. The cars were just parked, stopped dead in the middle of town. Some had people in 'em. That's a town pastime on summer evenings — drive downtown to see what's goin' on. I'd rather be home crocheting, watching *Three's Company*, or baking squares.

But some folks crave excitement and have to get out.

I headed on down the street past Stedmans.

I'm telling you it was a *scene.* I've lived in this town sixty-two years and never seen anything like it — except the day years ago when the Lewis Hotel burned down. Everything was at a dead halt.

The police were out, busy being important. I saw Sherman Lewis — that's Loraine's first cousin's husband — holding folks back behind the barrier set up in front of the PO.

I eased my way over there — past men with cameras, dogs, toddlers in strollers, you name it. I leaned over the barrier.

"Sherman," I called.

Sherman went with Luanne once. Past history.

He came over, important in his dark blue with the light stripe up the leg. Good-looking fellow.

"Hi, Glory."

"Anybody hurt, Sherman?"

"Not as far as we know." He pointed at a kid sneaking under the barrier. "Get back, fella. Stay back."

The boy stuck out his tongue and backed off.

I skirted the barricade — just a piece of rope strung between saw horses — and made my way past the PO over toward the far side of the store, the side that had fallen in.

Let me tell you, that was something! Folks say living in a small town can be dull, but you'd go far to find more excitement than our town had that morning. All's you had to do was move through the crowd and listen. Everyone here knows everybody else's business — or almost. If you can't keep your mouth shut and your ears open, you're dead. If anyone smiles at you or says good morning, say it back. That's survival.

Sam LeBlanc was talking to Carl Harris, the hardware store owner.

"Just dug too deep. Some stupid, I'm telling you."

"Wonder, does the insurance cover?"

"Depends on whose insurance. They say Mrs. Blanchard — "

"Did she get hurt?" I butted in. That's Auntie Bill.

"Nope, Glory. They say she was busy making doughnuts and heard this terrible roar. Saw the ceiling and wall start to come apart and felt a little bit of floor caving in. Hid herself under the table. Didn't come out till everything had quieted down. Then they heard her. 'Hey, get me outta here.' Not a finger hurt. She was holding the broom. Lost her pocketbook, though."

"Coulda been buried alive," Sam said.

"Yessir. Coulda been buried alive."

"Did you see her when she came out?" I asked Sam.

"Nope. They took her out of the back door. Some close call."

I could see old Auntie Bill clutching her broom, her face all screwed up like a squirrel's, her eyes shut. She's a case, Auntie Bill. Town do-gooder. Seems to be her life's work to get the food into people's mouths. When I was in Saint John with my nerves, she helped out my Luanne. Wouldn't take a cent, just saw a need and filled it. Packy had headed out to Alberta by that time, and Luanne didn't know when Chester would get back from wherever he was. All on her own with a newborn, Caesarian at that. So Auntie Bill moved in. And when her house burned to the ground, the town rallied. Gave her son Wally the crossing guard's job. It brought in a little. Auntie Bill, she never complained, just got out and looked for work. That's when she went into the bakery.

"Got your hair done, Glory?"

Leonard. He'd moved in right beside me. I hoped he'd be stopping by that night after supper. He seldom misses. It gives a point to things, somehow.

"Just came from Hazel's."

Sam, his brother, wasn't saying much but I could see he was taking it in.

"Did you hear that Josh pulled Mabel Straight's grandson, Terry, out of harm's way?"

We were all just standing there staring at that hole. Nothing going on at the store. Must of been five hundred people milling around talking, gaping at Pampers and Robin Hood flour and fifty-pound sacks of potatoes heaped in with rocks and boards and debris. A tractor sat there empty at the far edge of the pit.

"No, I haven't heard much." Len looked all scrubbed and freshly shaven. He's much cleaner than his brother. And never teases the way Ellard did. I knew I was getting pink. "Was Terry hurt?" I asked.

"No one hurt, far as they know. The cash girls were on their coffee break. The bad side of the store happened to be empty, excepting for Terry and Josh. Terry was stacking flour. Josh was over near the ice cream freezer studying the specials. Felt the floor shake. Grabbed Terry and ran." Leonard looked me over. "Guess it sometimes pays to indulge, Glory."

Now what did he mean by that? He's been coming every evening for a year. Just tea and squares. Maybe that's all her wants. If it's more . . . I'm ready.

"See you later," he said and moved off.

He was wearing his new windbreaker, light blue with darker blue collar and cuffs. He's long and lean, Leonard, not heavy as a bull like Ellard. I hope Weight Watchers pays off this time.

It was ten to twelve. I had just ten minutes.

Jack Ward, who takes pictures for the weekly paper, was roaming through the crowd shooting from every angle. The whole side of the store was exposed. You could see rows of canned goods — soups, fruits, vegetables — all neatly stacked, ready to go. They look undressed or something, all lined up along the shelves, and right beside them — nothing. Just sheer drop right into the pit outside, or what had been outside. The bakery, near the front end of the store, was gone completely, and the right front window had shattered and fallen in. The roof had caved down toward the hole, too, and there was the sense that at any moment more might go. Meanwhile, the soup cans stood ready.

"Gonna send this one to *The Globe and Mail*," crowed Jack as he passed me.

"Put us on the map, eh?" chuckled Carl from down the line.

CBC was there, holding a mike in front of Junior, who was over behind the barricade, right in front of the store, where they could get a good picture of him plus the damage. His lips were moving a mile a minute but I couldn't make out what he was saying. Later that night I saw him on TV, and Auntie Bill telling how she'd grabbed the broom.

Linda Stevenson, Katie's girl, had pushed her double baby stroller right up to the sidewalk's edge near the barrier, and the twins were goggle-eyed. "Some show, eh, Glory?"

Happy as a clam, Linda, with her babies. Loraine told me she got married in one of those "For the Bride Who's Beginning to Show" dresses from Sears. There's some think she's one brick short of a load, but she's doing just fine with her babies. Maybe this is what she's been waiting for her whole life.

The mayor and undertaker, Finley Cooke, arrived on the scene and moved over toward Junior to shake his hand, once CBC finished. Probably wanted to get his mug on TV. Wouldn't put it past him. He gets all the PC stiffs and Junior's a Liberal, but that day it didn't matter. No business for him outta this disaster. He planted himself in front of Junior and pumped his hand like the next thing we'd hear would be strains of "The Old Rugged Cross."

I stood around a few more minutes feeling good in my fresh perm, the town swirling around me, talking, swapping gossip, or just staring. It was like everyone felt they'd escaped from something. Leonard had gone down round the corner, probably to the Tea Room for a coffee. The morning was warm and mellow, glassy, like the last days of September can be around here. Some folks were in shirtsleeves, no jackets, and huge white clouds floated above the Stop-N-Buy. It was like a fair or something, everyone moving around that hole, talking about how lucky we'd been there were no injuries or deaths. Everyone gathered to see what they could see.

That night we were on TV. And next day it was in *The Globe and Mail*, the story plus the picture of the grocery store with its side off and the roof hanging down over the pit. Sam said the Tea Room sold out copies of the paper that morning before ten.

I watched TV and read the paper, but nothing caught it. There won't come another day like it soon, the whole town out there to witness disaster. Only you'd hardly call it disaster. Leonard tells me the insurance will cover. No one was killed, or even hurt. We made TV, *The National*, and people all across Canada read about us.

Best of all, a big new store, twice the size, will open any day now.

Portfolio

ALMOST FOUR-FIFTEEN. Julie would be on time. Never late. Five o'clock sharp, the hour every other Friday he dreaded. First, at four-thirty, Mrs. Lincoln. Would they collide? He'd never met Mrs. Lincoln but had his suspicions from the way she wrote — long involved sentences, poor punctuation. Probably huge, and a smoker. He disliked large women and hated smoke in the office. Once, to Howinger's disgust, he'd put a small sign on the door, "Thank you for not smoking." "Christ, Will," Carl said that afternoon after class as he blew flamboyant smoke rings toward the unblinking bust of Shakespeare, "who're you after? No undergraduate would dare smoke in here. If it's a mature student, why not? Why deny them one of life's smaller sins? A little smoke won't hurt you."

One Christmas Julie gave him a sign with a thick black line through a lighted cigarette and he pasted that to the door. With luck Mrs. Lincoln would notice. Her situation was touchy enough without added hassle.

At least Julie would be brief. She had it down pat now: "Here they are, Will, all yours. Bye, boys." Then off without a backward glance, swinging her tight little ass through the deserted halls as if to say, Who needs this? The boys would stand there strained and awkward. John should be less runny this weekend, the worst of his cold over. Eric would spend the first few hours zapping his father with that Bug Off look. Thirteen. His long-suffering sighs labeled parents a wart on the universe.

"Can't you even pitch a curve, Dad?" he'd asked two weeks before, as if the ability to project a spherical object through space certified masculinity.

"Never spent much time at it," he replied, calculating, then popped a halfway decent fly. "Too busy studying." He stifled the urge to say, Isn't Ben giving you guys a workout? Julie had specialized in the muscle-bound type for the past eight months. Ben was her latest.

Yet later that evening, after they had all settled in a bit and re-established their rhythm, the older boy grew conciliatory, wanted to talk all about his new school. He was reading *A Connecticut Yankee in King Arthur's Court* on his own. He was full of questions about math. "Why'd they put a dumb jock to teach grade nine math?" he muttered. A fine line of dark hair outlined his upper lip and he was biting his nails.

Nothing was simple.

Now — Mrs. Lincoln. Four-twenty.

He leaned forward at the littered desk and shoved aside today's papers — thirty-five essays on point of view in *What Maisie Knew.* Later. Sunday night, maybe, after the boys left, when rooms reclaimed their emptiness and the dripping kitchen faucet could again be heard. Routine, even a dripping faucet, could comfort. It drove Julie crazy.

Overhead the fluorescent light buzzed and in the far bookcase the stand-up cuckoo clock Julie had given him their second Christmas prepared to perform. The corridor outside was silent. You could almost smell Friday afternoon. What other fool would still be in his office?

He stared at the stuffed three-ring binder before him with a feeling of sadness. *What could he possibly say?*

"Madam, I respect your life experience but it just doesn't convert to academic credits. You can't make some of these equivalencies. Here, let's look."

He'd pick up something innocuous — the description of her trip to Ireland, say. "Now, let's look at this. Yes, I see you went to Trinity College. Saw the Book of Kells, yes. You even, you say, walked Dublin in the steps of Leopold Bloom? Yes, that would be educational. Now, have you ever studied *Ulysses*?" Melon, smellon. And if she had?

It would depend on how tenacious or fragile she was. Never could tell about these old ladies. Could be tough as nails. He'd already assigned the trip half a credit, largely on her description of reading

153

Riders to the Sea, then visiting the Aran Islands. She'd composed a long descriptive poem about Inishmore's "craggy hills and flinty gardens mocking wind and rain and sea" — all, she claimed, in iambic pentameter.

He leaned forward, opened the notebook again, and flipped past pages of photographs, drawings, and too-light type. A large middle section was labeled *Art.* She must have typed the descriptions herself — full of blotches and inserts.

"When I was in my sixties, after my husband died," wrote Mrs. Lincoln, "I studied watercolor for five years with an artist in Newport."

The next five or six pages showed photographs of watercolors mounted in neat little black corners. A scene on the Oregon coast. *My trip to Banff. Looking at the Snake River. The petrified Ginkgo forest at Vanguard.*

He studied a photographed painting of The Inn at Spanish Head. The perspective was from below, from the beach, looking up the cliff at the massive stucco resort hotel. He remembered too well . . . their room had faced the ocean, the third floor . . . a patio . . . Julie shy as a bride. She made him feel — capable. They'd go down the steep wooden steps to the beach in the evening and walk barefoot, wet sand pushing beneath their toes. Afterward, a little wine, a long night, the surprise of moonlight on flesh. That it rained for three days didn't matter.

He studied the other snapshots. She had a steady hand. Once, he'd fancied himself something of an artist, in grad school, before Julie. He'd survived Minnesota winters partly by painting all weekend while others skied. The girl upstairs in his apartment building offered lessons in watercolor. He loved that sense — quick, catch it now or never — and the delicate results. Whatever happened to those pictures?

"What've you got there, Will, new centerfold?"

He looked up at the dark paunchy man leaning against the door frame.

"Another one of those damned portfolios." Will flipped it closed. Somehow it felt like indecent exposure. She was late. Maybe she'd forget to come. Traffic. Red lights. Illness.

"Christ. Why'd you ever let yourself in for that? Did you hear about Charles Thompson's wife?"

No, and he didn't want to. Shame he hadn't closed the office door, not that that would have stopped Howinger. He'd had the office next door for fifteen years. They knew each other's coughs and sneezes, could tell time by each other's schedules.

"Decided she oughtta be able to claim some credit for their trip to the Greek Isles last summer. Got him going around in circles, poor fella. It's not like Nelda Thompson did anything serious there, if you know what I mean."

He knew. Nelda Thompson, campus bore. A woman with too little to do and too much to say. Had come snooping around the minute she heard Julie had left. Could she do anything? Didn't want to interfere.

"Look, Carl — "

"Yeah, I know. Julie coming at five as per usual?"

Son of a bitch. Was there anything he didn't know? "Yes. So I've got to finish this now."

"Okay, okay. Catch you for a beer Monday afternoon. Then you can tell me how it turned out with — what's her name?"

"Lincoln. Mrs. Lincoln." They'd already discussed the case over one beer. Carl failed to understand why it troubled him so. "Tell her no," he'd said. "Just no. Can't water these things down to no meaning, Will. Little old ladies are the scourge of the universe. Ever get behind one on the freeway?"

"Shut the door, will you, Carl?"

The steps echoing down the hallway beat in his head like some dull remembered pain. For how many Friday afternoons had he listened to the heavy steady fall of Carl Howinger's retreating heels?

Will opened the looseleaf binder again and stared at a photo of flowering plum trees. *Willamette Valley Summer* read the caption.

She had studied photography, had a darkroom. Soft shades of pink. Must have had someone else do the color developing. Maybe she'd be like that, soft pink. He doubted it. Her letter was too aggressive.

Dear Dean Thompson,

I have read in The Evening Star of Salem College's arrangement for evaluating a life experience portfolio. Many years ago I took some evening courses through Salem's program in our town. I have four credits toward a BA. I am older (seventy-four) and it is difficult for me to get out. I am a widow living in a senior citizen's complex. My children are grown, my husband passed away ten years ago. I have spent the past months putting together the enclosed portfolio of my life experience. As you can see, it has been varied. I feel that it has deep educational value. I have studied your catalog and applied beside each set of my experiences the number of credits I think it deserves. Would you ask your committee to review this? I will be eager to hear from you as soon as possible.

Sincerely,
Mabel Lincoln

"See what you can do, Will," said Charlie Thompson when he handed it over. "Thing weighs half a ton. Some life experience!"

He'd taken it with a feeling of despair. He was new to the three-man committee this fall. This, after arguing against the whole business in a faculty meeting last spring. "How can you measure life experience?" he asked them, embarrassed that some might know what he was going through at that very time. Not that *he* would have minded some credit. Who was to give it? What great academic dean in the sky was sending him down credits for trying to be fair, generous even, with a wife he couldn't fathom? He fought spreading anger the best way he knew, through work. It was not a method Julie respected, or even comprehended. "Where are you going to stop?" he asked his colleagues. "This granny knits intricate baby bootees so we give her credit for an aesthetic eye?" When it came to a vote, the majority prevailed. Continuing Ed was a money-maker in tight times. People living longer, looking to fulfill expectations, do something they'd never been able to do before for one reason or another. He knew all the arguments but still thought it dangerous. He could imagine all kinds of goofy abuse. This fall he'd been named chairman of the committee. "To protect academic values," Dean Thompson told him. "Wouldn't want to be in your shoes," said Howinger, when he heard.

The other two members of the committee had already evaluated Mrs. Lincoln's portfolio and handed it to him. His was the final word.

He turned pages and stopped at one entitled *Crafts*. A photograph of dolls faced him, there must be seventy or eighty, dolls of all sizes, round porcelain faces, unblinking eyes, curly hair, straight hair, dolls in evening gowns, dolls in overalls, dolls in frilly shirts, two dolls in sailor

156

outfits. Arms and legs stuck out stiffly in the doll rows, one above the other. Must have doll bleachers of some sort, he thought. Nothing else showed in the picture — no lamp, no chair. Not even a Cabbage Patch Doll, he thought wryly, suddenly liking Mrs. Lincoln.

She had collected cast-off dolls for years, scavenged local dumps for them, rehabilitated and dressed them, given them to the local mental hospital.

What could he do with that? Bill Edgett had inserted a caustic note: "This does not merit academic credit. Barbie never got a BA."

Sometimes he wondered what it would be like to have daughters. Howinger had two by his first wife, saw them every other month for a day or two. They seemed so much quieter than Eric and John, or was he so far removed he couldn't tell any more? Maybe it was sexist prejudice.

He took the white-out and obliterated Edgett.

⚌

A light knock at the door.

"Professor Harlow?"

"Yes?" He closed the portfolio and set it squarely in the center of his desk. "Come in."

Good God! Why hadn't anyone warned him? Who would have known? Her picture had appeared nowhere.

"Are you Professor Harlow?"

Her voice was low and steady. She seemed calm, standing there in the doorway.

"Yes, yes, come in. You must be Mrs. Lincoln."

Thank God he hadn't stood. She couldn't be more than four feet tall. Where (and how?) would she sit? Would he have to boost her into the chair? How could he? He tried to remember biographical details in the portfolio. Had something escaped him? Mother. Grandmother. Artist. Traveler. Not a hint of this. What a situation. Surely she would manage it. Lots of experience. Was he blushing? Please, Julie, be late. And the boys, they might laugh. He felt warm beneath his collar. His palms grew suddenly damp.

"Come in, Mrs. Lincoln, and sit down." His mouth was so dry he could scarcely speak.

157

She waddled in on too-short legs, watching him. The billowy white hair on her oversized head looked freshly done. All got up to meet the professor.

At the bookcase near his desk she paused and looked up at crammed shelves.

"My, my," her back was to him, "you've read *The Thorn Birds?*" Julie's. Left behind.

"Yes. Quite some time ago," he managed, allowing himself to stare while her back was turned. Her thick legs in seamed stockings plunged straight into her low-heeled shoes, minus ankles.

"I thought Ralph was a bastard," she said, turning toward him.

How would she place herself? She seemed untroubled. Then he remembered her letter. Little men have to be bullies to make up for their deficiency in size, his mother had once told him when he ran home from school with a bloody nose. Was it the same for women? He'd always been tall himself, shooting up in ninth grade to six feet. Recently he'd begun to go soft beneath the belt.

She surveyed him from behind frameless glasses. "Well, Professor, I came to see if you've finished evaluating my portfolio."

Her glasses bows were those crazy ones that go down instead of straight. What madness vanity, he thought, trying to look matter-of-fact, casual.

"I — "

She came round in front of the chair beside his desk.

"Could you hold this for a moment?" She handed him a bulging navy purse.

Leaning back, she placed her palms flat on the seat of the chair and hoisted herself with practiced ease.

"There." She reached over for the purse and placed it on her lap.

Her legs stuck out straight on the chair. Like dolls on bleachers, he thought, and tried to forget the picture. How her muscles must bulge beneath the long sleeves of her decorous navy suit. A lifetime of hoisting. Light blue ruffles rippled down her front between the edges of her open jacket, and her nails (he saw as she grasped her purse) were pale purple. *Seventy-four.*

"Well, Mrs. Lincoln," he began again, "I was just giving your portfolio one last look." He stared at the fuschia cover with its calligraphy title: *Life Portfolio.* Hopeless.

"And?" She pushed herself farther back in the chair. Her fingers clasped her purse. They were short pudgy fingers, a large diamond on the left hand.

Julie had wanted a diamond. He'd never seen his way clear.

"What did you think of it?"

He had this feeling she was testing him. "I found it . . . interesting indeed. You've had a lot of interesting experiences in your life, I must say." God, did he sound like a wimp. If only she could, would, *really* tell him. There was a whole world to be learned from her.

"Yes, you might say that, Professor. But what I want to know," she leaned forward and her voice took on a harder edge, "is what can it be made to count for?"

She was a bird, a plump full-breasted ruffled bird, searching for worms. He cringed inside. His neck was positively wet. Surely she was expecting special treatment. What had prompted her to contact Salem? Year of the Disabled and all that?

"I wondered if you might tell me a bit more about your trip to Ireland, Mrs. Lincoln." A stall. He hated himself as he leaned back in his chair and swiveled to face her directly. He could stall only so long. She had left the office door ajar. The hall outside was deserted and silent. Any moment — Julie.

Her small green eyes seemed never to blink. Without a word, she opened her full-sized purse with its shiny clasp, extracted a pack of cigarettes, and snapped the purse back shut. "Do you have a light, Professor?"

He yanked open the top drawer and rummaged. Exploring fingers grazed paper clips, rubber bands, dried-up ballpoints, straight pins, scissors. Matches, finally.

She took her time, inhaled, glanced up at the pale Shakespeare atop the bookcase behind him.

"Yes, about Ireland. I went with my son. My oldest boy."

Big or little? he was dying to ask. Was it hereditary? Did all little people come from little people? How did it happen, anyhow? Or could a little person produce a big person? How? What did you mate with to accomplish it? A world of munchkins housing a giant. He tried to focus on her story. He could feel the tabletop pressing against his chin. It would take all new furniture . . .

"He's a professor himself," she said.

Damn him. Didn't little people have conventions now, he'd read somewhere? Could she sue Salem College for discrimination? He saw himself in court pleading his case: *This has nothing to do with size, Yer Honor* —

"And so he took me around Dublin, you know, to all the places James Joyce wrote about in *Ulysses*" — here was his opening, he couldn't bring himself to use it, he let her go on, he nodded — "and we had a terrible time in some spots. You can't even find the house at Eccles Street any more, you know. And the door to that house, let me see" — she looked away from him a moment, trying to remember — "that house turned up at the oddest place, oh yes, I remember, at a restaurant, a really good restaurant on — "

"Grafton Street," he supplied. He'd insisted on taking Julie. Scorning his Irish stew, she'd ordered Coquille St. Jacques. "Yes, I've seen it. Was this the boy in the toga? He recalled the picture of a boy at a Latin Club banquet, decadent in a toga.

"No, no," she said in some disgust. "That's my grandson. The oldest. I've seven. I have their pictures . . ." She made a move toward her purse.

"That's okay," he said quickly. All the same, grandmothers. They'd buttonhole God Himself to show a picture of their grandson in hell. His own mother . . . hauling out snapshots of her professor son to bore the cashier at K Mart. Hard to imagine Julie —

"Tell me about your travels around Ireland," he said. Four-forty-five. Fifteen minutes. "Did you go to Yeats country?"

She fit herself snugly into the contours of the chair, took the plastic Disneyworld dish from the edge of his desk, pushed aside its paper clips and rubber band, and ground out her cigarette.

"They unloaded a busload of kids the day we reached the churchyard," she said, replacing the ashtray. "I'd already been disappointed at the Lake Isle of Innisfree. I'd wanted to see it. One of my sons is a beekeeper."

No hint of a smile. He held his gaze steady.

"Couldn't get over to the island that day. Boatman was sick. So when we got to Sligo I was determined I was going to make a rubbing of the tombstone. I enclosed a picture of it there — " she pointed to the portfolio. "You may have seen it?"

He nodded. He could remember nothing.

"I waited as long as I could for the kids to clear away. You know people don't *see* people like me," she said, daring him, he felt, to agree. "So then I just brought my apparatus and my son, he actually did the rubbing. You wouldn't take off for that, would you?" He shook his head automatically, wondering at the size of the son. Big? Little? "We got the whole thing. Have it hanging in my living room today. 'Cast a cold eye On life, on death. Horseman, pass by!'"

How could he take off for *anything* ? Her wrists were thick, as if she were meant to be another size. She wore plain, dark walking shoes, grandmotherly shoes. His own grandmother had worn the same, without the lifts. Was there a whole clothing industry, he wondered, for little people? She could have told him so much.

"You lost your husband some years ago, Mrs. Lincoln?" Was this a mistake? Four-fifty. He must get to the point. What was the point?

"Yes, he was my third."

Good God. Maybe she was fun in her day.

"Seven grandchildren," she reminded him. "They're proud of me. They'll be so happy to see me graduate."

He took a deep breath. No delaying longer. Julie would be there any minute. They hadn't even touched the portfolio.

"Well, now, Mrs. Lincoln . . ."

She moved about on the chair as if to resettle herself, while her face grew expectant.

He opened the portfolio randomly. "Now here," he began. The Inn at Spanish Head. Why that? "This picture — "

"We honeymooned there. Ralph, my second husband, and me," she said with a broad smile. When she smiled her eyes turned to slits and two gold teeth glittered.

For an instant he felt on the verge of something. It faded.

"Then, when I took up art — later, after we divorced," she hesitated, he nodded encouragement, "I went back there. We'd had such good times. That would have been around . . . 1960 or so."

She would have been fifty.

"He was your second husband?"

"Yes, a sewer surveyor in Portland. Made for the job."

Was she putting him on? He flipped hastily. He caught sight of dolls and kept flipping. He stopped. They were staring at a photograph of a small bungalow with pink shutters.

"Now that," she said, "I only put in because it's part of history. My history."

"I'm afraid, Mrs. Lincoln . . ."

She wiggled forward to the edge of the chair and perched there as if trying to decide something. For one second he feared the plump-breasted robin might turn predatory.

"I have to tell you — " he swallowed.

"I know what you're going to say, Professor." She edged forward more, almost teetering there, her toes brushing the floor. "I've more work to do. Don't you worry your head about that."

"But — "

"Surprised?"

"Yes. Truthfully, I am. You mean — "

"I didn't expect full credit for graduation."

What did she expect? Would he ever know? "I understood you wanted total credit for what was in the portfolio . . ." His voice sounded nervous. Was she kidding him? She didn't appear to be kidding. "You know, Mrs. Lincoln, there's such a thing as requirements, prerequisites — "

She slid from the chair.

"There are prerequisites for life," she snapped. "I could fit in your wastebasket and you could carry me from this office. No one would ever know."

Her eyes were on a level with his, inscrutable. He stood. Her head barely reached his chest.

"You could cart me outside," she went on calmly, as they moved toward the door now, "that is, if you found a way to put a lid on, look for the nearest oversized trash can, and dump me in, Professor." Her voice rose. "Prerequisites — "

The door opened.

"Hi — oh, I'm sorry."

Julie backed up, obviously confused. Behind her Will could see Eric's eyes widen.

"Perfectly all right, Madam. Your husband — "

"He's not my husband."

"Well, then, whatever he is — "

"Come in, Julie," he managed. "Mrs. Lincoln was just leaving. We were discussing her portfolio."

Julie had regained her usual control. She surveyed Mrs. Lincoln with a cool, curious eye. She wore red today, a knit dress; its ribbing clung to her curves. He kept his eyes on Mrs. Lincoln.

"You're an — *artist?*" Julie's incredulity was scarcely masked. She was more than a foot taller than Mrs. Lincoln.

"Mrs. Lincoln has brought me an impressive portfolio," he heard himself saying.

Mrs. Lincoln was buttoning her jacket. She looked at the boys. At Julie. Then, with the slightest gesture, she motioned toward the boys. "These must be yours?" She glanced at Will.

"Yes, Eric and John."

Julie's clock began to strike. A carved mountaineer leaned out the small doorway and bowed. "Cuckoo. Cuckoo."

"To answer your question, Madam," said Mrs. Lincoln, now at the top button. "Yes. I am an artist. An artist in life." She turned toward him. "With the striking of the clock no further comment is necessary. You've convinced me, Professor. There's more work to be done. I thank you for your time. I shall return."

Did she wink? Behind those glasses? He wasn't sure. He bowed.

Her steps echoed down the deserted hall, quick heavy thuds. Short legs.

Julie was busy looking around the office . . . posters, books, the mess on his desk. "Nothing ever changes here," she murmured. "It says you, Will." She turned her scarlet curves toward him. "Well, here they are. I'm off. Have a good weekend."

She opened the door and disappeared.

"Where to, Dad?" said Eric. He looked positively happy.

"McDonald's or Ponderosa?" said Will.

He was thinking of little people. Of how the whole world was organized for the big. Of how they must have to stretch and jump and slide and lift themselves where ordinary people just moved. Of how McDonald's or Ponderosa were scaled to the ordinary. Of how unreachable a salad bar would be for the likes of her.

"Forget it," he said. "Let's go out to Vecchio's and have a steak dinner."

They'd sit in a fancy dining room and he'd treat the boys like kings.

Another Country

MOTHER'S HERE. IT HAPPENS once a year and I dread it. I'm mesmerized by her foot, a size eleven in ragged sneakers, tracing a circle in the sand. We rest against this huge rock on the shore of Northumberland Strait and she traces that big foot in the sand. Around and around. She hates her feet.

"How long does it take the ferry to get over to the Island?" she asks, as we stare out at the white dot gliding across shining blue toward the horizon.

"Forty minutes."

She used to call it Prince Edward Island, like the tourists in summer when they roll down their window to ask directions.

"I want to get back to the whole question," she says, her toe tracing.

I could almost sleep, lie down in the soft sand, brush aside seaweed and pebbles, dig a nice warm hole, and rest. Not while she's here. My mother, at sixty-five, remains a dynamo.

"Why *doesn't* he speak, Ellie? Surely there's some medical answer. Surely doctors can offer you *something?*"

I look out at Gordie, a small five, floating in his tube.

"I've told you, Mother." I try to sound quiet and even, for I've learned any other tone backfires. She means well. She is a concerned grandmother. "There's nothing wrong with his vocal apparatus. Or his brain. Or his nerves. We've had the child tested to a fare-thee-well. *We have to trust.*"

I feel my own trust, now that she's been at me for three days, shaved to the thinness of that pink shell gleaming against the sand.

164

"Your mother," says Rob in his quieter moments, "has the affliction of most Americans. She wants instant results."

He forgets now and then that I too am American. Or was. How does one shuck off such identities? A little paper, a quiz, a book of history memorized, to say premier instead of governor, prime minister instead of president, learning not to notice the Queen's picture in the post office or the omnipresent Union Jacks. To my mother I'm certainly still American.

"Ellie, if you'd just let me take him back to Boston," she is going on, her foot moving slowly to rest against the sand. "I know he'd get help there."

"I won't have him a guinea pig, Mother." Can she hear my doubt? Or does she read it as one more don't-interfere gesture? Does she guess that one comes to prefer silence to the fatigue of constant explaining? She knows only part of our efforts to coax speech from this child in every other way judged "normal." What, we wonder, *is* normal? He can throw and catch a ball better than his fourteen-year-old sister.

"Surely your medical bills are enormous?"

"Medicare, Mother."

"I forget that. Canada is quite socialistic, isn't it."

She swirls in her prejudices against this country I've adopted, as if somehow the child of our loins, born in the States, might have talked on schedule and now be breaking the IQ record. My mother is used to bright children.

But look, he's limping toward us, one leg lifting as he walks like a lame ostrich, bright red blood dripping onto the sand.

"What happened, Gordie, what happened?" She is there in an instant, on her knees in the sand before him. "Was it out there?"

He waves a tanned arm toward the water, medium high tide right now.

"Probably jellies," I say, trying to stay calm. I can see a surface scratch on his leg, acquired no doubt as he raced for shore after the jellyfish got him. A circle of pink dots is beginning to appear on his chest.

He points to it. "Um, ummmmmm, um. . ."

His lips are tightly closed. Eloquent in his refusal to talk, he dances in the sand, pointing to his chest, waving at the sea, miming danger, hurt, fear — and above all what appears to be outrage. His blond straight hair is plastered to his high forehead and a ridge of salt lines the back of his neck. I see this as I wrap him in his towel and head him toward our blanket farther up on the beach, Mother following.

Moments later, calmed, he is back in the water floating about on the big black inner tube Rob inflated for him this morning.

"Now, Ellie," Mother continues, "about Boston . . ."

My mother has lived her entire life in Newton, Massachusetts. Her home — a modest colonial on a comfortable tree-lined street — she bought long after we'd grown and gone. It satisfies her. At last, after thirty years of hard work, she quit, splurged, and gave herself the setting she longed for — and deserved. She is disappointed in me, or perhaps baffled would be a better word. She tries to disguise this now, or maybe doesn't even feel it as we lie together on the moth-eaten car blanket, July sun warming us, waves lapping at our feet. This setting erases much. That's why I try to have her come in summer.

But she is still disappointed, and I wonder just why a mother's disappointment should be such a burden. I'll turn forty next October. I've made my choices, certified my own identity by being sure it's not hers. Yet every now and then when she's here I catch myself recognizing a movement of hers that is also mine — the way she dries a dish or makes a bed, or just the way she sits in a chair. As if the body repeated itself throughout time, insuring that certain simple things will last — a unique posture, a way of sitting in a chair.

"Mother," I say, "I'm firm." She turns to look at me, her gold earrings catching a glitter from late afternoon sun. "If anyone takes Gordie to Boston, it will be Rob and me. There's a superb children's hospital right in Halifax. But for this summer we're letting it go, trusting that in his own good time he'll find a way to talk. He has a year before he starts grade one."

I spare her details of frustrating sessions with doctors — pediatricians, psychologists, even a neurologist. She never took her child to a birthday party, stood in the doorway watching mothers and children babbling away beneath bright balloons, prayed her child would join in, then saw him squeal and squeal but never speak, his eyes growing bright with a pleasure he wouldn't — or couldn't — name. She never felt the shame of wanting to shout into well-meant sympathy, *Here, let me show you the pictures he draws for hours each day, beautifully shaded vistas and tightly coiled imaginings of a world I could never have thought up. Could you?* My two brothers and I got As in school, talked early and well. I had never expected to feel this loss.

What's really on her mind even more than Gordie, I suspect, is her furniture.

"All right, Ellie," she says. "I believe you. But if I can do anything . . ." Her voice fades as the turns again, earrings aglitter, to look at the sea, this alien stretch of Atlantic, this *not*-Cape Cod.

※

After supper we walk the beach again. Rob has taken Gordie and Sarah to the park so Mother and I can have this required talk. I know what's bugging her.

I watch her big sneakered feet flatten the sand. It amazed her that in Halifax we were able to find shoes she can't get in the States. Her feet have always been a problem. When I was a child she'd walk the floor at night with cramps, trying not to waken me with her groans. That was after Dad had disappeared into the blue, after she'd moved me into her room. I could hear her get up, though I never let on.

Once, when I was old enough to think the question, I was tempted to ask if they'd conceived each time he was home on leave, we three kids were so perfectly spaced — '40, '42, '44 — me, the only girl and last baby. But the subject was taboo. How explain to three small children that a man who'd distinguished himself for bravery in the war couldn't survive fatherhood, even without distinction? He walked away from it.

The evening air is warm and clear after an almost perfect day. Shiny beach grass waves on the ledge above us. The tide is in. The water would be warm after its long trip across the sandbars. We love to come down here on clear July evenings, build a fire, roast hot dogs and marshmallows, then swim. Gordie will sit by the fire, arms locked round his knees, the deep blue of his eyes glowing as he watches the flames. I sometimes think he's the happiest then, as if he and the leaping flames and lapping waves and dipping swallows share something our voices violate.

We pick our way over barnacled rocks, ignoring dead purplish jellyfish plastered against the sand. This is the season of jellies on the

Northumberland Strait. It has something to do with shifts of wind, though I've never quite figured it out.

"Well, have you and Rob thought about my offer?" she begins.

There is no way to be subtle about this. She can hardly say: *Well, now that you two have done your back-to-the-earth bit and found running water to be an asset, now that you've tried raising your own food and found buying vegetables at the grocery store more to your liking, can you bring yourselves to consider my furniture?* Actually, her irony is not that acid. She believes in manners.

She must know we've thought about her letter, talked it over.

"When are you moving, Mother?"

"Early October. I haven't set the exact date. The people want my house November 1. I start paying rent on my apartment October 2. There's a lot to get rid of, cutting down from eight rooms to three."

She isn't asking for pity. My mother is a strong woman. She cuts her ties. She raised the three of us alone, working day and night to give us the childhood she thought we should have. Only when that was over did she indulge her desire for the touches of gentility she'd observed in homes of friends — a small oriental rug, a silver tea service, special china cups. Now, after so few years, she must shrink her space to three small rooms. She will obey her doctor. She wants length of life more than teacups. But that a weak heart should so rule a life! How maddening it must be.

"There's the dining room set," she is going on, "all mahogany. We did some auctions right after the war, got good buys. And there's the drop-leaf table and the wing chair, and your old bedroom suite . . . I always felt you'd want it someday. Of course . . ."

I know what she's thinking. *I didn't think it would be this way, Ellie, twenty years later, you stuck up here in Canada living a life I don't understand with a good man you refuse to marry.*

She says none of this. She's much too polite.

"Where would I put it, Mother? The dining room table, for example."

"You could certainly get rid of that pine thing you've got."

"That 'pine thing,' Mother, represents hours of scraping and sanding. Rob found it in Cy Talbot's barn. We did it together."

She remains silent.

How tough to be in her spot — visiting mother, trapped here by economy restrictions of Air Canada, forced to sustain discomfort and stress not of her choosing.

"But the value . . ." She looks out to sea. Whitecaps dot the strait and the horizon is pale orange. "There's no comparison, Ellie. You know that."

"It means something to us."

"And doesn't my furniture?"

Furniture. It bores me. I cannot convince her of this. My child is five and will not speak.

"There's the sheer expense of moving it here, Mother, even if I had a place to put it." I shoot her a glance but her sharp, handsome profile reveals nothing. She has remarkably few wrinkles. "If you'd asked me eight or ten years ago I probably could have used anything, but we've managed to get the place together now and — "

"Somehow, Ellie, I always thought you . . . what of the children? Sarah is old enough . . ."

"At the moment, Mother, Sarah cannot see beyond the end of her fourteen-year-old nose. In time, maybe. She'd probably like something, that's true. But all those years in between . . . how do I know even where we'll be?"

She's silent a moment. "I suppose that's true."

It has taken her years to absorb that.

"Then there's always Customs . . ."

Now and then she sneaks things through. She can't understand that we can have trouble. It gets complicated — one child American, not Rob's but mine, the other ours, but Canadian. We must anticipate with passports, ID, have everything in order. Rob hates crossing the border.

"But surely they wouldn't make trouble if it was *my* furniture."

"Mother, they don't see things that way. It's American furniture being brought into the country by Canadians. We'd have to pay duty." I can't say, *It would be easier after you're dead.*

"It certainly wouldn't work that way in reverse."

Stubbornly patriotic, she kicks her American sneaker against a small striped stone. "Remember when you used to collect these at the Cape?"

"Uh-huh." I remember too well. Uncle Edward lent us his cabin for two weeks each summer. We had a fire every night — Jerry and Tim fought over who would light it — and I felt it was the snuggest, safest place in the whole world.

"Yooo-hoooo. Ellie. *Yooo-hoo!*"

Rob. Waving us to come back there, his arms moving frantically, saying *hurry*. His chest looks strangely pale and vulnerable in this evening light. He still has a farmer tan, even though he's given up farming and turned salesman. He's good at that, too.

We turn back and hurry over the beach toward him.

"Must be something about the children," murmurs Mother. "What could be wrong?"

He's half running toward us, still in bare feet, leaping over razor-sharp mussel shells.

"What is it? What's happened?" I call.

"Gordie's got a terrible pain. Lower right side. I wonder could it be appendicitis?"

Mother is almost ahead of us, ready to take over. I don't resent it. She's always been good in a crisis. Rob hates to see one of us in pain. When he takes out the children's splinters it leaves him weak. "Where is he?" she asks.

"Doubled up on the daybed."

Inside, we find him on her bed, moaning, Sarah sitting by him holding his hand, trying to quiet him. Lately she has discovered eye shadow and her gray eyes look large and terrified.

"Show me, Gordie. Show me where." I touch his forehead lightly.

He cannot straighten his leg. A bad sign. "Did you call the ambulance, Rob?"

Mother is fussing about the child's pillow.

"It'll take them longer to get out here than it would us to get into town. I'll start the car." He's pulling on a T-shirt while Mother begins looking for a blanket.

"You'll have to come with us too, Sarah," I say. "Get a sweater. No telling how long it'll be."

⁂

His moaning is low and steady. He's past crying, just quick shallow breaths against pain, as if he's afraid to breathe too deep. I hold him in the back seat, his head cradled against my jeans, while Sarah sits in front, stiff and quiet, between Mother and Rob. She has pulled her blonde hair into two clumps, each held with a yellow elastic around a pink ceramic bobble. The back of her neck is peeling.

"Good thing this road has finally been paved," says Mother.

I remember the first time she bumped down it from the airport, her brave effort not to say *You're living here?* when she saw what was then a sparsely furnished cottage, her attempt to be civil to this man not even my legal husband — because what else could she count on in family? A daughter, she'd always said, is different from a son. I remember her hugging Sarah and saying, "How's my only granddaughter?" Then the two of them went off down the beach kibbitzing. Five years ago. I was about to have Gordie and too sick to register much except relief that they clicked, that my mother's frustrations would not be vented on her granddaughter. She'll take Sarah back with her now, for two weeks with her father. Little enough to give. I can see in Sarah's head that other head shape, long and narrow, with flat ears. She is not pretty.

"What's that clump of wildflowers along the road?" Mother asks, above the muted groans.

"Lupine. It's all over the place." Gordie is quieter now.

"Never see it at home."

Suddenly Gordie lets out a long sigh and opens his eyes. He points a clenched fist toward his stomach. "Hurts," he whispers.

I want to shout: "Stop the car! He's spoken!" I swallow it, act as if this is all perfectly normal — *it is* — and whisper, "Show me."

He points again and I see in his opened palm dents from the pressure of his nails.

"Hurts, Mommy."

I stare out at waving purple and white and pink lupine and think this simple thought: He has called me Mommy. My son knows. He will talk.

"We'll be there soon, honey. The doctor will take care of the pain. It may be your appendix."

My mother is talking to Rob about Ronald Reagan. Sarah interrupts — a bad habit we're trying to break — to say, "But all he wants to do is start a nuclear war, Granny. He's war-crazy."

"Not really," says Mother. "He just wants us safe."

⚎

It's nearly ten o'clock. Outpatients is deserted.

Rob fishes out the medicare number and fills out papers while Gordie is wheeled away. Mother takes a straight chair beneath a picture of the Queen.

"You stay with Granny," I nod to Sarah.

Doctor Wilson is new in town this year. So far we haven't had to try him. His daughter will start grade one with Gordie next fall.

The examining room feels all fluorescence, gleaming metal, and white walls. As the doctor probes, Gordie is nearly screaming. The sound held behind his tightly sealed lips is like the high cry of an infant, coming from way back in his throat. Rob has him by both arms, trying to comfort and hold him still.

Doctor Wilson looks up at me as he runs an expert hand across Gordie's exposed stomach. "Appendicitis. It's not always so easy to diagnose, but I'd say this is it."

Gordie has opened his lips again. "Hurt. Hurt. Hurt." He repeats the word over and over, sucking it in with his breath.

Rob looks at me from the other side of the examining table, his skin yellow in this light. We must both be thinking, *He is talking.* How odd to find hope centered in a moment of such pain.

"I'll have to call in the anesthetist," says the doctor. "It may take a him a while to get here. We'll keep Gordie sedated."

The child has stopped speaking. He breathes hard, and little beads of perspiration line his forehead. His hair, curling and damp, is plastered down. The narrow Band-Aid from this afternoon still crosses his fragile leg bone. I think of the surgeon's knife and start to talk.

"When will we know, Doctor?"

"The operation's not complicated. We should have him out of the woods and awake but groggy in four or five hours. There'll be some pain and discomfort afterward. We'll get Gordie into a room. Then I'd suggest you all go out somewhere and have a coffee. Nothing more you can do."

172

He lies on his side, eyes shut, hands clenched. To straighten the leg at all is now impossible. Rob's gone out to tell Sarah and Mother that I'll wait here for a little while. After that, we'll all go out. Where? I can't put my mind on that right now.

The only room available is this double. Behind the pink dividing curtain lies an old lady snoring, her breathing heavy and regular like the snorts of a rooting pig. I peeked in after the nurse left, but didn't recognize her.

Gordie's going under, I can tell. His hands are beginning to uncurl.

Just this morning, those hands drew a wonder that intrigued even my mother. Jagged mountaintops formed his horizon, colored black and very dark green. He uses fine-tipped Magic Markers and goes through ten doodle pads a week. No trees on his mountains, no timber line, just bare peaks. One mountain gleamed white at the peak, silver streaks running down one side. In the foreground, at the base of the silver-sided mountain, lay a perfectly round pool of brilliant blue. Somehow, even with Magic Markers, he found a way to make the shiny blue water suggest both surface and depth. He's good at shadows. The mountains cast shadows like jagged exposed teeth across that pure blue. Against the water, the snow-capped mountain made a point of white. In that reflection, centered in the white, he drew a boat — not from pure imagining as the mountains must have been, for he's not even been to Cape Breton, but modeled on the lobster boats here at Murray Corner which we'll watch during August lobster season. The boat was perfect to the last detail, colored red instead of white, to make it show. Leaning over the side, a small dark figure hauled in something, no doubt a lobster trap. I couldn't see his catch. Too microscopic, if it was there.

Gordie ran to me with the finished picture. He was squealing with happiness and relief. I couldn't read in it any more than I saw, but perhaps I didn't need to. It was enough to hold it with him, and *look*. Our house is filled with pictures piled on bookcases, in drawers, beneath his bed. Sometimes I think if I could read them I would know him. Their beauty is undeniable.

He has Rob's ears, small and low. Now and then — I've never told her — I can see Mother in him, the imperious way he waves a hand or stalks away from us when he is denied. He has a trace of the dictator — a frustration, I think, that the world will not open for him, wordless.

The air here smells thick and sharp, like a mixture of alcohol and candle wax. Just outside the door nurses are talking softly. Gordie frowns, as if some ghost prowled his dreams.

From what reservoir of pain did he extract his first word this afternoon? We thought we heard him whisper *Sarah* once in the examining room. The lips have been so firmly closed we've almost adjusted to a silent son. I didn't think much about it at first. Children can be early or late to speech. Sarah was early, but those were other days. Now she talks too much at the wrong time, not enough when you want her to.

This is the last child I will have. It is enough.

He's sleeping peacefully. The perspiration has dried on his face. Curled up in a ball, face pressed in toward the pillow, he has gone beyond pain.

I must find the others, be practical. There won't be much open at this hour of night.

⧉

We settle on Martha's Place out on the Trans-Canada. A truck stop just outside town, it's the only restaurant open most of the night.

We knew Martha quite well. When I was pregnant and sick with Gordie she came and helped out, her husband driving her to the shore to stay over with us for two weeks before Mother came. Each morning she'd bring me a thick slab of her homemade bread slathered with strawberry jam and admonish me to eat up, feed the baby. When he was born, she sent us a hand-crocheted yellow baby blanket. Just three years ago she started this small restaurant and quickly built up a clientele. Everyone in town was shocked when she died of cancer last year, a young forty-two. Her daughter Laura has taken over — a tall, thin, round-shouldered girl with dark wavy hair and an awkward way of holding herself that is strangely disarming. There is a delicacy about her, unexpected in this small clapboard diner that smells, even now at eleven-thirty, of grease and gravy. Only she and the cook are on tonight.

"Would you like just coffee? Or maybe a nice piece of homemade

pie? We've blueberry, cherry, strawberry, and just a little lemon me-
ringue left." Laura stands by us in her light blue apron, her weight on
one foot, her voice tired after a long day. Her mother couldn't have
been twenty when she had her.

"Oh, heavens," says Mother, scanning the small plastic-covered
menu. "I couldn't eat anything. Just coffee, thanks."

Rob is ravenous. A cheeseburger with the works.

"Would you like your coffee in a mug or a cup?" Laura asks.
Mother is happy with a cup.

We're too spent to talk. One other table is occupied, with two driv-
ers from the Labatt's truck out front. The patter of their French is
comforting. I sit with my back to the counter and kitchen, facing past
my mother right into the dark. Lights outside shine against the windows and I see the back of Mother's silvery head, Rob's and Sarah's
profiles reflected in the glass.

"Could he die?" asks Sarah suddenly.

"He won't, honey." Rob's voice is tense.

"We caught it in time, Doctor Wilson said," I add. Her bangs hang
down in her eyes and her skin looks pasty. She needs sleep. I long to
make her feel secure but there are no easy ways. She sees her father
once a year — now that, as he says, he can "relate to her." She tells
me little about those trips and I've given up wanting to know.

"Used to be you panicked at appendicitis," says Rob, biting into his
cheeseburger.

"Well, I must say, Rob, we wouldn't have gotten any faster health
service at home."

"Helen, from you that's quite a statement."

"Don't be snide. I'm just saying I was amazed at how fast it was
done. Were you pleased with the doctor?"

"Absolutely."

Mother turns to me. "What did Gordie say in the back seat?" she
asks.

Until this instant I never knew she took it in.

"*Hurt, hurt, hurt.* That was all. And we thought maybe we heard
him say your name, Sarah, in the examining room." Should I let more
out? "And . . . he said Mommy."

No comment.

Sarah is busy with her apple pie à la mode. The pie here is terrific.

Martha used to make it all herself. When Rob started traveling with pharmaceuticals, he'd drive into town for breakfast. Martha saw that his coffee was full and hot, his eggs done right. She'd ask about me, concerned that a new mother forty miles out of town might go mad with loneliness.

"When do you think we'll know he's okay?" asks Sarah.

"Couple more hours." The tic in Rob's left eye has started and he's trying to keep from rubbing it.

I look through the dark window — past faces, backs of heads, the reflected cash register and counter. In front of the Sleepy Time Motel across the highway three flags hang limp in the night air: New Brunswick, Canada, United States. The murmur of French covers our silence.

Mother looks haggard, as if today has emptied her life. I can't remember seeing her look quite so worn. Her cheeks are growing thinner, and when she hurries she sometimes has to stop to catch her breath. It is as though the skeleton of age is peeking through, tracing on her features a hint of what is to come. She has deserved better than two sons who live far away and don't invite her . . . and this daughter.

"You mother almost died once — or so I thought," she is saying to Sarah. "She was only fourteen, no, eighteen months, a fat, healthy baby." She pauses, as if uncertain whether to go on. "We — your grandfather and I — had to rush her to emergency at Massachusetts General."

Sarah is all ears. She's never heard a word about her grandfather. I tried to explain once why Rob and I have never married. "To lay history to rest," I said. "This time it can't repeat itself." She looked baffled, and changed the subject.

"She was a great crawler," says Mother. As she talks, a flush darkens her cheeks. "She got in under the sink and opened some liquid cleaner. I was hysterical, sure she'd swallowed some."

My mother hysterical? I try to see her, a young mother, panicky, catching up the baby, calling for her husband, runing to the car, stalling it in her haste. Or did he drive? Who held the baby? Maybe they took a taxi.

"Your grandfather calmed me down. He . . . was good at that then."

I cannot see him. Blank. I can imagine her younger and prettier.

176

"We got there around midnight. They pumped her stomach. Such a little thing to go through that. Afterward, they kept her in overnight. We went out and got coffee, or maybe it was a stiff drink. I can't remember. Probably a drink. It wasn't . . . like this." She glances around the diner.

It wasn't like this.

꧁꧂

My mother's voice is low and steady, telling her only granddaughter something she has never uttered before, at least to me. She speaks without rancor, as though in this moment, here with us, past the crisis, warmed by coffee, she recalls not his desertion but something else I'll never know.

I look out at the limp flags, three in a row, the high yellow lights shining down on the driveway into the motel. Against that I see Mother, the back of her head as she talks to Sarah, the girl in the window listening and eating. At the same table sit two onlookers. We are faces in the window, heads, bodies, occupying some mysterious middle space between the sleeping world out there and the spotless counter behind me. A world of shadows and reflections, merging and moving, plays against the dark. Through it comes my mother's voice, low and steady. It teaches me something as she speaks to her granddaughter elaborating history, my history.

It teaches me that furniture doesn't matter, to her or to me. Not really. We can oblige her by taking a chair or two. Perhaps Gordie or Sarah will sit in it as she once did, bringing alive for an instant the trace of something long since gone. Or maybe we'll take nothing. We'll work that out.

What matters is this space we occupy now, here in the too-warm diner by the side of the highway, surrounded by the smell of fries smothered in gravy, the murmur of another language, the timbre of my mother's voice putting together her life, all of us held in hope for Gordie to pass beyond pain and find his voice. The voice of another generation.

Every generation is another country.

Why Eat Pot Roast
When You Can Sing?

I

THEIR NAMES WERE CHLORINE and Fluoride: twins. As their mother lay in the hospital listening to the monitored double heartbeat she heard, beyond the heartbeats, a radio blaring down the hall. Some kind of consumer program. *Chlorine, fluoride:* the words kept weaving through her gripping pain and release. *Chlorine, fluoride* — the cadence, the beauty of their sound floated through her delirium, and when at last high forceps and stern resolve enabled the second baby to escape the dark tunnel and follow her sister into the sterile light of the delivery room, Mrs. Keefe looked at her squirming progeny and whispered with her last breath, "Chlorine. Fluoride."

Chlor and Flor they were. Motherless, but not alone. They had each other. Identical twins. Two similar faces — dark hair, dark eyes, small thin bodies, and an innate sense of rhythm. They faced life together.

And life looked back at them more kindly than might have been expected. Their father had long since vanished; now their mother was gone. They found new parents, however, gentle people who raised them to young womanhood with understanding and tact. "Chlorine and Fluoride, our twins. Yes, odd names. They look alike, but they're not quite identical."

The girls were taught to curtsey when introduced. Eventually,

Chlor did a little step with her curtsey, just the tiniest chassé, while Flor stood there blinking.

Chlor was the leader. From the beginning, pushing forward into the light of this world, she was the more resolute. Flor trailed her about with quiet resignation: the follower. Slower, shorter, and quieter, Flor could catch the rhythm of the moment from Chlor. Who would say she was the lesser? She had the gift of responding.

What to do with their lives? That became a question when the girls, at seventeen, finished the required steps: schooling, puberty, rebellion against authority, the discovery of passion. Life certified them mature. They looked at each other and wondered: what now?

For them the ancient question held new complications.

"I want to keep house," said Flor. She had always loved to play with dolls.

"I don't," said Chlor. She had always loved to climb trees.

"Then it should work," said Flor.

"I'll dry the dishes," said Chlor magnanimously.

II

It was a small house, white with green shutters, on a shady side street in a town of fifteen thousand. Every day Chlor rose, dressed (she loved clothes), ate her porridge, and walked ten blocks to be a receptionist for Doctor Hadley, the town orthodontist. She hated wearing a uniform. White did not become her.

Flor, meanwhile, did the dishes, cleaned the house, and read. She went to the town library every afternoon. She read mysteries, romances, Gothic novels, historical sagas. She stretched and stretched her imagination. At four she would begin to think about dinner. She could do wonders with pot roast.

It went on like this for some time. Chlor grew tired. She took up jogging, tried in vain to persuade Flor to run with her.

"Round and round," said Flor. "It's idiotic. Besides, my heart and lungs are fine. I'd rather read."

Chlor stifled a spasm of irritation and kept on running round and round. Eventually her thighs grew hard. She sat less and less patiently behind her metal desk. Her fingers flipping through files grew slack.

"What am I doing?" she said to herself — and walked out, jogging all the way home in her flat white oxfords.

"I've quit," she said, bursting in on Flor, who was trying pot roast in beer that night. "Let's do something together. Any ideas?"

It was extraordinary. Flor was full of ideas. She could never remember having been the one to suggest anything before. Setting down the tasting spoon, she said, "We could write songs and sing them."

"Absurd," said Chlor, always practical. "I don't play an instrument. And who'd listen, anyway?"

"You know the scales and can read notes," said Flor stubbornly.

"How would we do it? And where would we begin?"

"Together. We can do anything together. Just make up our minds. I'll do the melody, you do the words."

"What kind of songs?"

"Newies but goodies," said Flor. "You know. The kind of thing people relax to. The kind of music you tap your foot to, remembering snatches of words here and there."

"But we've never done anything like this. Where would we start? And who'd want to hear *us* sing?"

"We'd start right here."

"Okay, then, you tell me — which comes first, the melody or the words?"

"Who knows? We'll have to find out."

The pot roast was done. Over it they grew sillier and sillier, making up words, looking for melodies.

"Tiptoe through the graveeee," called out Chlor, relieved to be done forever with white uniforms, low oxfords, x-rays of rotting bicuspids.

"Dada, dum de da da," chorused Flor, spooning gravy over rice.

It was a happy night. They sang all through dishes. They had saved money for three years. They were twenty. They would have an adventure. Who was to say they couldn't do it?

III

In a month they had written twenty-five songs. Mornings were spent at the public library in the music section. They read lives of the great song writers — Porter, Ruby, Gershwin, deSilva, Brown and

Henderson, Warren, and others. When afternoon came and it was time to sit down and compose, they had only their own resources. Not too meager, it turned out.

Sometimes Chlor got the words first. "Listen," she'd yell.

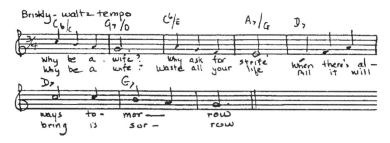

"What rhymes with *morrow?*"

"*Sorrow,*" Flor would reply, plinking at the keyboard of their secondhand upright.

They tried out combinations, testing for what rang true. Sometimes it came easily, words and melody seeming to meet in mid-air. so came one which would make them famous:

It was one of their first, composed the night Flor tried pot roast in vinegar and wine. Maybe that explained it: something tart, bubbly, and substantial — their songs seemed to blend all.

At first they were content just to enjoy their own music. Before long, though, they wanted more. They turned to the yellow pages to find an agent. They were innocent. What made it work? Was it the sight of twins — two young girls with dark hair, dark eyes, figures in perfect bloom, and folders bulging with homegrown tunes which were a mix of the same beauty and innocence? Whatever the recipe, it was right. He took them on.

"Can you sing?" he asked.

"We can harmonize," said Flor. She had a good ear and could hear what would go with a melody. "Can you find someone to play for us? We want to perform. It won't do to sing these only to each other. Can you find us bookings?"

Their luck held. In short order he found them engagements in small clubs, the two girls standing by the piano, accompanied by a young man with a light mustache and glasses through which he watched the twitching of their thin shoulder blades for cues. They had expressive bodies, and he was subtle and discreet. Leonard was his name, quickly changed to Learned by Chlor — who loved to tip words slightly and saw that Learned knew more than they. He had studied at the conservatory.

He was good at transposing.

Flor found something exciting about Learned. To Chlor he was simply background music. She sensed the difference and tried not to mind. "He's more than a beat to you," she teased.

Flor replied:

Cle - ver he may be, But he'll ne - ver do for me.

IV

Within two years Chlor, Flor, and Learned found themselves headed for the big city. People had said it couldn't be done. But they had played and sung all the spots about town and seemed to have exhausted their chances at home. "Where else to go," said Learned, "but the city?"

"The lights!" said Chlor when they arrived, charmed by the radiance of blinking neon. She'd grown used to the unblinking fluorescence of the public library, the warm lamplight of the white house with green shutters.

"But listen," said Flor. "The noise!" She was stung by sirens, screeching tires, whistles, screams, the cacophony of motors. "How will we ever make music here?" She'd grown used to the harmonies of small town living: one fire alarm a day, friendly mechanics.

"Easy," said Learned briskly as they each toted a suitcase into the cheap, clean hotel. "Carry it with you."

Again, their luck held. Down the hall, inside a small room with tan walls, sat a talented musician named Free.

"Free?" said Chlor, when they met a few days later in the hotel coffee shop.

"Free," he said, sizing her up. Still the same dark beauty with more than a touch of innocence. "That's right. My mother named me Freedom. She'd grown up in a strict, repressed household. This was the way she got back."

"Did it work?" Chlor was intrigued.

"It's complicated," he replied. "I shortened it to Free in high school and I've been Free ever since. Let's talk about you."

Free was a musician, the highbrow kind. He'd never quite made it but was a regular substitute in the symphony: double bass, tuba, and drums — an unlikely combination, but he was versatile and willing. Nights he played the clubs about town. He could also play jazz piano and swing, the real oldies but goodies. He shifted his several hats with aplomb. "Basically," he claimed, "it's all a matter of rhythm."

Chlor and Flor recognized the truth of that.

They became a foursome. Their ability to work together was extraordinary. Even the producers who watched them audition saw that. Chlor took the lead, Flor harmonized, Learned kept up a running accompaniment and watched for clues from shoulder blades. Free, meanwhile, announced songs and played drums or occasionally bass. They'd worked out one routine in which he and Learned played a two-piano accompaniment for the girls.

Girls. That was the problem. "You've got to move your bodies," said Free. "You're terrific, but too static. Rhythm means moving. Loosen up."

They did. It came easier for Flor, who'd always been the one to catch a beat and move with it. These days, she dreamed up the movements and worked at them with Chlor. Endlessly patient, Learned kept a steady beat going in the background.

"But it's not fun any more," objected Chlor as she bumped about the hotel room. "It's tiring." She was remembering file on molars. She'd begun to grow circles under her eyes. She'd stopped jogging.

"Takes work to get ahead," said Free. He had lots of push. "But you've got what it takes.

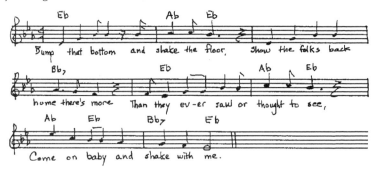

Soon, even the big city yielded. They became The Famous Four. It was something about the way they worked together — now one to the foreground, now another. Audiences wanted more. Feet tapped. Hands clapped. People raved about them. They put out their first golden disc. Teenagers plugged into them. Middle-aged couples found a beat they could hear. Even grandpas and grandmas tapped their feet as they rocked, whittled, and sipped their tea. "These sounds make sense," they'd nod, and sometimes they'd sing along.

V

They had been six years in the big city before Flor finally married Learned.

It was bound to come, thought Chlor, as she caught the bridal bouquet and turned back toward the studio with Free to work out a routine for the next three weeks. Flor and Learned had gone on their honeymoon. It was the first time the twins had been apart.

"Don't fret," said Free, buying her a posy from a street vendor and handing it to her with a flourish. "The song must go on."

"But I've lost half myself," she said — and tried to focus on the new tune he was humming.

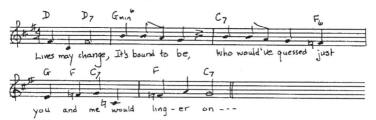

In the middle, for four full measures, nothing happened except brushes against snare.

"Might work," she said doubtfully, wishing Flor were there.

"Will work," said Free. "You've got to change your style now and then. Nothing stands still."

He started it major, ended it minor. People who heard it detected a new element in their song. Younger listeners liked it — a touch of melancholy. Grannies said, "Give me back the lightness and beat." Teenagers loved the brush against the snare. They discovered novelty in a pause.

Flor and Learned returned, Flor somehow older, subtly matured. Happy, no doubt about that. Flor was happy. Learned had always been discreet and remained so. They took an apartment one flight up from Chlor. Free still lived at the hotel in his tan-walled room.

Audiences grew.

"Isn't it time people got sick of us?" Learned mused to Flor.

"Why stop to wonder?" she said. "We'll know when it happens."

"Shift your style and you'll hold your audience," said Free.

"That's all I can shift now," said Chlor. "I can't do anything else but sing."

VI

Years passed. They remained The Famous Four. Learned and Free multiplied arrangements. Free learned how to play cello and French horn. Learned became expert at reading shoulder blades. Chlor and Flor refined their rhythm and song to a subtle play of body and voice. Chlor's wrinkles were deepening. Free had a streak of gray. Learned was into bifocals. Time, it seemed, was catching up.

One day Flor called Chlor upstairs and showed her something she was knitting.

"Guess what?"

"What?"

"Bootees."

"Oh, nw. What of our music?"

"Don't worry," said Flor. "It will go on. Meantime, wish me luck."

She began to expand. She carried the baby high. "A boy," nodded grannies on the street. "It's bound to be a boy." "A girl," said Learned when the heartbeat was monitored. "It beats in three-quarter time."

As Flor expanded, clouds were gathering. War. What place had darkness in lives so golden? Free was drafted, Learned was exempt.

"I'll go with you," said Chlor, surprised at herself.

"Don't be silly," said Free. "What would you do?"

"Maybe we can sing to the boys. I'd be a better entertainer than aunt."

It took some arranging, but they did it.

Over the next few years Chlor learned to sing and bump in the most unlikely locations: on raised platforms in large tents, in open fields surrounded by tanks, in deserts beneath beating sun, on shipboard. She belted it out to khaki-clad men and practiced being a woman. They loved it. Free was always with her; they were still a team. People thought things about them, but people were wrong. Free was affectionate toward Chlor, and she was devoted to him. "Just good friends."

But devastation affected them both — the sight of all that waste. Into their music, hard as they fought it, crept more shadow, a lingering blues note.

Chlor often sang against the bass alone. The space between her voice and that steady strum, the silence itself, became part of her music. Still, they continued to shout for the *old* songs, those men in khaki. Free and Chlor obliged, knowing their own music was changing again.

These days Chlor had more hip to bump around. When they hugged at the end of a show she could no longer feel Free's ribs. They bickered about the future, which was growing alarmingly foreshortened.

"Tastes have changed," said Free. "And so have we. We may find we've lost our audience."

Eventually, from platforms and maimed bodies and ravage and ambiguous victory at best, they returned. Free was maimed. "A freak accident," he said, "not even a proper casualty." He would write a song about it later, when he had distance. His hearing had been affected. A dull rumble troubled his inner ear, constant and annoying.

The time had come to go home.

Where was home?

They found Flor and Learned back there — not the same house, not the same shutters, but housed and shuttered, or so it seemed to this couple fresh from the open fields of death.

Their child, small and dark as Flor, subtle and humorous as Learned, was already walking and talking.

"He's tone-deaf," said Flor, as Robert bowed to his newfound aunt and uncle.

"How come?" asked Chlor, only half expecting an answer. Free could only partially hear now, and for the first time she found herself searching for songs.

"We're teaching him to dance," said Learned. "Next best thing."

Robert got his top hat and cane and jigged a few steps for them on nimble feet.

"What a future," said Free, with more enthusiasm than Chlor had seen in months. Suddenly she felt old.

Still, she went on singing. It had become habit now. And it was true, what Free had said long ago: before many days the sisters again caught their rhythm and set about creating new songs. Their sounds were different now. Learned was fond of analyzing reasons for the change.

"War," he said. "It does it to everyone."

"What about you?" said Free. "You weren't in any battle and your harmony has changed."

"How do you know I wasn't in any battle?" asked Learned, and went on fiddling with the keys.

A new element had entered their song. In the intervals between lyrics on their records now, one might hear the sound of taps — the waltz time-clog of Robert filling in, syncopating, sliding, clicking his feet to the rhythm of Chlor, Flor, Learned, and Free's song.

These days Free suffered. The buzz in his ears grew stronger, the pluck in his fingers feebler.

He retired.

"Entirely too soon," people said.

"Only from music," he insisted.

"From life," said Chlor. They had been performing together for twenty years.

"I can still listen," he insisted, contradicting the truth they both knew.

Free died the next year.

VII

That left Chlor. Auntie Chlor.

"What good is a musical aunt?" she complained to Learned.

"As much good as an educated brother-in-law," he said. "Watch Robert do this one. He's just learned the maxi-ford."

The child *was* extraordinarily nimble. In spite of herself, Chlor felt drawn to him. Free was gone. She missed the old bickering and laughter. But here was Robert . . .

"Let's see you do the grapevine, Robert," she said sternly.

Robert eyed his overweight, bossy aunt. What did she know about dancing?

As she watched his feet moving across the room — *back, side, shuffle, hop, back, side, shuffle, hop* — she knew there was a future.

Chlor began to compose in a new way, to hear songs against the sound of Robert's tapping feet. Rhythms shifted. She and Flor still sang, though less these years, for Learned was at last finishing his degree.

"What for?" asked Chlor.

"Just to have finished it," said Learned.

"But life is so short," said Chlor.

"I'll be around for a while yet," said Learned, and opened his book.

Into Flor and Learned's living room every other night waltzed Auntie Chlor to train her nephew. "Listen, Robert. *Listen.* Hop, tap, move to the music."

These were quiet years. Once, Chlor would have thought them too quiet. But it took time for her to leave behind the images of war and carry into her own music the spirit of Free.

They had their royalties. Flor was into pot roasts again. Chlor lived down the street from Flor and Learned in an apartment. She'd had it with shutters and clapboard forever. She ate out a lot, never having conquered pot roasts herself. Some evenings, as she chewed her crab Louie or fish and chips, she'd hear from the jukebox music she knew all too well:

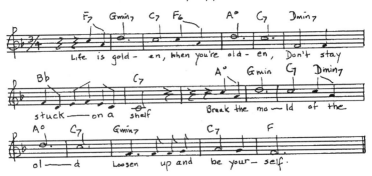

She paid little attention. She was moving into a new song these years, catching a new rhythm.

Sometimes when they practiced they drove Learned and Flor crazy. Robert flipped and glided and shuffled while Chlor hummed and beat time and played the piano. He learned his steps from an outside teacher, but evenings at home he put them together a new way with Auntie Chlor.

At eighteen they declared him raised. After all, hadn't the girls themselves set out earlier than that? And they had turned out all right.

So Robert danced out of their lives — with so much talent, so much will, such delicate rhythm that they trusted he wouldn't lose step.

VIII

Then Flor hung her apron on a hook behind the kitchen door.

"What're you doing?" asked Learned.

"Signing off from pot roasts," she replied.

"What next?" he asked, putting his index finger in the book to hold his place.

"Let's have an adventure."

"As soon as I finish my thesis."

"Thesis, bleesis," said Flor. "Books can't hold all your spirit. Remember Free."

"Write me a new song," said Learned. "In two weeks I'll be done.

Then I'll go wherever you want," he promised, hoping he could detect her shoulder blades.

So Flor hunted up Chlor, who was busy on the telephone with Robert. He had just won first prize in a talent show.

"I told you," said Chlor. "He's launched."

"Let's go," said Flor. "I feel a new song coming on."

Chlor and Flor and Learned set out again to find what life might hold.

IX

Learned is a little stooped now, squinting through his trifocals at their hips and elbows. He's given up on shoulder blades.

They can still pack in audiences. They can still pull melodies out of thin air, it seems. They've never lost their talent for creating rhythms — though now they lean toward more syncopation, delighting in delay and suspense. They love to make people move. There are subtle differences between Chlor and Flor. There always were. Together with Learned, however, they remain a team that's hard to beat.

Now and then when they come to a city or town they find the main auditorium booked ahead. Robert. He's making his way.

"He defies gravity," people say, breathless at his light feet, his perfect rhythm. "How does he do it?"

One night they wonder, too, the three of them sitting in the back of the darkened auditorium, unknown to Robert. They don't trail him. They want to leave him free.

Here he come: cane, top hat, flickering feet.

Auntie Chlor swells with pride, recognizing a trick or two.

"It's not quite how we did it," she whispers to Flor, on her right. "He's added a couple of things."

"Shhhh," whispers a bleached blond in front of them.

Learned, on Chlor's left, pokes her with his elbow.

The stage is bare. One figure commands it — tall, graceful, elegant. A single spotlight follows his flashing arms, clicking feet, his folding knees, as he tells a story, transforms himself through sheer movement: now a soldier, now a bum, now an astronaut, now a student, now a lover.

"I like the lover best," says Learned, adjusting his spectacles.

"*Shhhh,*" hisses the blond.

Flor is silent, mesmerized. It had never occurred to her until this moment. *Look. Watch those feet, shiny black toes cutting air in swirls. See the design. Air. Grace. Melody. Humor.* Free understood, of course. He must have. And maybe Learned. They'd studied theory, could transpose.

Her heart pounds. She leans forward to whisper across Chlor to Learned.

"Do you see, Learn? Do you see what he's doing?"

Chlor shifts her weight so as not to miss a thing.

The blond turns around. "Will you *pleeese* keep quiet?"

"Learn," says Flor. "Can you hear it? Listen. He's changed the beat. The orchestra's shifted some chords around, but can you hear it, Learn? He's dancing to our song. *It's our song Robert is dancing to!*"

Learned leans forward slightly, distracted by the blond's twitching shoulder blade. He stares at the gray-streaked hair of Flor, his wife of many years. Her round dark eyes.

"Of course," he says calmly. "What else did you expect?"

Season of Apples

BEFORE MRS. LEORA MAY goes to town she thinks about what she should wear. She might meet someone at the post office or the grocery store. You never know. And that somebody could be anybody — the mayor, the president of the college, the minister, the undertaker, anybody. Actually, she's already met most of them picking over cabbage or fingering mushrooms at some point in her thirty years of selecting produce at the town's better grocery store. Nonetheless, possibilities remain.

She goes to town at least twice a day with a submerged sense of expectation. It shows in the way she dresses: the perfectly pleated skirt, the coordinated blouse, the ruffles, the heels. You can count on her to dress in style. Many women go slack in this town. Not Leora May. She avoids synthetics, hates polyester. She used to be embarrassed to wear her fur coat downtown, but this winter fur is not only acceptable but shown in all the better fashion magazines.

You might pass Leora at ten in the morning, one foot raised, about to step from the curb at the traffic light intersection. If your eyes meet, she smiles a haven't-we-met-somewhere smile and waits for the light to turn. She crosses quickly, swinging her skirt, as if someone waited for her on the other side.

Then again, you might meet her mid-afternoon. There isn't always a second mail delivery but Leora likes to check. There could be a letter in their box, masculine writing across the envelope. As she turns the key she sometimes dreams of a lover, laughing inwardly all the while at her foolishness. Her name will be in dark blue ink, tall strong letters.

Of course it never happens. It's usually a bill. No one ever writes to her.

When she catches herself emerging from this wayward dream in the darkness of her early morning bedroom she rolls on her side, nestles in behind Mr. May, clasps his loosening waist, and thinks of daisies. Fields of white daisies in the wind. It's a trick she learned years ago, she's forgotten just where. She hugs that reliable back, smells the dry fresh cotton pajamas, and counts her blessings — among the daisies.

She has been freed of many things: financial worries, parental responsibility. Her one daughter, Margaret, has grown up and moved away. Leora once thought it would be nice to be a grandmother. She'd be a trim, fashionable Nana. She's kept her figure and has her hair done every week. But she's been denied that chance to prove herself. Her daughter never speaks of the possibility, and Leora knows better than to bring it up. Her son-in-law is a realtor and they live in Ontario. He seems to be doing well. They've never had to ask for money. As for Leora's own parents — they died at exactly the right time, leaving her a reliable income in dividends. She is enviably free, as less fortunate friends sometimes remind her, to wander untrammeled among the bending daisies of her imagination.

It is late fall now, and cool. Those who garden (Leora does not) have taken up the harvest and finished with pickling. The long winter season is about to begin. In March, weary of snowblowing, curling bonspiels, bridge, coffee, evenings by the fire, and *Hockey Night in Canada*, she and Arnold will leave for a week or two in Florida. That is still far off.

She wonders if she should put on her new leather boots this morning, they pull so at the calves. They *are* neat looking, though, and she wants to look neat. As she comes out the back door she sees a skin of ice on puddles here and there. Boots are appropriate.

Besides, there are other more important things to think about today. Whether she'll tell Arnold after it's over she hasn't decided. He did not see the ad in last night's paper, she's quite sure. She watched him carefully from across the living room and detected nothing new in the way he threw the paper aside when he'd finished, stretched his legs, yawned, and wondered aloud, "Think it's too early for a fire, Lee? Got the whole winter ahead and only one cord o' wood this year."

As she opens the car door and slides in behind the wheel, she checks to see that the clipping is still in her pocket. She's put herself together with special care this morning: new pleated tweed skirt, Ultrasuede jacket (dark brown, fall), matching purse and boots. The blouse, she decided after trying three, has just the right amount of frill.

They want a teacher. The notice did not specify what level. There are many kinds of teacher. Surely this one would not be too glamorous. Sedate, say, yet still attractive. They also want *Grandparents, Teenagers, Children, Housewives, Executives,* and one *Napoleon.* She has no interest in being cast as a housewife.

All evening — through supper, stacking the dishwasher, watching the news, listening to Arnold snore softly in the recliner — she'd hugged the question to herself. Later, welcoming Arnold's bulk during the night, she'd decided. Yes. She would go. It would take nerve. It was unlike her. Yet just the notion of it — stepping before the camera, suffering the glare of lights — made her feel different already, lying there in the dark, hugging Arnold's waist. What if people in town actually *saw* her? What would she say? How explain? Surely it would never come to that. *Yet if she didn't secretly hope it would, why go at all?*

Morning light dissipates such questions.

Leora presses the sole of her new boot on the accelerator and sets off for Moncton.

⊰⊱

The building is tall and square, gray concrete with windows on all sides. A vertical barracks. She maneuvers to find a space in the already crowded lot, then checks her watch. Nine-thirty. Auditions begin at ten.

Outside the revolving door she takes a deep breath, then pushes through. Just inside, a tall blond girl in a powder blue suit, white stockings, and powder blue shoes almost bumps into her.

"Oops, sorry," smiles the girl, and disappears around a corner swinging her white briefcase.

Suddenly Leora feels her lipstick is not right — too bright, too shiny, something. She slips into the washroom to check. There may be others after her slot. Perhaps she should be carrying a briefcase.

Freshly scrubbed tile and chrome announce a Monday morning in the ladies' room. Leora May surveys Leora May. She straightens her collar and squares her slightly padded shoulders. The salt-and-pepper hair waves back neatly, the eyeliner is discreet, delicate bows of gold brighten her earlobes. Yes, businesslike but not severe. Blotting her lipstick for the final time, she turns away, pushes through the door, and turns down the corridor toward the elevator.

Here, a small crowd has gathered. Pushing inside with the others, she squeezes between a plump grandmother type smelling of coconut and a tall thin man with sharp elbows. Something hard digs into her hip.

"Anyone for three?" calls a voice from the front.

"Everyone for three," laughs an oily male voice behind her. Perhaps it belongs to the knees pressing against her pleats. "Three's where it's at today, man."

Three. The doors slide open.

Already a line snakes around three sides of the third floor. Leora takes her place.

Ahead of her, two young mothers in loose print tops and dark slacks hold squirming toddlers, two little girls, one dark, one blond, each in ruffles and shiny black pumps.

"Brad would kill me if he knew," whispers one mother.

"When I told Jack he said, 'Don't tell me you're goin' up there fer that. You ain't got no acting experience.'"

"Do you think experience really counts?"

"How could it? They know we don't have no acting school here."

"Cah-cah," wails the chubby blond toddler, "cah-cah."

"Soon, Tiffany, soon," whispers her mother, releasing the child to the floor. "Try to hold it a little longer."

Farther ahead, two teenage girls, their eyes ringed in black, peach blusher burying acne, shift from one foot to the other as they chew gum.

The one in filmy transparent pink says dreamily, "Do you think this is how Cheryl Tiegs got her start?"

Her companion — tight royal blue jumpsuit, spike heels — creates a small pink bubble from her mouth. It explodes against her blusher.

The line inches forward.

Leora speaks to no one. Had she imagined it like this she might not have come. She is shy. Life has never forced her to push. She'd expected some tension, but this . . .

Behind her, a man with thinning brown hair and unshaven, pockmarked neck leans in too close to people, talking incessantly. Above his green jacket (a shade darker than his green trousers) shows the soiled collar of a gray shirt. He moves up and down the line.

"Twenty-five dollars an hour," he announces to the girl in blue. "Never get things like that round here. Must be from Toronto. Might have to go to Halifax to shoot."

Leora looks away. Her eyes have begun to smart. He smells of tobacco and alcohol. His pale eyes, passing over her, look bloodshot and hungry.

"You mean we might have to go out of town?" The mother of the blond toddler fishes in her purse and hands a Kleenex to her friend. "The train to Halifax isn't cheap. What's it up to now, anyways?"

"If I was making twenty-five dollars an hour I wouldn't worry about train fare," says the girl in pink.

"Nothing to worry about," says he, nudging the girl's elbow as she slips a hand beneath her blouse at the shoulder to adjust a dark strap. "Once you sign the contract, they're stuck. Just do a lousy job. Two hour minimum the ad said. Stretch it out."

Leora shuts her eyes.

❀

After an hour they round the first corner. Another half hour, then the second. People are wilting. Children whine and complain, pounding up and down the corridor, mussing ruffles, tugging at elbows. One towheaded miniature sailor has fallen asleep face down in the middle of the floor. As the line advances, his mother, plump in fuschia, bends over him. "Samuel! Samuel! Wake up!" She hoists him upright, then lifts him to rest his head against her shoulder. One elderly man, his head aglow with perspiration, leans against the wall penciling in a crossword puzzle. Leora never thought to bring a book.

Finally, up ahead, the office door opens.

The two teenagers disappear inside.

A lanky sour-faced man carrying an attaché case emerges. Deaf to whining children, he strides past. Executive, thinks Leora. Prime minister descending to his bulletproof limo. The backs of her knees ache and her eyes feel weepy.

⚌

Here are the teenagers again, giggling. One catches Leora's eye. "A breeze," she whispers as they pass.

"When did they say they'd let you know?" calls the man in green after them.

The young mothers and toddlers have gone in. Leora is next.

⚌

She enters the outer office. One child has just spilled chips all over the carpet. Flushed and glassy-eyed, she cries quietly.

"Here, Sarah, come look at this." Her mother picks up a magazine from the low table and leafs through it.

Smudged and suspicious, Sarah looks at her mother, then dashes over and struggles onto her lap.

"What's that animal, Sarah? Can you tell me?"

Leora, on the chair opposite, studies the secretary. A pasty-faced blond of indeterminate age, her woolly blue sweater molds small pointed breasts above the keyboard as she types. She turns to Leora.

"Mrs . . . ?"

"May. Leora May."

"Fine." She hands Leora a sheet of paper. "Fill this out while you wait, please."

Name. Should she put another, become someone else? But what if they call her? Could she be sued for traveling under false pretenses? Isn't she doing that anyhow? Hours in the steamy corridor have melted down the walls of her mind. She stares at the form. What has she in common with this sniveling toddler, these anxious harried people waiting to make their twenty-five dollars an hour?

Leora May she writes — and hopes, almost, that she never hears from them.

198

The man in green (would-be Napoleon?) stands by the desk breathing at the secretary. She ignores him.

25 Fairview Drive, Tantramar, writes Leora.

Telephone. Chancy. But Arnold is at the office all day, every day. *555-3357.*

The form asks nothing else, not even her social insurance number or her age. She hands it back to the secretary, noting in the upper corner a square for a photograph.

A mother emerges from the inner office holding her child's hand.

"You may go in now." The secretary nods to Sarah and her mother.

Napoleon flops on the vacated chair and stretches out his legs, exposing a large hole in the sole of one shoe.

A child's high frantic cry erupts from inside the office. Sarah and her mother reappear.

"Couldn't do a thing with her," snaps the mother to no one in particular. They hurry out. "There'll be no ice cream today, Sarah. I told you to behave!"

"You next, Mrs. May."

⁂

It is a corner room with windows along both sides. A green plaid chesterfield has been placed with its back to one wall of windows. Near it stands a girl with dark fluffy hair holding a camera.

"Please sit here," she directs Leora briskly and hands her a wrinkled sheet of paper. "Read this in the voice you think right, when I tell you. At the end I'll take your picture."

She stations herself opposite, Polaroid to her eye.

Leora skims the mimeographed sheet. *"Oh, at last a plumbing store that has everything I need. Tubs. Sinks. Faucets. Even toilets. I'm never going to go to another plumbing store!"*

As she reads, she feels herself watched. To her right, behind a partition of windows, a man sits at a desk in another room. Directly ahead of her, behind the girl with the Polaroid, windows reveal still another room with a man behind a desk. Both men have their heads down, as if reading. Are they, somehow, listening in?

"Please begin, Mrs. May."

199

She reads the ridiculous passage. What on earth are they after? Perhaps this is just to see if she can read. Her mouth goes dry. Her brain is stuffed with cotton. Her voice sounds too high. Girlish.

"Thank you." The girl opens the door. "You'll hear from us in a day or two, Mrs. May, if you're chosen."

"My turn," announces the man in green, brushing past her.

The air outside is heavy and stale. The line still winds almost to the elevator. She passes them, eyes forward, bracing herself against unspoken questions: What's it like? What did you have to do?

Release, freedom itself is stepping outside into drizzle that falls cold and steady against the flesh, chilling bones against the warmth of too much desire.

⁂

Tuesday morning, Arnold delays over a second cup of coffee. A man of regular habits, he leaves the house at eight-thirty and walks the five blocks to his work as sales manager for a wholesale distributor in town. In four years he will retire. Leora, ten years younger, anticipates Arnold's late sixties as something dark and heavy that will swallow her. He, too, is nervous about the future. He takes long walks, putters in his flower garden, plays chess. They are not used to full days together and it seems he will have little to turn to except Leora when retirement day arrives. This prospect alarms her, lest moving more fully into the closet of herself he should discover its empty corners. She's tried to interest him in woodworking (they've a shed full of unused tools) but he's hostile to hammer and nail.

As he leaves the breakfast table to get his winter jacket, the telephone rings.

"Mrs. Leora May?"

"Yes."

"Research Associates, Incorporated calling. You were here yesterday for an audition?"

"Yes."

Arnold is coming back through the kitchen. He looks preoccupied. Today he has a big meeting with salesmen from all over the province. He opens the back door.

"We're calling to tell you, Mrs. May, that we're considering you for the female professor. Would you be able to come for a second interview tomorrow at ten-thirty?"

The bland cool voice shoots panic through her. "Just a moment, please."

Arnold is closing the back door. She shoves it open and steps with him onto the small porch.

"Arnold — "

"Touch o' frost last night, Lee."

"I — " Cold dry air shocks the bare flesh inside her loose housecoat sleeves.

"Want something?" His mind is on sales.

Everything, she longs to whisper. She draws his smooth shaven cheek close.

"No . . . it's okay. I — I'll take care of it later. Good luck today."

He gives her a peck on the cheek and bounds down the steps. Arnold works to stay fit.

⁂

This time the elevator is empty, as are the corridors on floor three.

Behind the desk in the corner office sits the dark fluffy-haired girl who took her picture. The blond has disappeared.

"Mrs. May?"

"Yes."

"Please take a seat. It shouldn't be long."

From the other side of the magazine-strewn table, a scrubbed, rugged-looking young man with thick light hair combed straight back glances at her, then quickly away. Leora crosses her knees and reaches for *Fortune*. The pleats on this new tweed skirt are satisfyingly sharp as they fan out across her lap. She is wearing just what she wore last time. Arnold will already be at his meeting.

The click of the keyboard fills the office. The young man crosses, then uncrosses his clean running shoes. Their silver and blue match his silver-lettered sweatshirt: Edmonton Oilers. Athletic, thinks Leora. Definitely athletic.

Suddenly a short stocky man in a light jacket bursts into the office.

"Cindy?"

The typist looks up. "Yes? Oh, what a relief! I'm so glad to get you. I knew when I saw you. I said to myself, 'That's my Napoleon.' But you hadn't filled out your address for us and I never got your picture. Ran out of film, remember? We'd never expected so many people." She swivels around to face him. "Know how I got you?"

He leans forward, pressing his palms against the desktop. Pale lining shows beneath the back of his jacket. "How?"

"I called Zellers and asked who was in charge of the Phentex department."

He chuckles. "When my boss called me in, I couldn't imagine. What do I do?"

"Just take this," she hands him a yellow sheet, "and go over there behind the partition and fill it out. Not your whole life story." She turns to the athlete. "You may go in now, David."

⚜

Not your whole life story.

What are their stories, these pathetic hopefuls? Leora flips pages, blind to print. Marriage to Arnold has held its surprises. Behind his steady patterns she has found, at times, the balm of understanding and the risk of passion. These moments are worth waiting for. You cannot force them. Once — was it twenty-six years ago? twenty-seven? — she knew the pain of impossible desire, the need to possess — or give, which was it? — that sucked her strength at the end of a school day, made her lean her back against the classroom door, clench her fingers around the doorknob lest she open it, roam the hall, find him and declare what there, in the light of day, the solidifying stillness of the emptied school, would have stripped her naked, defenseless, exposed to what she knew would come: rejection. He was married. A father. And did he even see her — the young new female teacher from Halifax struggling to cope with phonics and snowsuits, leaving school in the afternoon to return to her rented room, her spelling and reading workbooks, her discovery that a teacher's certificate and location in a new town did not guarantee adventure or even spice? Those were the first months.

After a time, life evened out. She made friends, took up curling,

202

came to know the town through its children. And after a year he was gone, moving with his wife and two small children back to Prince Edward Island, his home, to teach math in a junior high. A step up, a step away. Did he ever sense the beating of her heart as they passed in the halls? Remote now, that question, tamed to memory, reduced by time, habit, and the strategies of survival to a shadow you learn to live with because it can never be turned to light.

Leora uncrosses her legs.

⊰⊱

David opens the office door and emerges. Eyes on the floor, hands in pockets, he passes her.

"Now, Mrs. May. Please take this with you." Cindy hands Leora a sheet to which her Polaroid picture has been stapled: a smiling, gray-haired stranger.

A man with sad eyes stands waiting by the door.

"Mrs. Leora May? For female professor?" He takes the sheet of paper.

"Yes."

"I'm Mr. Martin." A low pleasant voice and tight smile offset the large Adam's apple working as he speaks. "I was so glad we reached you. We've had trouble finding some."

Mr. Martin closes the door and slides behind his desk, waving Leora into the chair opposite.

"Now then" — he looks quickly at the sheet before him — "Leora . . . you must wonder what this is all about."

"A bit."

The office is large and sparsely furnished. It has the feel and look of something hastily assembled for the occasion: his gray metal desk, two chairs on her side, bookcases along the inside wall, windows to her right and behind her. Except for five green apples in a row, the painted black shelves are empty. His desk is almost bare. On the blotter lies a large sheet of paper. Between him and Leora, at the edge of the desk, sits one apple.

"Well, I may as well tell you now that we're promoting New Brunswick apples. It is Mrs., isn't it?"

"Yes."

Perhaps at this very moment Arnold is addressing salesmen, a task which unnerves him. He imagines her, if he imagines her at all, walking to the post office, collecting their mail, meeting a friend for coffee. Why does she think of the clean cotton smell of his pajamas as she faces Mr. Martin, whose dark suit has a slight shine?

"Now, I have here an ad we've developed for apples." He picks up the paper, the corners of his narrow mouth curling almost to a smile. His eyes never smile. "It really is, I hope you'll agree, quite clever."

The lone apple sits there, three tiny brown spots on the side toward her.

"The ad goes like this." He leans back in his chair and reads in a low even voice. "We have a football player — you may have seen the fellow who just left, he's one possibility, although we haven't yet decided. Today is simply the final audition for two candidates. Anyhow, this football player is in his outfit, he's just come off the field, he's tired, he takes an apple, holds it up, takes a big bite, breathes and says emphatically, in a muscular sort of way if you know what I mean, *un-beat-apple*. Get it?" He looks over the top of the paper at Leora. "*Un-beat-apple*. Then we have an executive type who has an apple on his desk. When no one is looking, after a board meeting, say, he takes a bit, looks up and says, *un-sur-pass-apple*. Get it? Now then, we have a housewife. She's in the middle of her morning, beds made, dishes done, ready for her break. She pauses a moment, sees an apple on the kitchen counter, takes a bite and smiles, *delect-apple*. Last but not least" — he leans forward and actually smiles — "here we come to you."

She has lost her tongue, her mind, on some distant beach. Can he be serious? She tries not to stare at his working neck. The fascination of it.

"You are a teacher. It is the end of the school day. You're still in the classroom. Everyone's gone home. Some student has left an apple on your desk." Mr. Martin reaches forward and picks up the apple. She sees the ring. Do he and his wife eat apples, munch their way together through long winter evenings? "Now you just bite into this and say with a smile, *in-cal-cul-apple*. It's not easy, I realize. *In-cal-cul-apple*. Get it? Now. . . would you mind picking up this apple, Leora?"

Should she do it or walk out?

She picks up the apple.

"That's right. Now hold it near your mouth. Perhaps you'd like to practice saying the word a few times. *In-cal-cul-apple.*"

"You actually want me to take a bite?" She sees her predecessors of the morning sitting here biting. His basket beneath the desk must be full of bitten-into apples. Perhaps beneath her desk, Cindy has a bushel. Perhaps —

"Yes. Just take a small bite, then say, '*It's incalculapple.*'"

She bites. The apple is hard and tart. His eyes are on her. What to do with the piece in her mouth? She pushes it aside with her tongue and manages "It's incalculapple."

"Wonderful!" The corners of his mouth curve up in a tremulous U, his eyes sadder than ever. "That's really excellent." He moves out from behind the desk.

She stands also, shaking down her pleats. Over. So simple. So stupid.

"Now, we're considering two persons for this part, Leora. I'll call you this afternoon. We shoot next Wednesday. Could you make it?"

She's gone this far. She nods.

"Good. He opens the office door. "Thank you. Thank you very much. We'll be in touch. You may come in now, Mr. Simpson."

⚓

Leora and Arnold May have been married almost twenty-five years. Long enough to experience the limits of compromise, the persuasions of love. She met him at the Curling Club one bitter cold January night in her second year of teaching third graders in Tantramar's one elementary school. 1955. He was slicing roast beef at a bonspiel buffet, a tall chef's hat covering his already graying hair, his smooth cheeks pink from kitchen steam. She offered him her plate and saw the care with which he sliced. "That do, Miss Edgehill?" He was, she later learned, already widowed, alert to possibilities but not aggressive. He knew her name. Quiet and steady, a good businessman, honest to a fault, he'd lived in Tantramar all his life (except for the war) and his father before him. Any newcomer was soon spotted and identified.

He has always, in his way, appreciated his wife. He never forgets their anniversary. For the last he bought her a string of real pearls.

When Leora fingers her pearls she knows she is loved. They have a comfortable home and have raised a child without dramatic mishap. They have traveled some — France, Mexico, Bermuda, London, and now, every year, Florida. The social life of Tantramar may lack glamor, but the Mays enjoy good friends, well-mixed drinks, summer lobster feeds at the cottage, Saturday night curling. In late spring, when nights are clear and peepers start up out back, Arnold and Leora will sit of an evening on the patio, look out on the lilac hedge, the soft blue carpet of wild forget-me-nots spreading beneath the budding apple tree, and know contentment.

Of late, though, Leora has felt something missing. It's nothing more than a vague sense she has, like an echo in the mind of music heard once long ago. Imaginary daisies soothe her less and she sometimes wakes in the middle of the night with the fear that she is going blind. Irrational. Not a feeling easily shared.

She keeps her counsel, walks to town, visits friends. Until now, one way of coping has been to tour her closet. She loves shoes. She has a whole closet of them — high, medium, low-heeled, open-toed, closed, strappy, sling heel. Arnold calls it her Shoe Emporium. These days, however, rows of shoes neatly placed, toes forward, cannot reach her. She rarely visits them.

⚍⚎

Sunday morning, Arnold surprises her.

"Lee, let's go out for brunch," he proposes as he stands before the mirror knotting his tie.

From her pillow she surveys him against the light of the window: tall, white-haired, gentle. "Ummm."

"There's a new French restaurant over in Shediac. They're supposed to have a terrific Sunday brunch."

"Would they be closed for the season?"

"No. Sam Billings was in the office Friday and told me about it. Champagne brunch every Sunday."

He bends over her, his tie grazing her neck. "How about it?"

⚍⚎

206

The restaurant looks out on Northumberland Strait, cold and choppy today. They've had frost but no real ice yet.

Arnold chooses a table near the window. The large dining room resounds with nautical motif: plastic lobsters here and there, fishing net draped over the rafters, a lobster boat in one corner of the room. In it, watercolors of the New Brunswick coast are displayed. Every picture shows a lighthouse. At the center of their table a small carved lobster fisherman holds the brunch menu.

They nibble quiche and sip champagne, looking at the ocean. In the distance, Prince Edward Island, a dark strip along the horizon. Shifting clouds lay dark streaks on the water and whitecaps dot the harbor. Far out from shore one boat rides the waves. Impossible to see figures from this distance.

Arnold has worn a dark suit, a white shirt, and the silk paisley tie she gave him for his birthday. He looks almost handsome. Should she tell him of her adventure? No. Too soon.

"Lee?"

"Umm?" Nothing must jostle this peace.

"I've been thinking, Lee. What would you like to do for our twenty-fifth?" He lifts his champagne goblet toward her in a mock toast.

"Don't know. . ." She is aware of a couple seated three tables away. The man has his back to her, but his neck —

"How about a little cruise, Lee? We've never taken one, you know."

The neck looks familiar. The collar, what she can see of it, is gray. The hair grows unevenly in back.

"Tom Melanson at the office took one last year with his wife. Said the food was terrific. Dancing on board ship, too."

Napoleon. The man in the green jacket. Only today he wears deep maroon. *Napoleon*.

"Anything wrong, Lee? You seem distracted." Arnold sets down his champagne.

"No. That's fine, Arn. You know I'd love to take a cruise." What will she say if the man sees her, speaks to her?

"Lots of dancing. Sounds like fun, eh?"

Throughout the winter there's dancing every Saturday night at the Curling Club. Arnold's mother, once an elocution teacher, insisted her two boys learn to dance. She trained them to be gentlemen.

"They were paying twenty-five dollars an hour," booms the familiar voice.

His companion, a small woman in purple, leans toward him, listening.

"Where did you think we'd go, Arn?" She must concentrate. Arn is fidgeting. It's clear he's been preparing for this moment.

"The Mediterranean, maybe?"

"Let's. By all means. *Anywhere*." She focuses on him, his recently trimmed mustache, his kind blue eyes. He keeps his shoes polished. His collars gleam. On the back of his right thigh he has a war wound, a long thin white line which magnetizes her fingers. He never speaks of it.

Two gulls out in the bay wheel above a floating morsel, cutting crazy circles high in the sky, then diving toward frigid blue.

"Arnold," she says suddenly. "Let's go. Now. I've had enough. I'd love to drive down near the water. It'll be our last chance before winter. What do you say? Right now.,"

"But — " He nods toward half-empty champagne.

"Come on." She lifts her napkin to the table. "Just drink it down. Never mind. . ." She leans forward and covers his hand with hers. "I want to be with you."

He pushes back his chair.

They must pass Napoleon's table. Leora stiffens her back. She moves by quickly, half expecting: *Hey, wait, you there. Haven't I seen you —*

Nothing.

His companion's fifty if she's a day.

⚜

Wednesday it rains, hard gray rain that pounds the car roof and windshield as she drives again to Moncton. She's thrown Arn's extra-large umbrella into the back seat in case she needs it. She's to meet the crew at an elementary school. Even the word "crew" excited her when Mr. Martin said it on the phone. "We've decided you have the part, Leora. We'd like you to wear just what you wore to the audition. Meet the TV crew at the East End School on Mountain Road. Can you find that? Yes, well, they'll be there on Wednesday at three-thirty in the afternoon."

It is an old-fashioned square brick building on a busy street. She pulls in behind the school, pops up Arn's umbrella, and dashes in the back door.

Empty halls smell of dampness and dust, the residue of children recently gone. From somewhere in the distance comes the rhythmic swish of a floor polisher. She hurries past a bulletin board display of children's drawings, her heels echoing. The office must be in the front of the building.

"Looking for someone?"

A white-haired woman has opened her classroom door to identify the clicking heels.

"Yes. I was to meet some TV people here."

"Oh, you must be Mrs. May?" Smiling, the woman opens the door wider. "I'm Mrs. Smythe, the first grade teacher. They're going to use my room. Our principal just told me. I'm so excited. They're due here any moment. I've just finished cleaning up. They didn't say what part of the room they needed."

She speaks shyly, waving Leora into her room.

An ancient world, timeless, one Leora recognizes with an odd pang as she steps into it: orderly rows of miniature desks and chairs, blackboards with borders of pressed leaves, Best Work on display, vowels and consonants and numbers and pictures promising little minds entry to the vast, elusive, depthless world of knowledge. Red, blue, and green paper balloons line the upper sections of the high windows, each balloon displaying a big black capital letter. Square yellow cards with numbers dangle from a piece of clothesline strung across the back of the room. Every corner calls forth its promise, the very one she herself once made, day by day, in a room much like this: life, its colors, its shapes, its numbers and sounds, the subtleties of its arrangements, the waywardness of its denials, the whole swirling faceless grip of it, can be *mastered*, oh yes it can, *if only, children, you will take hold and apply yourselves.*

In this moment, as Leora drips on the freshly waxed floor, all of it — teacher, classroom, vowels and consonants, the promises they hold — strikes her as the ultimate vanity. The final seduction. A fool's task. *What has she learned? And what has she taught?*

"Just set your coat over here on this desk," Mrs. Smythe is saying.

"I hope everything looks all right? I wish I'd had time to do a new border of leaves or something."

"Heavens. I'm sure it doesn't matter. It's just an ad."

"Must be some exciting, still." Mrs. Smythe ties a transparent plastic hood beneath her chin. "To be on TV. I can't wait to tell my
grandchildren. They'll watch every night until they see you." She
moves about collecting books, papers, briefcase, and — unbelievably
— the apple.

"It's not exactly exciting — "

"Here we are!" booms a man's voice, as the door bursts open.

Suddenly the room buzzes with three people lugging cameras,
cords, lights, equipment.

Mrs. Smythe nods and leaves.

"Here, Ed. Put one here. Another one over there, John."

Two men in jeans and nylon jackets move about the room placing
cameras and lights.

"You're here." Mr. Martin offers Leora a sad look.

"Let's see," says one of the men. Short and muscular, with greased
black hair, he reminds her of someone on that crowded elevator the
first morning. "You must be the teacher?"

"Mrs. May," says Mr. Martin. "This is John, the director, Leora."
He might be announcing the cast for a funeral.

"Now if you'll just stand over there," says John, pointing to the
scrubbed blackboard. "We'll see how that looks."

She moves to stand beside Mrs. Smythe's immaculate desk.

"That's fine. Just a little to the right, please. Fine."

A tall slender girl carrying a bulging purple tote bag swings into the
room. "Hi, all. Everyone make it okay? I've got the apples." She
glances at Leora. "You must be Mrs. May?"

"Leora," mourns Mr. Martin.

"Ah, Leora. Well, I'm Nan Fisher with the provincial department
of agriculture. I promote New Brunswick products, hire marketing research people to create commercials, and if I like them, we fund them.
Pretty neat apple ad, eh?"

"Over there, Ed, push it a bit . . . No, not you Leora, you're fine.
The camera. Better angle from there. Good!"

For several moments they shift equipment, discuss possibilities.

"Leora, face straight forward, please," urges John.

The cameraman has disappeared.

"Fine. Ready?"

She nods.

Light blasts her eyes shut. Electric red zaps her eyeballs, leaving black and white dots playing crazily through retinal dark.

"You'll get used to it in a few minutes," calls Nan from outer darkness, "just keep your eyes shut, Leora. These lights are terribly bright. They'll get hot, too."

The world has dropped off. Somewhere outside, voices murmur like water over rock. She is the rock, immobilized by light, voices flowing over, around her. Who are those strangers beyond her rim, outside the edge of this new world?

"What about color?" asks a male voice.

Ten years ago, on their tour of Rome, Arnold and she visited the Colosseum. Their guide, a tall, dark, voluble Italian, led them through the arcades, his long manicured fingers flashing exotic-looking rings as he described Doric, Ionic, Corinthian columns and recited the horrors of early Christian martyrdom — savoring, she felt, the imagined crunch of lion teeth against pious bones. From an open spot on the third storey, while sirens screamed outside on the Via di San Gregorio, he pointed out how once, long ago, the huge amphitheater could be transformed into a lake on which miniature naval battles were staged, how gardens and forests had been simulated there to fool imported wild beasts into a hunt. Then he led the footsore tourists down to the very center where they stood for a few moments looking up and around, dwarfed and silenced by that vast crumbling ellipse of blood and circuses. Two silver planes spread fading vapor trails overhead in a faultless blue Italian sky. She could almost hear the roaring crowds, smell the sweat of gladiators, bleeding Christians, and lions. Hot dry dust filled her throat. "Dare to be a Daniel," she murmured to Arnold and they snickered. He too had suffered through Presbyterian Sunday school. The dust and heat and shimmering haze of midday Rome had left her with a splitting headache and back at their hotel she'd gone to bed for the rest of the day.

"Color's definitely off. Must be a combination of the blackboard and jacket. Can we adjust?"

"Do a white center."

She is a white center. The Italian guide had dark sideburns and wore a wide black sash with a buckle.

Voices buzz. Leora opens her eyes. Faceless dark shapes move about uttering sounds. Balloons have become black circles.

"Should she smile?"

Does she have lips? She licks them.

"Turn a bit to the right, Leora, please. That's it."

"Should the edge of the desk show?"

"What about her hands?"

Light burns her face. Her armpits grow damp.

"The earrings, Bill."

"What about 'em?"

"A teacher wouldn't wear earrings like those."

"Hey, you guys, what century you living in?"

"Well, let's try it without them, anyhow, Nan."

"Okay, okay."

Leora removes the gold bows (24K, fifth anniversary) and leans over to set them in an extended hand.

"Yeah. That's better."

Rain pelts the window. Her legs have begun to ache. Pain caps her head, tracing a line from ear to ear. How long has she been standing here? Ten minutes? Fifteen? One foot has gone to sleep. She presses her boot against the floor.

"Sorry to keep you standing like this," says Mr. Martin. "We're getting some strange interference. Have to pull the plug and try another outlet."

"Relax, Leora. It'll be a few moments,"

The balloons regain color. Ronald McDonald grins from the side bulletin board, framed by fall leaves. Her daughter Margaret used to press leaves. Hot iron on waxed paper. Was it grade one? Was it every grade?

Mr. Martin approaches, holding an apple.

"Here we go, Leora. You're looking great. When we get the lights back on, you start."

She takes the apple. How round and smooth. How solid.

"Light flashes. Darkness.

"Now, Leora. Think of your school day. Think how tired you are, how your back aches and you're so glad the students have left, you're alone in your classroom, you look down and see this apple on the desk, you pick it up and think, ah, you'll have it now."

Ah, to be out in the soft splashing rain . . .

"What we want you to do it hold the apple, look at the camera, say toward it 'It's incalculapple,' then take a bite and smile."

She bites. Juice dribbles down her chin.

Laughter.

Margaret, a teething toddler, wore something they called a dribble bib . . .

"Now, Leora, that's fine. Don't worry. Just try it again. Maybe a little less juice, if you can manage it."

She spits the bite into her hand and drops it into the wastebasket. She takes another apple from the hand extended into her light.

"It's incalculapple," she manages, tart juice tickling her tongue.

No laughter. She must be doing better.

"Could you turn to the right, Leora, and look over here? Good. We'll go again."

Where is Napoleon now, her Napoleon? "Louse it up," he said to them. Could it possibly be worth it?

She bites a smaller bite. "It's" — she smiles, making her eyes bright, "incalculapple."

"Better. Coming. Close."

Someone turns off the blinding light. The world returns.

"Would you like to come over here and see yourself on video?"

Who is this biting woman in brown (everything greenish on screen) and tweed looking so idiotically pleased, saying "It's incalculapple" over and over? No wonder they laughed. Human emotion has been distorted to a pitch beyond control. These smiles are grotesque.

She returns to her pool of light. Oh, to be out of here, far from these people, not to see an apple for a month, forever. The back of her neck is soaking.

She bites. Sweeter. A bit of skin goes under her bridge. "It's incalculapple."

An hour and a half. The longer she stands there, the more clearly she sees one thing: she has ceased to exist for them. Perhaps she never did. She has left their shore forever. They could never follow her. The journey is hers alone. Again and again she bites, with each morsel leaving them farther behind. She thinks in different colors. *Once, at the Tantramar Frolics, they bought Margaret a pair of play glasses with moveable lenses of different colors — red, blue, green. With a mere flick she could alter the color of her world.*

"Incalculapple," says Leora — surprised.

"Incalculapple" — refreshed.

"Incalculapple" — gratified.

She does it automatically, flicking the colors of her mind. She has left them, she has entered a mammoth cave where human forms float and voices collide in a darkness emptier than any she has felt in her life.

Margaret was Caesarian. Arnold (those were the old days) waited outside. He lost five pounds that day. Just before she went under there came a moment like this, only white. A cruel light flooded her as she lay clamped against pain. Masked faces looked down, voices murmured, asking for instruments, discussing her. She looked up at their fading eyes and felt hatred, pure animal hatred for those sterilized hands which would extract from her throbbing body new life. She was nothing to them. A slab of flesh. An object. Flat on that table, about to give birth, she felt what she feels now — that she doesn't exist.

Between takes, the round dark shapes on the windows intrigue her. *Margaret loved balloons. Always, for a birthday, balloons floated about the house. . . . If she could just catch a string now, hold on, float out of this room, up and away forever into cleansing rain, float high above them all, soar lazily as she looked down at the top of Mr. Martin's grieving head, wave coyly at the two Napoleons, swerve wildly, float back, yes back . . . over the miles . . . to Tantramar . . . to the solidity of decaying patio, the bare maple near the shed, the defunct daisies . . . the cinnamon warmth of Arnold, the dry fresh smell of his pajamas, the secret of the white line on the back of his thigh . . .*

"That's it, Leora."

The blinding light is doused.

They are all still there.

She says nothing.

She has no time to lose.

She moves toward the desk, takes up her coat and umbrella. Her hands tremble. It might already be too late.

"Now, if you'll just sign this."

Mr. Martin stands between her and the door, shoving a paper into her hands.

"This?"

"The release."

"What does it say?" She struggles with her raincoat, pushing into the sleeves.

"Routine, Leora. This give us permission — "

She scans the paper. "But this gives me away."

His eyes grow pained. "Gives you away? I don't understand."

Silence gathers in the room. John is chewing a toothpick. Nan, stuffing papers into her tote bag, stops. Watches.

"Does this allow you to use my picture for any purpose you wish?"

"Now, Leora — well, you might say — but you'll be well paid, and it isn't likely — "

She sees herself beside a bottle, cigarettes, pantyhose, the eighteen-hour Wonder Bra . . .

John has shifted his toothpick. The cameraman has folded his tripod. Nan is picking up her trench coat.

Leora tears the form in half.

"Here." She hands the two pieces back to Mr. Martin. "Write one that includes a clause 'with my permission.' That's all I ask. You have my address."

"But there's a matter of time . . ." Mr. Martin's eyes are sad. Disbelieving. "The apple season, Leora, it doesn't last forever — "

"Exactly." She may never hear from him. His mouth is still open as she pushes past him, through the doorway, Arn's umbrella in hand. "Exactly, Mr. Martin. You are so right."

Breathless, her heart pounding, she hurries through the empty, polished hallway, opens the front door, closes it behind her, leaves the school, and re-enters the world.

A world of rain, splashing gray rain.

She lifts her face to it, heedless. Her throat is chalk dry.

The car is still there, over at the end of the lot. She half expected it to have vanished. She turns her key in the ignition. It starts.

She pulls out of the lot, enters the stream of crawling cars, aims her headlights into the long road home.

She must concentrate. Not get distracted. In rain like this, headlights coming toward her blur. The world grows fuzzy. She must navigate with care. As Arn would say, "You never know what the other fellow might do." *Swish swish* go the wipers as she peers out at the streaming world. The pain in her head has disappeared.

It will be a while, though, before her heart stops pounding. A while before she loses the sensation of narrow escape.

It will be a while before her world contracts and rain again feels ordinary.

She presses her booted toe on the gas pedal. Caution.

The apple season doesn't last forever.

She heard him. *Swish swish.* She peers through the windshield. Yes, dammit, she heard him. Saw his eyes as he said it. His sad, disbelieving eyes. Pitiful man.

The apple season doesn't last forever.

She's heading home. Still in season. Too early to wither and hoard. By any calculation, still in season. It's too early to mourn.

Time yet to savor many a juicy bite.